HOME RUN ENCHANTED

FAIRIES AND FASTBALLS
BOOK ONE

BRIGID COLLINS
RON COLLINS

SKYFOX PUBLISHING
Fantasy

Home Run Enchanted

Cover Design by Brigid Collins & Ron Collins

Cover Images: depositphotos.com
Magic morning at the park - shock
White baseball isolated on white background, object, sport - samurkas

SKYFOX
PUBLISHING
Fantasy

(In Trade Paperback)
ISBN-10: 1-946176-46-X
ISBN-13: 978-1-946176-46-2

(In Hardcover)
ISBN-10: 1-946176-47-8
ISBN-13: 978-1-946176-47-9

CONTENTS

Do you believe in baseball magic?

CHAPTER ONE

Baseball was so entrenched in Emily DeWitt's blood that it was currently causing her the most acute agony she'd ever experienced.

Well, not baseball itself. The game was a balm for most hurts, and the simple feel of a ball in her hand often calmed her when things got to be too much. She'd spent many an evening working out a difficult geometry problem or agonizing over her wording in an English essay while absently running her fingers over the well-worn stitching of her mom's old baseball—a foul ball caught at a Cubs game long before she'd ever met Emily's dad.

Emily was eighteen years old, now. The past few years had made her grow accustomed to things getting to be too much.

She frowned at the shelf over her desk in her bedroom.

More specifically, she frowned at the empty space on the right end of it, where the line of fake-gold trophies petered out. The left side represented her years in Pee-Wee Tee Ball, crammed first with participation trophies, but quickly shifting to markers of genuinely successful seasons. Emily's team had won a lot once they got the taste of victory, and that flavor had followed her as she progressed up into Little League. The middle portion of the shelf held much nicer trophies representing the best of her kid years.

But then she'd hit middle school, and Mom had gotten sick. The trophies tapered off, then ceased entirely the year Emily had started at Pattersonville West High School and joined their team, the Unicorns.

To be fair, that first year she hadn't exactly been playing her best. Most of her energy had been devoted to getting through wave after wave of teachers exclaiming how much she looked like her mom when *she* was a freshman, how wonderful it was to see Meredith's daughter in the good ol' Unicorns jersey, gosh your mom must be so happy to see that, since girls weren't allowed to join the team back in the day no matter how much she begged to be allowed to try out, and how *is* Meredith doing these days, anyway?

Once Emily got used to delivering a quick "she's dead," and moving on to asking about the homework she found more energy to focus on the game.

But the Unicorns, she'd found, were long past their glory days. In fact, the last time they'd made any sort of consistent waves was a hundred years ago when their star player had hit the State Championship-winning home run and promptly disappeared. Legend said he literally vanished, right as he was crossing home plate. But most people believed Adrien Thorn had just left town quietly because he couldn't handle the pressure of being scouted for the big leagues.

Mom always said she believed the more fantastical version. Probably because Mom certainly had believed in the magic of baseball.

But baseball's magic hadn't been enough to help her pull through cancer, and now Emily was afraid it wasn't going to be enough to let her see her mom's dream to fruition. The calendar was moving toward spring now, and Emily stood on the cusp of her senior season. The right side of her trophy shelf remained as bare as it had when she'd started high school.

She had one single season left.

One year to bring Mom's beloved Unicorns to victory, and she couldn't shake the feeling she was already blowing it.

A quick knock on her open doorframe jarred her from her dark musing, and her dad poked his head in.

"Hey, hey, baseball princess," he said, grin wide across his red face. "First game of the season! I made your favorite, blueberry pancakes, bacon, and OJ. Champions can't win on an empty stomach! Come get 'em while they're hot."

Emily bit back a sigh. Now that he'd mentioned it, she did notice the telltale scents of his cooking. Normally, she'd be delighted. This morning, the aroma just made her stomach flop over. "Thanks, Dad."

Dad frowned. "Hey now, what's with the black mood? You haven't even got your uniform on yet."

"I just..." Emily glanced first to the blue and teal jersey still hanging in her open closet alongside all her shirts and pants — a wardrobe fit for picking up a game of catch at any time — and let her mind picture the dark number eleven that, if it could have been, would have been her mother's before hers, then let her gaze return to the shelf with its accusatory gaping hole. "I'm not sure I believe...anymore."

Her stomach writhed again as she vocalized her internal, baseball-induced pain.

"Ah," said Dad.

He sat beside her on the bed, taking pains to avoid mussing the bedspread.

Silence rang in Emily's room. From downstairs, the murmuring sound of the television tuned to the upcoming White Sox game floated up to join the miasma of suckage. Grief was a familiar visitor in their house, but it didn't make it any easier to deal with each time it stopped by.

Had Emily really just admitted she didn't believe in the magic of baseball?

She'd spent months wrestling with that truth.

Dad must be so disappointed.

She rushed to fill the silence before he could react. "It's just, Mom talked about the Unicorns' Golden Olden Days so much you could feel how hard she wished she could have experienced them herself. She told those stories like they were old fairy tales. And then she never even got to see me make the team. I don't think I can handle the idea of having wasted four whole years."

Dad broke the silence with a cough, then a breath.

"You know your mom is already proud of you—I am, too. Always. Neither of us will think less of you if the Unicorns don't ever win a trophy. That's not what she wants for you."

"Yes, it is," Emily said, ignoring the way Dad continued to speak about Mom in the present tense. "She wanted a Unicorns trophy as much as she wanted the Cubs to win another World Series. Probably more. Heck Dad, she used to *joke*," Emily did the air quotes around the word joke, "about being the witch who stole the peasant couple's first born so she could train me up to be a star baseball player. It's a *million percent* what she wanted for me."

Dad laughed, which ticked Emily off even more.

Completely missing the angry energy she was throwing off, Dad reached over and plucked Mom's ball from the corner of her desk, where it rested when Emily wasn't holding it. He held it in one hand, smiled a much softer smile than his game-day-dad grin, then tossed it up once and caught it again with a quiet smack.

"Your mom wanted you to play your best with a team you love. Nothing more, nothing less."

He stood up and set the ball up on the shelf in the empty space with a fond little pat, then clasped his hand over Emily's pitching shoulder. "That, and she really, really wanted you to beat the pants off that snotty Callie McMasters again."

Emily couldn't hold back a giggle at the mention of her long-time rival. The Pattersonville West Unicorns played McMasters' Marion High Bulldogs today. The Bulldogs were big. It was an important game.

"Yeah. Maybe that's what's got me messed up today. Haven't managed to win against Callie's team since Little League."

"Exactly. And today's as good a day as any to get your mojo back. The Bulldogs may have pulled victory out of the jaws of defeat every game of your high school career so far, but that'll just make today's win all the sweeter. That's the kind of thing your mom's baseball magic is all about."

Emily nodded. "Thanks, Dad."

"Now, come on. You're supposed to be outgrowing this teenage mayonnaise by now."

Emily rolled her eyes, mostly for his benefit. "It's *malaise,* Dad," she said, repeating their ritual.

"Knew it was one of the two. Come have your breakfast, eh, slugger? I want to spend some quality time with you before I head to work."

"I'll be down in a minute."

Dad gave her one final squeeze—held it for an extra fraction of a second, just long enough to let her know he wasn't making light, but not so long as to overwhelm her delicate teenager senses—and headed back downstairs.

She waited until his footsteps reached the first-floor hallway, then reached up and took the baseball down from her trophy shelf.

She let her fingers run along the seam of red threads before setting it back in its place.

She liked the idea of it coming to rest there — once she'd earned it. For now, it belonged on the desk.

Was that self-torture? She couldn't tell anymore. But before setting it on the desk, she'd let her hand curl around it in her best curveball grip and tried to let the magic her mom had believed in trickle into her, just a little.

It wasn't much. But it worked. Well enough, anyway.

She grabbed her Unicorns cap and set it firmly on her head.

She had a game to win.

CHAPTER TWO

Despite Emily's lingering sense of despair, the sunshine, blue sky, and clouds over Unicorn Field made it a decent day for baseball. A lingering winter chill made the air snap, which meant she needed to get her shoulder good and warm before the game started.

Especially if she meant to start this final season of her high school career off with a win.

Warming up in the bullpen, Emily gazed into Jake Nesbitt's mitt and did her windup.

With an easy motion, she finished her toss, breaking off a sharp curveball that she envisioned smashing into Jake's catcher's mitt with a satisfying pop.

In reality, Jake fumbled the catch and had to go frog-hopping off after it to scoop it up.

"Nice," he said, tossing the ball back with an air of *nobody saw that, right?*

She tipped her cap as she caught the return toss, indulging his silent wish and pretending she'd been looking the other way.

She ran the toe of her cleat over the red scruff of the bullpen mound. She loved baseball fields, and Unicorn Field was a good little field in its own way. It was a beautiful place. All green and brown, marked with its perfect chalk lines and surrounded by stands of wooden benches along each baseline and behind home plate. There was a feeling of history around the whole field. Or maybe that was just a whiff of the popcorn that the concession stand was selling. Popcorn and rainbow ice slushies for the total win.

Of course, Unicorn Field reminded her of her mom. This was the place where all of mom's hopes and dreams came to a head, and thus it was the place where Emily felt closest to her.

This was what her mom had loved. Whenever Emily stood on the mound and breathed in the cold, early spring breeze, she heard her mom's voice in her mind. No words, of course. Just her tone. The musical lilt that would come out as she described the way the field made her feel, the way the crack of the bat stirred her heart. The way she would have played any position if the team had only given her a chance back in the day.

An unbidden smile split Emily's lips.

At least she'd managed to fulfill that part of Mom's dream. She played shortstop when she wasn't pitching.

If someone asked her whether she preferred pitching or hitting, she'd say it depended on which one she was doing right then. Everything felt good when she was on Unicorn Field.

The colleges would make her specialize, but that decision was a year away. Assuming, of course, that some school decided to offer her a scholarship.

She tried hard not to focus on that, but it was the problem with being a big fish on a ceremonially bad team. As much as she loved her teammates, the Unicorns were never very good as a group—and Emily tried to tell herself it wasn't her fault.

As if that mattered.

Any scouts that came around today wouldn't be here for her. They'd be here for Callie McMasters.

She threw another pitch, then caught another return toss from

Jake and, rather than throw again right away, she gripped the baseball hard.

Unable to stop herself from glancing across to the other dugout where Callie McMasters threw her own warm up tosses, Emily felt a sizzling bolt of competitive fire slice through her body. The Bulldogs were good. Always at the top of the rankings. McMasters, their pitcher, and sometimes shortstop or center fielder, was their best player. She could hit. She could field. She could run. To make it worse, Callie McMasters knew it, too.

Those scouts here today would *see* Emily, but they were *here* for Callie because Callie *always* led her Bulldogs to the State Finals.

She was also the daughter of the man who owned McMasters' Ball and Glove, the local manufacturer of quality sporting equipment, so it was a general expectation that Callie would live up to the family name, as it were.

Emily's skin itched to beat her. Her fingers twitched around the baseball.

"You done warming up, then?" Jake asked, standing behind the bullpen plate, mask in hand.

"Ah, yeah. Sorry."

"It's cool."

Down the foul line, decked out in his blue and teal Unicorns windbreaker, and with his white cap with its gold bill pushed up over his forehead, Coach Amabe clapped his hands and gave a bark that he thought was demanding, but actually came out as a happy bellow.

"Time to take the field, kiddos! Let's get at 'em!"

As good as her last curveball had been, Emily was glad he hadn't seen it.

You are too young for the twisty stuff! he'd always say. *Don't hurt your arm!*

But Emily wanted to win. If it took the occasional curve to do the job, she was willing to chance it.

Besides, she knew her limits better than he did.

"Take the mound Emily!" Coach A called, almost singing her name as Emah-lee.

"On my way!" Emily yelled.

She pulled her hat back onto her crown and set her mind as she jogged to the raised mound of dirt in the center of the diamond, taking in the sound of her cleats swishing through infield grass.

Mom's voice was in her ears again, delighting in the crunch of the dirt up on the mound.

Did Mom ever talk to Dad this same way? Emily'd never asked. But she only heard Mom this strongly out here on the field, and right now, like many of her early season games, Dad was at work. When he got home that night, win or lose she would tell him about every play. He would make some quip about how she had probably struck out her future husband, and she would roll her eyes.

But she wouldn't talk about how she'd felt Mom.

Yes, being here today felt good, but she wasn't sure she could roll her eyes at Dad for much longer. There was a realness to Mom's version of baseball magic. Of course there was. But it was just a feeling. A memory of happier times.

Real baseball magic, whatever it was, she thought now, came from grit and determination. Nothing more, and nothing less. For all her mom's poetry when she had spoken about the game, at the end of the analysis, winning was about skill and about practice.

Doing her best to ignore those thoughts, Emily stood tall on the beautiful white pitching rubber and breathed in a lungful of springtime air. *All right, Mom,* she thought as she brushed her hand down the number eleven that ran below her jersey's left breast. *Let's do this.*

Mom's voice faded, and the Unicorns infielders chattered as they took grounders from Patsy Pell at first base.

Jake took his position, squatting behind the plate, and she bent to take her last few official warm ups.

A few minutes later, the umpire yelled "Play ball!"

THE GAME WAS long and hard fought.

Emily struck out the first two hitters, but Callie McMasters caught a fastball at the knees, and with one swing it was 1-0.

Emily bore down from there, giving up only one more run in the third inning when Benji Amberman threw a ball into the dugout rather than to Patsy at first base, and Callie McMasters pelted a double to score it.

But in the Unicorn half of the third, Emily singled and used an elegant slide to steal second base. From there she was enough of a distraction that Patsy managed a hit. Emily ran like the wind and scored to make it 2-1.

Two innings later, Emily led off and found a sweet pitch to her liking — a slider maybe that didn't slide. It hung up in her eyes and she didn't miss it, depositing the baseball well past the fence in left field.

As she rounded the bases, Callie McMasters caught her eye and tipped her cap.

If there was anything that made her not *completely* hate Callie McMasters it was that, despite her attitude, Callie wasn't above acknowledging good plays by the other team.

Sometimes anyway.

A few moments later, Emily rounded third and arrived at the white pentagon that was home plate, touching it for the second time and officially tying the score.

Later, when she was sitting alone in the dugout, Coach A came to her. Next time she went out there it would be the seventh, and theoretically last, inning.

He sat down quietly beside her and said the words Emily figured he was going to say.

"You play shortstop now," he said.

"I'm going to pitch," Emily replied.

The coach shook his head. "You've already got too many pitches on your arm."

"No, Coach. I don't think you understand. It's my last season as a Unicorn. This is my game. I'm going to pitch."

Emily knew what was going to happen, though. Coach A was the guy in charge. It's my job to manage the game, he would say. Emily would be moved to shortstop, and Jamal "Jammy" Douglass would be brought in to pitch. Jamal wasn't terrible, but Callie would murder him on the mound, the Bulldogs would score, and that would be that. One game, one loss.

Instead, Coach A was completely silent.

When Emily raised her gaze to look at him, the coach's eyes were direct, but not sharp. Assessing more than judging.

"All right," he said. He picked up her glove, clapped it softly on her knee, then handed it to her. "It's your game."

Then he stood up, cheering as Patsy made the last out on a grounder to third base.

THE FIRST BATTER POPPED UP. The second grounded out.

Callie McMasters was next up.

She stood at the plate, waggling that bat and staring at Emily like she owned her. Which, Emily had to admit, with both a homer and a double in the game, Callie could stake that actual claim. Now she looked at Emily like she intended to put the next one over the fence, too.

Emily picked up a handful of dirt to dry her hand, then used a sleeve to wipe her forehead of sweat.

"Whatsamatter, DeWitt," McMasters said. "You're just delaying the inevitable."

She gave a what-the-hell chuckle.

Lovely.

Emily missed with her first pitch, though. Too far outside.

The next was inside.

Callie plastered the third, a slow changeup, but got too far ahead of it and pulled it a city block foul.

Maybe the umpire gave Emily a break on the next pitch. The called strike evened it up.

Emily curled her fingers around the ball as she held it in her glove. This next pitch was it. She could feel it. The key to the Unicorns' whole season. Either she'd toss the lever that would send them into competition, or throw the spark that burned their first game to ashes.

The expression on Callie McMasters' face said she felt it, too.

Emily bent to take the sign. Jake Nesbitt suggested a fastball, away.

Emily shook him off.

All right, he seemed to gesture, changeup, still outside.

He pounded his mitt and waited, but, again, Emily shook him off.

Curveball, she thought. Curveball, down and in.

Finally, he called it.

She wound up and delivered.

Callie started to swing, then froze, and as she ducked to avoid getting beaned in the head, the ball caught air and dropped perfectly across the plate. To his credit, Jake caught it.

"Strike three!" the umpire called.

"Yeah!" Emily called, pounding her fist into the glove. "*That's* magic!"

"WE STILL GOT A GAME TO WIN!" Coach Amabe called to his rowdy team as they bounced around the dugout. "We need a run! We need a run!"

Emily stood at the edge of the dugout. Her every nerve was jangling with adrenaline. They had a chance. She would bat fifth in the inning. Assuming it got to her.

After a walk, two outs, and a dribbling infield hit, it did.

This time she was the one who strode to the plate, waggling her bat.

She took in the field around her — the skies darkening into that twilight moment that was always so marvelous, that moment when the field lights came on and the daytime and nighttime worlds collided. Standing by the batter's box, she heard Mom again. More than that, she *felt* Mom. Here, waiting, watching, hoping for a Unicorns win.

She gritted her teeth.

"You got this Emily!" a voice came from the backstop.

Dad.

He'd taken off work early.

She used the bat to lightly tap her batting helmet, ensuring it was on right. Then stepped in to wait for the pitch.

This is my game.

When the pitch came, the ball seemed as large as a watermelon.

Emily swung, and knew it was gone the moment she hit it, knew when it had impacted the bat in that sweetest of sweet spots, the swing so perfect she couldn't even feel the ball coming off the bat.

She trotted around the bases, listening to voices scream and cheer.

They'd won. The Unicorns. Finally.

She rounded third base, and the smell of mown grass and raw sawdust grew thick. A horn blew somewhere distant, and Emily felt as if the universe was actually pulling her along the baseline, drawing her towards home.

Her teammates were gathered around home plate, corridoring it off, giving her space to get to the base before they would swamp her in a delirious celebration. Each of them held one finger up off the brim of their cap — the Unicorn Salute. The Unicorns were starting the season 1-0!

Maybe... Maybe she could still believe in her mom's magic.

The five points of home plate sparkled in the evening gloaming.

Two more steps.

The smell of wildfire came to her. Of cinnamon and spice. Of something old and ... so sweet it was almost rotten?

One more step.

Voices. A song? The patter of an ages old rhyme.

For the third time that day, Emily DeWitt's foot came down on home plate.

CHAPTER THREE

The instant her foot touched the plate, warmth spread throughout Emily's body. Her lungs squeezed like she was at the edge of a door, about to jump out of a plane, then rapidly filled once more. The taste of honey and spice flooded over her tongue. A deep quiet fell over her then, leaving her ears ringing in the absence of her teammates' cheers.

The disorientation of it left her stumbling.

A firm hand caught her elbow, allowing her to regain her equilibrium enough to keep from faceplanting into the grass — much longer grass than should be.

"Careful there," came the soft voice at her shoulder. "Mind your footing."

"What the—" she cut herself off with a gasp.

Standing taller, she took in her surroundings. She was definitely *not* in Unicorn Field anymore.

The long grass wasn't the worst of it. The finely raked dirt and pristine white lines of the diamond were completely replaced with tiny, pale shoots of grass and white flowers. The bases were blobby slabs of white stone rather than the traditional bags. Where the stands should have been was now a thick growth of silvery trees. The dugouts were shadowed places under heels of moss-covered rock.

And lights twinkled everywhere she looked — absolutely everywhere — scintillating in lazy waves as they moved through the twilit air. Lights that fluttered tiny iridescent wings and scattered sparkling dust in their wake.

The hand on her elbow squeezed lightly. "There, now. Getting your senses back?"

Emily whirled about to look at her companion. Her jaw dropped.

He wasn't human.

From the waist up, her new companion looked like a man, and he even wore something like a baseball jersey, buttoned neatly all the way up to his bearded chin. Atop a head of bristly black curls sat an old-style baseball cap at a prim angle. But below the waist, the thick brown fur covering his goat legs made any garment unnecessary. Still, he'd obviously combed his fur until it shone, maintaining a fastidious appearance. The only thing that hinted at any nervousness was the way one of his cloven hooves tapped rhythmically against home plate as he continued to hold her steady.

Home plate is the same, Emily noticed idly.

"I don't understand," she said, shaking her head, still getting her bearings. She had intended to ask where she was, but then she looked at the creature more closely, trying to remember stories from somewhere ago. "You're a faun?"

"That I am, lassie."

Emily closed her eyes in disbelief. "I'm going insane."

"The step from your world into ours is Adoo Zee, which can lead to some wooziness, or so I've heard. It's been some time since anyone was able to use this old fairy ring to bring anyone across," said the faun.

Emily closed her gaping jaw. She whipped her head from side to side, searching for hidden cameras. "What is this supposed to be? Like Narnia? Is someone playing a big joke here?"

"Oh, no. No joke. We're quite serious about improving our play," said the faun. "We wouldn't have spent the power needed to call for a skilled player for a mere joke."

Emily stopped scanning the strange field and turned back to the faun. She looked him up and down again, took in the strange garb — strange for a fairy, she'd think. A brown jersey with black and white trim. Clean and proper, if not on the edge of threadbare.

"You... you play? Baseball?"

The faun tipped his head back and let out a soft, almost wistful laugh. "Me? Oh, no, no, no. I don't like to get much dirt on my fur anymore. But I still run the team the Small Folk have put together this season. Manager, I suppose you could call me. Or General Manager. Though, really, all the team leaders here probably prefer Duke, Lord, or just leader. Except, of course, the King and Queen themselves."

Emily was gaping again. She put one hand to her head, where her fingers bumped up against the batter's helmet she still wore. "Mr. Tumnus is a general manager?" she muttered.

"Mr. Who?" said the faun. He shook his head. "No, I'm afraid I don't know any Tumnus. You may call me Fennoc."

He gave a little bow.

"And what may I know you by, player?"

Uncertain how else to respond, Emily opened her mouth. "My name is Em—"

"Shh!" said the faun, Fennoc. "Not your true name! Myself and the rest of the Small Folk players are trustworthy, but you never know who might be listening. And there are plenty of teams throughout the Realm whose rulers you would not want to have any power over you."

He shuddered and glanced over one shoulder. But he quickly shook his head and smiled once more, expectantly.

"Um." Emily didn't like the sound of this. "I guess you can just call me Em, then?"

"Excellent! Miss Em, welcome to our humble baseball team. The

Small Folk are grateful to have your aid in our quest to win the Web Gem for the first time in many a season!"

He bowed once again, this time a more sweeping gesture as he swung his arm to encompass the strange field.

"Uh, just Em is fine..." Emily started. But before she could ask who the Small Folk were, people began emerging from scattered hiding places. A willowy nymph and a pair of short, red-cheeked elvish waifs stepped cautiously out from among the tree trunks, followed by two dryads who walked literally out of the trees they embodied. Three gnomes unfurled themselves from what Emily had mistaken for a pile of rocks by the dugout, and a pair of sparkling pixies swirled down from where they'd been perched in the boughs of the trees, scattering their dust over the long grass as they descended.

A second faun came to stand beside Fennoc, tossing a baseball in one brown hand. He, too, wore an out-of-date baseball jersey, but his was unbuttoned at the collar, and he wore his hat sideways so one stubby horn showed poking up from his curly hair.

"Oh my god," Emily said with a hoarse whisper. "I really am in Narnia."

"This is the Fairy Realm," said the second faun. "Specifically, the Other Field and its surrounding Glades, where all of us Small Folk live and practice. Though, the practice has been pretty poor up to this point, yes, brother?"

He nudged Fennoc with his elbow and cocked a lopsided grin at Emily.

Fennoc adjusted his hat, though the jostling hadn't dislodged it from its perfect angle.

"My brother," he said to Emily with a sniff and a dismissive wave. "You may call him Maddoc, if you ever wish to engage in inane conversation. He serves as our first baseman."

Maddoc stuck his hand out to Emily for a shake. "Pleased to have you join the team, Miss Em. It'll be nice to have a chance at the Web Gem for once."

Though Emily didn't remember giving him her hand to shake, he was already pumping it up and down vigorously enough to make her shoulder ache. Luckily, it wasn't her throwing arm.

"Uh, I kind of already play for a team... back home..." she trailed off as, emboldened by Maddoc's forwardness, the rest of the fairies pressed in around her.

"What position do you play, Miss Em?" asked one of the pixies, her voice just shy of too squeaky for normal human hearing. "We need a good left fielder."

"Nae, child! 'Tis third base we need covered the most," said one of the gnomes. He held his green wool cap in his hands, smearing dirt around the brim as he shuffled it around.

A little brownie clambered out of the nearest elf's breast pocket, crossing her arms and scowling at everyone. "Whichever spot she plays, she'd better be able to care for her equipment better than you lot! I'll not be running meself ragged no further repairing cracked bats and restitching mitts than I already do, ye hear?"

"I think she'd make a lovely shortstop," said the nymph dreamily.

Emily felt the air constricting her lungs again. The press of strange folk was too much, too close. She stepped backwards from home plate and raised both hands to ward the overeager fey folk from following.

"Hold up, hold up!" she said. "First, really you don't need Miss Em, all right? Em is just fine. But I'm very sorry, but I never agreed to play with you. I already have a team of my own, and I promised my — my mother I'd see the Unicorns to victory just once, so I'd prefer if everyone could just—"

"Unicorns haven't walked our fair Realm since the Ancient times," said the elf who was now cradling the brownie woman in his cupped hands. He squinted at Emily as if she were a particularly tricky calculus problem. "You do not look the way I've heard unicorns described. Too few eyes, I think it is. But enough to play catcher, I suppose."

Fennoc cleared his throat with enough authoritative rumble to gain everyone's attention instantly. "Miss Em will pitch for us. She's our *only* chance of striking out the Unseelie Queen's Designated Hitter."

A heavy silence fell over the gathered fairies. All joviality drained away, the pixies dimming, the dryads hunching in on themselves as if preparing to weather a storm. Even Maddoc pressed his lips into a thin line and clutched his baseball tight enough to turn his knuckles white.

Fennoc alone kept his shoulders straight and his chin up, though Emily caught the way his beard trembled. He met her gaze with his own piercing black eyes, then continued speaking.

"No team in the entire Realm has been able to field a human player except the Unseelie Court. Since the Queen no longer need bat for herself, she has been able to focus on perfecting her fast ball until it's impossible to hit. They've been unbeatable ever since. We just want a chance to win. Thus, I have scouted you."

"Everyone knows the Queen cheats with her magic, too," the dryad said. "All that extra time goes into finding more ways to hide her curses from the umpires."

A certain revulsion churned in Emily's gut at the thought of a dark fairy queen abusing the designated hitter rule, but she couldn't let herself give in to the urge to right that wrong, nor to the pleading looks the Small Folk were leveraging against her now. Even though she couldn't deny the little thrill that went through her at being scouted before Callie McMasters, she couldn't stick around in the Fairy Realm for even a day, let alone a whole season.

And she didn't particularly want to tie herself to yet another scrappy-yet-hopeless team, especially now that the Unicorns had finally beat the Bulldogs.

"I appreciate the compliment you've paid me here, really, I do. And I wish you all the luck possible for your play against the Unseelie team. But I have to go home. My team needs me, and I can't leave my dad. So, if you could just do whatever you did to pull me here but in reverse or whatever, I'd be super grateful."

But Fennoc was already shaking his head. "I'm afraid it doesn't work that way, lassie. I've already added you to our roster, ye see?"

He snapped his fingers, and a thin slab of stiff tree bark appeared in his hand. Clipped to it was a fluttering sheet of paper showing a list of names written in a dark red color.

There, at the bottom, read "Miss Em. Number 11. P."

Emily felt the tips of her fingers, her toes, and the end of her nose go slightly numb, not like she'd lost circulation, but like she was gaining it. She drew in a harsh breath through her nose, filling her lungs with air that still tasted like honey and spice and something a little more. The lights dancing around the field gave a bright, almost dazzling, flare.

"I..." she started. But her perception sharpened into a distracting haze of details. She could make out the individual fibers of the red threads on Maddoc's baseball. She could count the veins running through the pixies' wings even as they fluttered at hummingbird rapidity. She clamped both hands against the sides of her batting helmet and pushed it hard against her skull to block it out. "Stop that. I'm not playing for you, okay? I have to go home."

With that declaration, she stepped back again, and again, until she was stumbling along, running sideways away from the fairies and their strange Other Field.

She crashed through the underbrush and into the stand of trees growing where the concession stand ought to have been.

"Wait, Miss Em," called Fennoc. "I don't advise traveling the hunting trails alone!"

But Emily didn't care what he advised or didn't.

It wasn't the right call, just as Coach A's call to pull her off the mound hadn't been right.

She pressed on deeper into the darkening woods, her cleats kicking up clods of decaying leaves. Bare branches slapped at her face as she ran.

She had to get home.
She had a season to win, damn it.

CHAPTER FOUR

The woods got dark fast, far faster than should have been possible. What little sense of direction Emily had was lost almost as soon as Fennoc's voice faded behind her.

Not that she'd ever known where she was going.

Why had she run this way? The field was where she'd come into this world — where she'd been pulled in against her will. She should have investigated home plate, or maybe poked around the weird stone dugouts to see if any secret portals could be found there. But she'd been overwhelmed, and all those fairies had been crowding her, looking at her with their dark, pleading eyes.

Win this for us, those eyes had said. *It has to be you!*

Emily squeezed her eyes shut as she ran on through the grasping branches of trees. She already had one floundering team putting all their hopes on her shoulders. She didn't need another! She didn't care about any Fairy Realm Series or Web Gem or whatever. She cared about the Unicorns, about getting that long-coveted win for them. About getting them to the State Finals.

She cared about not letting Mom down this one last time.

She'd done this to herself, hadn't she?

She'd wanted to find a way to believe in her mom's baseball magic again, but she'd never envisioned the magic could get this real.

All at once, she realized she was crying as she ran. The tears dripped down her face to stain her Unicorns jersey. She wiped them away hastily, furious with herself. There was no need to cry.

Real baseball magic comes from grit and determination, she reminded herself.

She'd force her way home if she had to.

She just needed a place to start looking for the road back.

Maybe she should loop around and head back to the Other Field. Surely by now the Small Folk would have gone back to wherever their homes were. She would be free to examine the space on her own.

She slowed her pace to a jog, keeping her limbs moving to avoid frozen muscles before coming to a full stop. The woods seemed to lean in, around, and over her. Instinctively, Emily hunched her shoulders against their oppressive presence. Panting, she came to a stop and spun in a slow circle, trying to get her bearings but realizing she had no freaking clue where she was, or how to get back to the Other Field.

A breath of wind set the dry grass around her rustling. The sound was a harsh cackle in the dark of night, but the grass's motion drew her attention to the presence of a faint but distinguishable trail winding among the trees.

It was somewhere to start, anyway. Though she didn't love the way the trees bent and twisted further along the trail or how the dark curls of mist beckoned her onward.

The story of Hansel and Gretel washed over her.

She thought she smelled the Big Bad Wolf.

She gritted her teeth and adjusted her batting helmet, a movement that somehow made her feel safer, then stepped purposefully along the start of the trail. It had to lead somewhere, and as far as she could tell, anywhere had to be better than right here.

She'd taken about ten steps when she heard the chuckle.

"Little hunter stalks the night," said a gravelly voice from right behind her shoulder. A horse whickered, and she felt its hot breath against the back of her neck.

With reflexes honed from dodging tags at second base, Emily spun around to find herself face to face with an enormous black horse. This was no normal horse, either, given the eerie white glow of its eyes or the way wisps of fog curled off its skeletal flanks.

The man riding astride it was likewise unnatural. Though the breeze had died away, his ragged wrapping and cloak still billowed around him with an ethereal aura. There was a golden, wolfish quality to his eyes, and a sharp gleam to the crooked, toothy smile he tilted down at her.

Behind him, a full host of other riders and runners melted out of the gloom. Before Emily could even think to gasp, she was once again surrounded. This time, though, there were no red-cheeked smiles, and no willowy nymphs or pretty pixies. These were wild things, sharp-toothed and long-clawed. Terrifying little men with caps the color of fresh blood wriggled amongst the thick-muscled legs of centaurs who grimaced and made the bits of bone braided into their hair clatter together. The eagerness she read in their gleaming eyes spoke more of an insatiable hunger than an eagerness to play a good game.

In the dark distance, hulking masses shifted unexpectedly, sending wafts of mud-stench over the gathering.

The common thread binding them into one cohesive group was how every single one of them made Emily's brain feel less like it belonged to a star baseball player than to a powerless first year.

"What does the little hunter seek, we wonder?" said the leader from atop his horse.

Emily swallowed. "I'm... I'm looking for a way home. Do, uh, do you know where I can find a portal back to the real world?"

"Oh, yes. We know where most things can be found."

Behind him, the gathered riders set up a high-pitched keening that raised every hair on Emily's neck. Reflexes or no, the ruckus left her paralyzed with raw fear.

She tried to power through it anyway. "So, is it just down this trail, or...?"

"You will not find what you seek. Not on your own. Such things require greater power than any individual could ever wield. This "real world" you speak of... to open a way back would be something of a team effort."

The leader leaned over the pommel of his saddle as if he were leaning against a bar. "The Wild Hunt seeks to field a team this season. We would like you to know how *invigorated* we'd be to see a mortal player join our roster."

Emily's ears throbbed as the keening rose in volume, and as individual yips and howls added sharp percussive notes. Was this it? Trying to get through them would be dumber than throwing a fastball down the middle to Callie McMasters. Even if she could move, she'd never be able to outrun a mass of hunters with their blood up.

The leader of the hunt laughed — a definitely not-nice laugh. "You're good enough to have a chance against even the Unseelie Queen. We can smell it on you."

And, as if Emily needed more reasons to be utterly creeped out, he drew in a loud sniff, making his nostrils squeeze and flare as he took in her scent.

The sniff echoed through the host of hunters as each one copied their leader.

"O-o-o-okaaay, then," Emily said through chattering teeth. She tried to clamp down on it. Didn't want to let him know how scared he'd got her, but it didn't really work. "W-w-what is everyone's deal with this queen, a-a-anyway? I mean, I hate the designated hitter rule as much as the next player, but—"

The hunt leader drew back to sit tall in the saddle, his lips pulled back in a snarl of pure intimidation.

His horse shied under him.

"Come, girl! Do you take us for fools? The Web Gem sits in the

Unseelie Court! We seek its power, the same as you! We have it scented, too, just as we have marked you! Do you fail to swing at a favorable pitch? No! You do not! Because you are a hunter! Thus, you shall join our team, or else learn how the Wild Hunt runs down its prey."

Emily was shaking in her cleats again.

"Come," said the hunt leader, pulling the most humongous knife she'd ever seen from his wrappings, its edge gleaming with the glow from what was now a silvered, nearly full moon. "Let us add your name to our roster."

"Stop!"

A brown blur shot out from the trees, and a moment later, Emily was shoved aside. She caught her balance in time to see Fennoc standing in her place, his little faun nose twitching in indignation, his arms crossed over his tidy jersey.

Mostly tidy. There were twigs poking out from the collar and sleeves now, remnants from his own dash through the dark woods.

The hunt leader snarled again, his teeth glistening wetly in the foggy night. "Do you stand between the hunt and its prey, leader of the Small Folk? Little fool."

But Fennoc stood his ground without even a shuffling of his cloven hooves, and Emily's respect for him shot up multiple notches.

"You cannot add her to your roster."

"And, why not?"

"Because," Fennoc said calmly, "by authority of the Other Field, she is already on ours."

The leader of the Hunt's dark form sat upright as stiffly as if a bat had been run up his spine.

"You wouldn't seek to oppose *that* mandate, would you, hunter?"

A rustle of leaves announced the arrival of another figure. "If you do," said Maddoc, taking a stance beside his brother, the tough beside the polish, "you'll have all the Small Folk to fend off, first." He'd replaced his baseball with a sturdy wooden bat, and the sound of it smacking the meat of his palm was a decent match in intimidation factor to the animal sounds of the hunt. A soft, sizzling rustle came from deep in the forest foliage, and Emily felt a new presence in the woods. "We brought the contract, if you need to see it."

Emily recoiled at the word, *contract*, but this didn't seem to be the time to stutter and stammer like an idiot, so she kept her mouth shut.

The hunter's snarl became a pained grimace, and he snapped his jaws as if he wished he could tear Fennoc's face to shreds. But he kept his place astride his black horse.

"It seems we are beaten to the mark, then."

All around them, the host of the Wild Hunt growled and hissed. The centaurs gouged great gashes in the ground with their hooves, and the Red Caps gnashed their teeth so hard they sent sparks tumbling to the wet leaves below. But the leader raised his gloved fist, and a shivery silence like a taut string waiting to be plucked descended.

"But remember, little Fennoc, that the hunt never loses its prey. Until we meet again on the baseball field, leader of the Small Folk, human player." He touched two fingers to the brim of his hunting hat. "We ride."

Like a line drive coming off a Louisville Slugger, the host sprang away, flying into the woods with a clamor of screams, bugling horns, and thundering hooves.

Emily stood alone with the faun brothers, feeling as if she'd just survived a tornado and an earthquake at the same time.

"Miss Em, I am dreadfully sorry we weren't able to catch up to you in time to head them off," said Fennoc.

"You're very fast," said Maddoc with a grin. He slung the bat across both shoulders and hooked his wrists over it. "I like that in a human."

Emily adjusted her batting helmet again, just to have something to do with her hands while she sorted out her frazzled nerves. "Was it true what he said about opening a way back being a team effort?"

Fennoc had the grace to look a bit guilty. "I'm afraid so. The power of the Other Field is old, and rather difficult to control. Getting you here was harrowing enough. Taking a chance to ask your permission before bringing you across would have wasted much of our ability, if not outright ruining the spell."

"But if we had the power of the Web Gem in our hands," Maddoc cut in, "we'd have much finer control of the Other Field and its whims. So, what do ya say?"

Emily didn't know what to think. She was out of her league here, trapped in Wonderland, or whatever this was, away from everything she knew. Away from real, solid baseball. Away from the Unicorns.

And Dad.

She had to get back. He must already be shouting Coach A's ear off demanding to know where his little girl had disappeared to.

Instinctively, she curled her fingers as if she were preparing to throw that curveball again. If the only way back was through the Web Gem, then through the Web Gem it was.

But it would be *her* game.

She stuck out her hand to shake. "I say, we play ball."

CHAPTER FIVE

On one hand, Callie McMasters understood the sudden rush of news stories. Especially at the beginning. Girl Gone Missing was sure to create a fuss and, to be sure, she was on board with it.

But now?

The police were scouring the streets every day. Posters had gone up all around. And, yes, Mr. DeWitt was everywhere, pleading with people to provide any information they might have. Callie had already given a hundred interviews to everything from old-school television stations to VR slots, all of them about Emily DeWitt rather than her own team. But despite how bad she knew this kind of thing could look to the outside world, Callie just couldn't buy into it.

Given that these investigations had been going on for days and no one could find anything at all to suggest how a teenaged girl had disappeared from under a mound of her celebrating teammates, Callie figured it had to be an elaborate stunt on DeWitt's part.

Sure, her dad had a right to pitch the fit he was pitching at anyone and everyone in search of answers to her weird-ass disappearance, but Callie really thought the way *nobody* could find anything else to talk about a whole week later was sad. From the way the entire population of Pattersonville was freaking the hell out, though, you'd think Emily DeWitt was someone worth making a fuss about.

The girl was a decent ball player and the only one in town who could give Callie an interesting game, but with the Unicorns weighing her down DeWitt would never get attention from the scouts without showing some real flare, and she knew it. Callie knew it. Everyone knew it.

DeWitt could have enrolled at Marion High and played with the Bulldogs like Callie, but she'd made her choice. She should have to live with it.

Which just made the ruckus going on about town even more grating.

At this rate, Callie didn't think her headache would ever fully subside.

Worse, the whole thing was starting to affect her game. She'd let the Central High Hedgehogs load the bases yesterday, and she was still ticked off about it.

She told herself this was a good explanation for why she was about to do the thing she was about to do.

For someone of DeWitt's athletic talent to turn thespian to draw attention to herself would be a crime akin to using a signed foul ball as a paperweight, but Callie had to admit the stunt a week ago had clearly done its job. In a few days' time, when the Unicorns were set to play against a team they had a decent chance of beating, sure enough Emily DeWitt would reappear in a magical cloud of smoke and confetti with some crazy story or other. Then she'd play a showy game, probably hit another home run, and bask in the attention of the scouts who should have been looking at Callie.

Well. Not if Callie McMasters had anything to say about it.

It was the dead of night, cool fringing on cold enough that she wore a pair of wrap-around earmuffs that ran around her neckline. The air held a sharp hint of rain that made fuzzy rings around the streetlights and turned the reflections on the black pavement of Pattersonville West High's parking lot into soft glowing streaks. The Audi her dad had bought her as a Senior year present was the only car there, and she'd made sure to park it far away from any of the lights. Just in case.

Stuffing her fists into her letterman jacket's deep pockets and twitching her loose hair so it fell over her face, Callie hunched her shoulders and headed for Unicorn Field.

It was stupid, but ever since DeWitt had done her disappearing act straight after beating Callie's team at the season opener, Callie had had this feeling. About Unicorn Field.

A sense of suspicion.

Sure, the cops had investigated the place, but she fully expected tonight's bout of trespassing would yield proof of some excellent stage trickery. There had to be something here. And if a high school senior could pull it off, maybe it took another high school senior to root it out.

The fences around Unicorn Field were high, but as part of her normal training routine, Callie did her time at the rock-climbing gym every Thursday afternoon. Even in the dark of night and without any safety gear, the fencing wouldn't pose any challenge.

She flexed her fingers to make sure they were warmed up, then leapt to grab a spot a third of the way up her climb. Reaching the top, she'd just swung a leg over, twisted her hips, and set her foot into a firm foothold for the climb down the inside when the first hitch in her plan came.

"What the hell are you doing up there?"

Callie managed to keep her hold on the thick aluminum tube at the top of the fence, but only barely. Dammit, she could really use someone on belay for her.

Tilting her head around, she picked out a shadowy, teenaged-boy-shaped figure standing on the grass by the foul line, shrouded in wisps of fog.

Great. One of the Unicorns was here, doing who-knew-what, and Callie was caught.

She might as well finish her climb down. He probably had one of the gates open somewhere she could leave by. Safer, of course, but much more humiliating if anyone ever caught wind of it.

Her sneakers hit the frosty grass with a crunchy thump.

"Callie Mc*Masters*?" said the boy in a tone that hovered somewhere between awe and disgust.

Callie elected to tip his scales towards awe.

"The game's up, bud," she said, flipping her hair back over her shoulder like she wasn't embarrassed to be seen in the company of a Unicorn. He *was* dressed in regular teenaged-guy jeans with a dark hoodie over a T-shirt that had a Taylor Swift lyric printed on it rather than the teal and blue Unicorns uniform, so that helped. "I admire the drive to help DeWitt catch the scouts' eyes," Callie said, continuing, "but enough is enough."

The boy frowned, less in awe and more in confusion. "What? What does this have to do with the scouts?"

Callie chuckled. "Nice try, but I really think it's time you brought DeWitt back from wherever you've got her squirreled away. Some motel out in Bradford, I'm guessing? Now listen, I'm willing to keep everything quiet if this stunt really means so much to your little team, but—"

A girl wearing a bomber jacket over a ruffled black mini-skirt and sheer black tights emerged from the shadows of the nearby dugout. Makeup dark. Very goth. An expression of impatience made her thick eyeliner wingtips flutter like raven feathers.

"Jake? What's taking you so—"

When she saw Callie, the impatience instantly turned to outrage.

"Callie McMasters? What the hell is *she* doing here?" The girl turned accusingly towards the boy, Jake, who threw up both hands to fend off her anger.

"Lay off, Patsy. Like I have any clue? She was climbing the fence, and now she's talking about Emily hiding in some motel out in Bradford for some reason."

Patsy twisted an accusatory glare onto Callie that was as sharp as that damned curveball DeWitt had pitched to her last game. Callie fought the urge to flinch away.

"Sohoho. *You're* the one who's responsible?" Patsy said, stepping forward so boldly Callie took a step backward. "We get *one* freaking win on you and your precious Bulldogs, and you spirit our girl away to some dirty-ass motel in *Bradford* of all places? What the actual hell is wrong with you spoiled rich kids at Marion?"

Callie put up her hands as Patsy advanced on her, one sharply manicured nail pointing directly at Callie's heart. "Calm the hell down. I haven't done anything to DeWitt. It was you pulling some kind of theatrics with a... a trapdoor under home plate, or smoke and mirrors, or something! I'm here to expose you for the frauds you are."

Patsy kept up her advance, until Callie's back was pressed against the cold fence she'd just climbed over.

God, this night had gone so wrong already.

And it was getting worse, as more Unicorns appeared out of the darkness to investigate the clamor. Was their whole dumb team here in the middle of the night? No wonder they couldn't play worth anything.

Hell. Maybe DeWitt hadn't had their help in doing a runner. Maybe she'd finally snapped under the idiocy and skipped town on her own.

Kind of a shitty thing to do to her poor dad, though. Especially since he was always clearly making the effort to *be there*, which Callie'd always thought was cool of him.

Whatever.

Patsy's nail jabbed hard against Callie's sternum again. Even through the letterman jacket, the pressure was uncomfortable.

"Your name is mud, Callie McMasters, until you bring our girl back."

Another voice rose from the small cluster of Unicorns, quiet in a way that made Callie want to listen harder.

"Callie didn't do it, Pats. But she's going to help us fix it."

Patsy twisted to look at the speaker, and her stabbing nail let up some. Enough for Callie to wriggle sideways a little, anyway.

Six Unicorns in total stood gathered in the grass of the foul line, and in the middle of them, the shortest held everyone's attention rapt upon them. For once, Callie didn't need the Unicorns' announcer using they/them pronouns to identify this kid — Benji Amberman, Callie remembered — as an enby. She found it awkward to see individual Unicorns dressed in their normal street clothes rather than the personality-erasing teal and blue uniforms, but she had to admit Benji's unapologetic rocking of a masculine gray sport coat and slacks alongside a "braids piled up high on their head" hair style, and a get up that included tasteful pink lipstick and blush was empowering just to look at.

But it was more than the makeup that drew Callie's eye.

Even in the dark of night, Benji seemed to glow, somehow. Their skin carried a certain golden luminescence that made it hard to look away from. Callie got the feeling that glow was happening on purpose, and that they could achieve the opposite effect just as easily, if they wanted.

The thought made her own skin tingle.

It also made her flash on her dad, who had no patience for the Amberman family and who made little effort to hold it back whenever they were alone. She didn't need a compass to tell her that seeing the Jewish enby glow like that would spin him off in directions she didn't want to go.

Jake shook his head. "Benji, my dudeling, you're doing that thing again."

Benji smiled apologetically. "I can't help it. Not if we're going to open the fairy ring and get Emily back."

Callie coughed in derision, but the Unicorns stood in deadly silence.

"You think that old story is true, then?" said Patsy.

"I believe it," said the kid Callie recognized as "Jammy," the Unicorns' sometimes-pitcher. "I've seen sparkly lights and heard something like giggling in center field sometimes when a nice pop-up fly comes my way."

"I know I've felt things," said one of the others. "Like something big is just about to happen. But then it never quite does."

"I'd say Emily evaporating was pretty big," said Jake.

Benji shook their head. "Emily did not evaporate. She crossed through the fairy ring. I'm sure of it. My family has stories."

"Stories?" Callie said.

"Yeah. They say Unicorn Field is built on top of a really ancient fairy ring, and while it's mostly inactive, sometimes... sometimes things come through."

Like a choreographed move, the rest of the Unicorns shuddered.

"Okay, Kiddos," Callie said. "Enough is enough. I'm at my wits' end, and I don't have time to sit around being punked or whatever this is. You caught my attempt at a break-in fair enough. You want me to get real with you? Fine. I came out here because I'm trying to be the best, right? And the only way to be the best is to play against the best. No offense, but DeWitt is literally the *only* competition in the tri-county area. So do me a freaking solid and drop the fairy tale bull. Just bring her back, okay?"

Everyone turned to look at her. Their various expressions of insult and pity made Callie's blood reach a decided simmer.

Benji was the worst. "Callie," they started, voice warm and soothing.

"McMasters to you, please. I'm not your friend."

"Fair enough," Benji agreed. "But if what you just said about Emily is also true, you'll be our partner, at least."

Callie scoffed. "Partner? In spinning fairy tales? I'll be a laughingstock."

"That's not what I'm talking about, but they're not fairy tales. They're history. At least, they are for some of us here in Pattersonville. We don't tell anyone, of course. But you might be surprised to hear we've got fairy blood scattered in places throughout the whole town." Benji paused to tilt their head back as if scanning the sky for an augury. "Although, most of it is pretty diluted by now. My great-great-great grandmother was a changeling, but all I can manage is the whole 'weird and spooky' thing."

Which they promptly exhibited by making their skin's luminescence flare just enough to set sparks dancing in Callie's eyes.

"Agh," she said, holding a hand up to block the brightness. "Okay, okay! So you're part fairy, then."

When the golden blaze faded, Callie inhaled a breath of cool nighttime air. It smelled fresh and filled her with a bold energy. She boggled at herself. Could that really be true? Could Benji really have magic in their line? That she was even considering the idea made her want to gag, but the sense of truth around the idea hit her like a line drive to the chest, and she couldn't doubt what she saw. The little Unicorn was still glowing around the edges.

Through darkness, she lifted the brim of her cap and peered closer at Benji.

"You're not joking, are you?"

Beside her, Patsy Pell smirked. "Unless you wanna give Benj a poke to see if they got any smoke and mirrors going on."

She said it like it was a dare but, though Callie still wanted to take a good hard look at home plate for hidden hinges, she had no interest in taking the bait. This whole night was already so far beyond her normal tolerance for weirdness.

"Never mind," Callie said. "Just... Ugh, just tell me what kind of witchy ritual or whatever we have to do to get DeWitt back. I'd rather get this over ASAP so I can forget all about it. Also ASAP."

But Benji was already shaking their head sadly. "It's not going to be anything we can manage tonight, I don't think. We're doing surveying right now. Nobody on this side of the portal has woken the power in...actually, I don't think anyone on this side has ever made a transition through the portal all by themselves. I certainly don't have any idea how to do it. Maybe it's not even possible."

Hell, these kids. Callie was even more insulted they'd managed to get the win over her team. "There's totally a way to do it. You just have to want it bad enough."

Benji's unfurling smile told her she'd just stepped straight into it. That, more than the razzle-dazzle a moment ago, fully convinced her of the truth of their claimed heritage.

"So, Callie McMasters," Benji said. "Do you want it bad enough?"

Callie ground her teeth so hard her jaw ached. She clenched her fists into her pockets tight enough her nails broke the skin.

She thought of the way DeWitt's curveball had caught her unawares, and how, over the past week of listening to everyone around her talk and talk and talk about the missing player, she'd turned at least ten ideas for how to counter that pitch over in her head. She'd never get a moment's peace until she had a chance to try them all against the real thing.

She pushed away from the fence to step into the circle of Unicorns.

"I want it," she said through clenched teeth. "Bad enough."

Benji's smile turned sweet as they held out a hand. "Then welcome to the Unicorns, Callie McMasters."

"Purely on a hush-hush basis, though, right?" said Patsy Pell. "I'm not cool with having my name and hers coming out of people's mouths in the same sentence just yet."

"Oh, don't worry," Callie said, trying to ignore the deeply slimy feeling of even temporarily being associated with such a mess of a baseball team. If any of her teammates heard about any of this, she'd never, ever live it down. "I'm not telling a soul."

CHAPTER SIX

Baseball in Fairyland, Emily decided, was going to take some getting used to.

The dugouts at the Other Field were both more primitive and more intimate than others Emily had been in. They'd been dug into the ground a couple feet and built with thick slabs of river rock jutting overhead to provide shelter. The stone was black and smooth, but it also glowed with some kind of power that got under Emily's skin and stayed there.

The benches were sawn tree stumps, their warm, golden rings gleaming like they'd been polished by the backsides of player uniforms for centuries. At each end of the line of stumps, mystical devices sprayed refreshing water. In the middle were bat racks contrived of a meshed tangle of deer antlers. A youthful brownie dressed in a meticulously patched brown uniform sat on the ledge looking out over the field.

The Bat Brownie, she thought.

Almost like the big leagues.

It was brighter now than when the Small Folk's ballclub had called her here.

Fairy lights still danced over the field, mostly in the outfield and in the space between the fence and the thick woods of sycamore, holly, and oak that grew up around the field. The air was fresh under a muted blue and gray sky. Banks of lights flickered with real fire from pikes that rose over the long green grass, and the dirt seemed so rich and dark Emily thought sliding might taste like chocolate.

A set of stands had materialized while she was off running into the woods, but they were built more like the seating at renaissance fair jousting reenactments rather than classic baseball bleachers. Multicolored awnings stretched over benches of polished dark wood to provide shade from the afternoon sun, and an impressive line of pennants with intricate, embroidered logos — clearly representing the various fairy teams — flapped gaily in the breeze.

Despite the differences, Emily still experienced a severe case of *deja vu*.

Baseball fields were beautiful no matter where she was.

And once again, she was preparing to play the first game of the season with a team full of, to describe the Small Folk charitably, underdogs.

Their opponents for the first game were the River Kin, which as far as Emily could tell were a group comprised of every watery fairy she'd ever heard of: silver-haired sirens humming to themselves in the opposite dugout, sleek selkies bouncing balls between themselves with seal-like playfulness, pure liquid undines slithering through the dirt between first and second base to form mud puddles, and even a single, ravenous-looking water-horse, a kelpie who Emily did not want to cross in case he somehow found a way to drag her down into the depths of his pond despite said pond being nowhere near. She hoped he was going to play in the outfield.

Despite all this seeming chaos, the River Kin gave off an air of control and coordination.

Their manager, Lady Marne, was a woman of slight, but somewhat human proportions, though the iridescent scales running up her legs gave her away as a mermaid in land-going form. She wore an expression of cool satisfaction as she watched her players flow over the field. All of them, including her, had on crisp uniforms that glittered like sunlight on water as they warmed up with sprightly games of pickle and long toss across the field. The occasional prismatic flare of green or purple rose in their glare.

In contrast, the Small Folk were shabby, sloppy, and apparently incapable of moving like a team.

Emily's heart sank as she turned to watch Maddoc attempt to catch a simple toss from Nash, their gnome catcher. Meanwhile, the two pixie players, Mellica and Jessebel, were too busy weaving daisy crowns from the flowers that made up the baselines to even bother throwing warmups. Over in the batting cage, the elf Greeven was grumbling levitation spells meant to hold a ball in place before him, but the ball kept tumbling out of his magical grasp before he could swing his gnarled bat at it. Even the uniforms were disheartening to look at, all rough woven and covered in stains that said they hadn't been properly cared for since the previous season.

She thought of the poor brownies and their complaints.

Emily held back a sigh. She had her work cut out for her, that was for sure. But she'd do it, somehow. She had to. Technically, she was under contract — though she'd shoved the glowing paper Fennoc had handed her after the encounter with the Wild Hunt into her pocket unread. Why bother reading the details when she had no ability to negotiate them, anyway?

But it was more than that.

Her freedom was on the line.

A soft clicking of hooves announced Fennoc's approach to where Emily sat on the bench. A sprig of fresh grass drooped like a wavy toothpick from one side of his jaw, and a pure white baseball stood perched on his fingertips, its crimson threads as bright as fresh blood. *His* uniform, at least, looked pristine, if rustic.

When he drew even with her, he held the ball out wordlessly, and she remembered his pointed declaration that she would be their pitcher.

"I can't pitch today," she said automatically. "I just went seven innings."

Fennoc's tiny black eyes drew to pinpoints. "Oh, go on out there," he replied. "Time is different here. Your arm will be fine."

A shock of fear jolted through her. The sudden weight of time pressed down so hard it felt like it had been a month since she'd struck out Callie McMasters. Unconsciously, she rolled her arm to discover that yes, he was right. Her arm felt better than fine.

But how much time had she already lost here?

"Why me?" she said, staring at Fennoc now.

"Don't be silly," the faun replied. "You've got the baseball magic inside you."

"Why do you say that?" Even though she was here, practically drowning in real, live magic, she didn't feel any different than she had before.

"Couldn't get through the plate gate without it," he said matter of factly. "No one gets through without it. When I was scrying through ahead of our summoning, I saw you throw a bendy pitch without even applying a curse beforehand."

"I do have a good curveball," Emily replied.

"So go on and get out there," Fennoc said. He turned to watch his team with a hardness in his black eyes. "The River Kin are ready to hit, but this time, the Small Folk will finally get a win."

Emily followed his gaze in time to see Maddoc bean little Nash with a return throw. She held back a wince.

This was not going to go well.

She couldn't delay any longer. The River Kin players were filtering into their dugout to line up in batting order. She was going to have to carry this game, and clearly, that meant she was going to have to pitch.

With a sigh, Emily took the ball from Fennoc's graceful fingers, grabbed a mitt, and, grateful she was still wearing her Unicorns uniform, stepped onto the field.

The grass whipped against her cleats with each stride.

In the stands, which were draped in dark shadows from the trees that towered overhead, a wild array of creatures were taking seats to spectate. Hard to make them all out, she thought. But there were beings of all shapes and sizes, from bull-sized amalgams of humans, to slim elven figures, to awkward, twiggy beings. There were even some things Emily thought of as "normal" humans — whatever that was. Weaving through the motley crowds were gnomes, elves, nymphs, and pixies like the ones playing on the team, except these were dressed in serving attire rather than baseball uniforms, and they were burdened with trays of delicacies and refreshments. They flinched and recoiled as the creatures they served snatched at the food carelessly.

It was a lot to take in.

Arriving at the mound, she tightened her grip on the baseball and realized her fingers felt numb. Nash, the gnome, squatted behind the plate and motioned her to warm up. His grubby cap poked out from under his woven mask, which was on crooked.

Anxiety flooded over her. She pounded the ball into her mitt, heart racing. Before she could begin, however, a commotion came from the crowd.

What now?

She looked into the stands just as a woman who practically shone with dark power was climbing up into the tallest, most luxurious box.

The woman stood regally tall, wearing a midnight black gown that flowed with a life of its own. Her face was pristine, smooth and pale, with cheekbones forever and a set of pointed lips painted blue. Her eyes, when Emily glanced at them, held her attention so firmly she thought the woman was going to speak to her, even across all this distance. They were as dark as her dress. Deep as an ocean.

"That's the Unseelie Queen," said Nash, now standing beside Emily. He'd obviously come over when she hadn't begun warming up. He stood at his full height, which was just above Emily's waist, holding his basket-like mask in one hand. An aroma of dry soil wafted from him. Twigs and dirt matted his dark, blue-tinged hair.

Emily bit back the urge to tell him to wear his mask straight if he wanted to catch anything properly, and instead looked back up at the stands.

The queen had taken her seat in a throne that rose above everyone else, and Emily watched as she beckoned someone to come sit in a second, smaller throne beside her — a partner draped in darkness so deep she couldn't make out any features, but who she saw wore a tattered baseball uniform that had, at one time, been white.

"That's the Designated Hitter," Nash said, wistfully.

Emily peered harder but had no success making more features out.

So that was the fabled pet human of the Unseelie Court. Her Majesty's Designated Hitter.

As the shadowed player took his lesser throne, the Unseelie Queen smiled gloatingly down at the pedestal by her feet, where what might have been the most beautiful trophy ever created sat on display.

Crystal and silver melded into one another like a living creature, glowing from within with a pulse as strong as a live heart. Twisted threads of holly and dark red berries wound between the crystalline core, and, under the tone of the noise around the field, Emily thought she could hear music wafting across the field from the trophy, low and bold, a victorious sound that seemed to come from an instrument like a violin, but not quite. It was a magnetic sound, though, strong enough that for just a flicker of an instant, Emily almost wished she'd been dorky enough to join the school's orchestra. Simply looking at it made Emily want to play hard and fast.

"Is that the Web Gem?" she asked.

"Indeed, it is."

"I can see why everyone's lusting after it. It's so far beyond amazing."

"It is a beauty, that's for sure. But that's not why everyone wants it. Or at least it's not the real reason."

Emily gave the gnome a sharp grimace to continue.

He took to his role with a flourish. "Ah, Miss Em. You look upon a fabulous jewel of ancient power. One that can break and protect against curses, as well as give the holder the right to ask one ruler from another team for a single boon before the start of the next season."

"Yowza."

"Yowza, indeed," Nash said. "The Unseelie Queen has been in control of it for longer than most can remember, though. Until now, their team has been impossible to beat because the queen used its magic to ensnare the only mortal player the field has allowed onto it. Until now, of course."

The Web Gem caught her eye again. This time, Emily felt power radiating from it, and the bits and pieces she'd heard about it finally fell into place. If she won the Web Gem, she could ask a boon of any team leader. Including the Unseelie Queen.

If she won the Web Gem, she truly could go home.

"That's what the leader of the Wild Hunt was talking about when Fennoc saved me," Emily said, still distracted by the power of the trophy.

"Indeed," Nash replied.

She gritted her teeth, feeling warmth coming back to her fingers.

"Let's get this done," she said.

But as Nash trotted to take his position behind the plate, Emily looked to the Web Gem one more time.

Its power whispered to her.

She could feel it in her bones. Hear it in the tones of her mother's voice as she thought about the baseball magic.

The Web Gem was her ticket home. And Emily had no intention of playing a whole season to punch that ticket if she didn't have to.

And then the umpire growled "Play Ball!"

For the first time, Emily took in the umpire's presence. It was a thick being who wore nothing but a loincloth and a set of padded armor. Its mouth was large, its face chiseled as if it were almost made of stone. At the center of its forehead sat its only eye.

"You're kidding me, right?" she said. "The umpire is a cyclops?"

The first hitter, an undine who spread tiny puddles in her wake, slithered into the batter's box and tapped the outside part of the plate with a bat that was a twisted and bent piece of tree limb.

Nash put two fingers down — the universal sign for the curveball.

Emily blinked several times, still honestly trying to get a grip on her sense of reality. Things were moving so fast. How long ago had her dad's champion blueberry pancake breakfast been? It felt simultaneously like a few hours and a few months since she'd eaten it.

But there was nothing to do but play the game.

Standing on the mound, her gaze went one more time to the Unseelie Queen, to her shadowy companion, and to the Web Gem.

"All right," she said to herself. "Let's do this."

THREE INNINGS later it was clear the Small Folk would not be winning this game.

Emily didn't need to feel her mother's tone or hear Dad's voice to know she was trying too hard. Over-throwing everything. As a result, her curve ball either didn't curve or, when it did bend, did not wind up over the plate.

The River Kin scored two runs in the first inning.

Another in the third.

Two more in the fourth.

With every pitch, she felt the Unseelie Queen laughing at her. Or was that the Web Gem itself?

Though she spent altogether too much time trying to separate the two, from the mound she couldn't tell the difference — and as the game progressed, she felt the queen's smile grow both deeper and more full of delight.

Her hitting was no better. When she stepped into the box, she felt the power of the trophy behind her, and found her mind running through ways she might steal it away between innings

She struck out the first time she tried to hit, grounded back to the pitcher the second time, and popped up to second base the third.

But it wasn't all her fault. Not by a long shot.

The Small Folk were worse than a hot mess.

Nash couldn't catch a single thing the River Kin hitters let through, no matter what pitch Emily had thrown. Their pixies in the outfield kept getting distracted by the fairy lights that still danced by the fence line. And when the Small Folk were at bat, Greeven, bless his enthusiastic little heart, couldn't help swinging wildly at *everything,* no matter how far outside the strike zone. He never, ever connected.

By the end of the sixth inning, Emily knew she was going to be trapped here in fairy baseball hell for absolutely the rest of time.

The final score was 7-0.

"I don't understand," moaned Nash from his bench stump, glancing at Emily. "We've got a mortal! How could we lose?"

"We just need to get tighter," Fennoc said as he flipped through the papers on his slice of bark. He pointed to the elf who'd played second baseman. "Delananey, we needed to turn that double play in the first inning. And Shady Marie," he turned his finger on the dryad hunched dejectedly in the corner by the bat racks, "you missed a cutoff that should have stopped a run. We got unlucky with hitting, but we know that will turn around."

No one on the bench seemed convinced, though, and many of them gave their manager dirty looks as if he'd personally let them down. Emily felt the pressure build even more as Fennoc spoke. He could give the team the old "it's a long season, and we'll get them next time" line. But Emily knew better.

She sat on her bench, stewing and stewing, until finally, she couldn't hold back any longer.

She stood, stripped off her pitcher's mitt, and flung it at the bench.

The hard slap of it striking the wood was a little satisfying, but not enough. Not nearly enough.

"This team is a joke," she said as everyone turned to stare at her. "And I'm the punchline. If you want to win, you have to win as a team. It can't all ride on just one player. It's not *fair,* and it won't even work."

Fury pulsed through her veins like fire as she glared at each and every one of her unwanted, unasked-for teammates. The way they goggled at her, as if the thought that *she* might be upset about this turn of events hadn't ever occurred to them, made her even madder.

"You wanted this thing so badly you dragged me into your mess. Well, I'm not here to do all the hard work for you, okay? I've already tried that for three seasons of high school, and it's gotten me absolutely nowhere. I'm done with that."

Silence rang in the dugout. A bench creaked as someone shifted uncomfortably.

Fennoc cleared his throat. "I'm sorry, Miss Em. We simply thought, with your baseball magic—"

"There *is* no baseball magic, Fennoc!" Emily shouted. One of the pixies jumped at the volume, and Fennoc pressed his ridiculous clipboard tighter to the breast of his un-dirtied jersey, but Emily didn't care. She hurt too much to care. "All there is," she said between clenched teeth, "is grit and determination. That's all it's ever been. And *stop* calling me 'Miss.'"

She pulled her cap off and ran her fingers through her sweaty, bedraggled hair. Then she jammed it back into place, bent to sweep her mitt back up off the bench, and pulled a deep breath in through her nose.

It smelled like failure.

"Come find me when you're all ready to be serious about this. I guess I'll be around, won't I?"

She climbed out of the dugout and didn't look back as she walked into the deepening twilight.

It was going to be a long, long night.

CHAPTER SEVEN

Even at night, the fairy lights never stopped twinkling over the Other Field and its surrounding meadows and glens. Emily had had to stomp over quite a few charming little hillocks and through cozy copses of birch trees before she found a small hollow full of enough shadow and murk to match her black mood.

Still, tiny glow spots winked in and out of existence to disturb her brooding.

She'd discovered one singular thing she liked about this whole place, though: the magic in the air allowed her to call a ball she'd already thrown right back to her hand, all ready to throw again without the need for a whole basket of balls to work through.

So, she stood, working out frustrations by hurling her single ball as fast and as far as she could into the darkness beyond the trees, taking great satisfaction at sending the little lights scattering like ripples on a pond, and then snapping the ball right back to do it again.

And again. And again.

But she'd made no progress on working through the fury burning inside, because no matter how hard she threw, her arm never built up that tell-tale ache that said she'd pushed herself hard. She was exhausted, but not in the way that felt good after a long day on the practice field. Instead, she felt like she'd been drawn but not yet quartered. Like she'd constantly studied, but never taken the test. Like she was a pot of water someone had boiled, but never poured over their tea.

That was it. She felt tepid.

And she knew it was at least partially her own fault.

She shifted the ball further into her palm for a changeup. Those sparkles were starting to get wise to her fastball.

Yes, she thought, watching the lights dodge prematurely as her changeup cut a leisurely path through the trees. The Small Folk weren't a very good team. But that could be excused, fixed, even. They just hadn't had much practice or quality coaching.

Emily, though. *She* had played a bad game.

There was no I in Team, as the gratingly popular saying went, but if she didn't get her *I* in the right headspace, she would rightfully be the one on the receiving end of a chewing out like the one she'd given back in the dugout.

The ball snapped back into her palm with a hard *thmp,* but instead of throwing another changeup, she held onto it, turning it around in her fingers as she stared vacantly into the darkened woods.

She couldn't stop thinking about the other human player she'd glimpsed.

The Designated Hitter.

Was she destined to become like him, trapped here until she became little more than a shadow, a tattered, worn-out version of herself, forever playing baseball at the whim of a fairy who hadn't asked before carving her name onto the roster in blood? Even if she didn't — couldn't — believe in baseball magic anymore, she loved the game too much to endure that kind of life. Which meant she needed to keep herself together. Keep herself going of her own free will. No matter how much her homesick heart longed to simply detach from this situation, she couldn't let herself become a wraith, just going through the motions out there on the field.

And, no matter how much she felt that her poorly disciplined teammates would never make a winning team, she had to keep trying.

If she wanted to ever get home, she needed the Web Gem.

If that meant she had to do it herself, so be it.

Her internal musings created a lapse in her throwing, and the winking lights out in the darkness now hovered close again. Their tiny glows highlighted small patches of detail in the gloom: the rough, mossy bark of a tree, the glint of an owl's eyes as it scanned the ground for prey, a tumble of rocks providing cool shelter to a cluster of purple mushrooms. This was a beautiful place. Emily could tell that objectively.

It was the kind of place you could feel pride in claiming as your home turf if you truly looked at it.

Of course it would be beautiful.

This was Fairyland, right? Narnia? Wonderland?

It was meant to be beautiful.

And, out here all alone, with her eyes closed and the soft, soil-scented breeze running over the drying sweat on her skin, she felt similarities between it and her own home. Not just Unicorn Field. Pattersonville.

The thought made her feel weird. Out of place, maybe. Like she'd remembered being a freshman on her first day. Still, the idea of this place made her uncomfortable in a different way.

This place...it didn't feel entirely alien. Instead, it felt like it had always been there, lurking just out of view, leaking its influence over everyone, faintly, subtly, almost negligibly.

Was the stress of senior year getting to her?

Was she going crazy?

She hadn't seen any real magic in Pattersonville, of course. She hadn't been consciously aware of it, anyway. At least she wasn't *that* bad off.

But she had felt it sometimes.

Mostly whenever Mom had talked about her baseball magic, but sometimes on Unicorn field, too.

Emily opened her eyes again, peered into the murky darkness, and threw the curveball she'd come to think of as her specialty.

The lights scattered once more.

But instead of a distant rustle of leaves as the ball whistled back to her, the soft slap of a ball meeting a bare palm came.

Fennoc emerged from the darkness, still prim and pristine, tossing her ball up and down and catching it with a smooth motion that spoke of timeless patience and a real, innate skill.

"Am I welcome at your practice session, Miss Em?" he asked.

Emily nodded, making space for him in the little hollow.

"My thanks," he said, stepping daintily around a slick spot of mud she'd unconsciously let her cleats sink into.

"I was serious about dropping the *Miss*, though," she said.

"Why would I do that?"

"I'm not exactly Miss material."

Fennoc looked up at her. "You can be several things at once, m'dear. Never limit your range."

Emily found her lips forming a twisted expression that was half-grin and half grimace.

"You sound like my mom." *Try out for pitcher,* Mom had said all the way back at the transition from Tee Ball to Little League. *But don't neglect your hitting skills!*

She'd also taken Emily shopping for big occasions, getting her prettied up for Uncle Jimmy's wedding and for her graduation from elementary school before middle school... before she got sick and lost that kind of energy. That was Mom in a single pill. *You can do it all*, she'd say. Never mind that the kids in middle school and now Pattersonville West were very clear about her place. She was the cute, not pretty, scrappy girl with gumption and a fastball that no one could hit. She was also not a scholar, despite the fact that she liked music theory and physics — though some of that was because it seemed to apply in some way to baseball. She was not funny. Nor quick of wit. She was not a school leader. Not an influencer. No one followed her social platforms if it wasn't baseball season, and no one invited her to any of the posh events held for advanced placement kids of junior youth leadership.

Her lack of likes was a measure that went on forever.

No, she thought, *I am most definitely not Miss material.*

To be fair, Mom hadn't been either. For many of the same reasons, and, Emily knew, many more. At least, Mom had never cared that she could be pretty when she wanted to.

"She would have made a fine third sacker, now, wouldn't she've?"

Emily did a literal doubletake. Third base, the hot corner, was her mother's favorite position because she liked the challenge of catching the hardest hit grounders.

Fennoc tossed the ball to himself once more, considered the darkness Emily'd been pitching into, and then threw a decent fastball of his own.

"Nice," Emily said as she watched the fairy lights dodge the pitch. It wasn't as good as she could do, but it was solid enough to give a batter a challenge, anyway. "Any reason you don't play on the team?"

The ball reappeared in Fennoc's hand with a little burst of fairy dust — Emily was glad that part didn't happen when she used the magic — and he looked at it with a sigh so deep with pathos Emily could see his true desire shine through.

"I'm no spell caster. Maddoc got all the family ability there. Plus, he's much more comfortable with dirt than I." He chuckled self-deprecatingly, and Emily couldn't hold back a half-smile of her own. "Besides, I'm much more intrigued by the numbers of the thing these days. How many times has this player successfully hit, or gotten on base, or tagged a runner out, or helped another runner cross home. That sort of thing."

"You're a statistician," Emily said.

"Is that what you call numeromancers in your world?"

"I suppose so. Or maybe sabrmatrician is better. They study baseball."

"That does sound better, then." Fennoc rolled the ball to his other hand. "There's a kind of magic by proxy, I suppose, through watching the numbers. I feel like, if I just watch them closely enough, if I track everything our team does down to the tiniest detail, I might be able to discern a pattern that would help us finally succeed in the tournament, to get the Web Gem, and so get the Small Folk out from under the thumb of the Unseelie Court after all this time."

The memory of what she'd seen in the stands flashed through Emily's head — the frightened, flinching way the non-player Small Folk had served the other fairy spectators, gnomes scuttling between the aisles with trays of refreshments, pixies swooping in between innings to collect up refuse that had been carelessly discarded into open spectator aisles. She recalled a whole battalion of elves working endlessly to adjust seats and rearrange boxes as the sun travelled its course, working diligently to protect the Lords' and Ladies' delicate eyesight from Fairyland glare.

The uncaring slashes of claws and teeth as refreshments were snapped up.

"We're the serving class here, you see," Fennoc continued. "The only reason they even let us field a team is because we're meant to serve as easy fodder for exhibitions. We're not meant to win. Not expected to, anyway. Why, if we won, who would serve at the end of season festivals?"

He gave a bitter laugh and shook his head, making his neatly trimmed beard sway. "More the fool I am for thinking that if I work the numbers hard enough I might be able to touch the baseball magic myself. But the more I look at the numbers, the more it becomes apparent that the baseball magic has simply ignored us. Abandoned my team."

His posture beside her remained composed, but she saw how

he'd curled his fingers around the ball so tightly his knuckles had gone white. "Losing time and again gets frustrating, especially when you've got people counting on you."

Emily pictured the empty space on her trophy shelf. "Believe me, that much I know."

But did she, really? Her trophy shelf *did* have trophies on it, after all. Quite a few of them. She'd tasted victory enough to grow accustomed to the flavor of it. Enough that its over-sweet flavor had soured the simple, refreshing fare of the game itself.

She thought about her mom, who never got a chance. And she thought about her dad, working hard every day on a job he could do well but clearly didn't want to be doing.

She'd been raised to be a star player.

What if she'd only ever subsisted on defeat, the way the Small Folk had?

Clearly, that was also a poor way to live. The players she'd seen on the field today had been bitter, or disillusioned, or just completely out of touch with what baseball was as a whole. As if they'd carefully cordoned themselves off from the full realness of the game to avoid the sour aftertaste they knew was coming.

The taste they'd come to associate with baseball.

When she arrived, a star mortal player of their own, they must have felt a blanket of despair lift from their lives, though. Her presence must have given them a little appetizer of the joy that could come with the game.

They had been honestly excited.

Losing with her had brought the reality of their lives — that they were nothing more than servants and punching bags — crashing back down twice as hard. Their plight was, if she could believe it, much worse than that of the Unicorns, who merely wanted another trophy to put in the sparsely filled cabinet in the gymnasium hall. At least her human teammates would graduate and get on with their lives.

But neither the sourness she felt now nor the sugar-rush sweetness she'd experienced before high school were what baseball really tasted like.

What baseball really tasted like was a hot summer wind through fresh green leaves, new-raked dirt over oiled leather, and the cool burn of muscles ready to run, ready to jump, ready to catch and throw and slide into home, safe by a hair's breadth.

And more. So much more, Emily remembered now.

So many things she'd stopped tasting for herself once Mom couldn't taste them anymore either, first because Mom was trapped in a hospital bed, and then because she was gone. And because Emily couldn't bring herself to keep believing in that airy-fairy baseball magic woo-woo when it had left Mom to suffer like that. Standing here in this not-so-gloomy hollow, though, with the fairy lights blinking and the owl hooting and Fennoc holding that ball and wishing so hard for a victory for his team she could feel it radiating off him in waves, she tasted it again.

It was the same here as it was in Pattersonville.

Something deep. Not magical so much as poetic.

"Well, Fennoc," Emily said. "If there's one thing we can agree on, it's that there is no such thing as baseball magic."

The faun twitched, and the long blade of grass dangling from his lips drooped. "'Tis true, I think."

"But that doesn't mean we can't shake things up."

"What do you mean, Miss Em?"

Emily started to correct him again, but decided it wasn't worth fussing about.

"Fennoc," she said, instead. "When was the last time the Small Folk played a good game of baseball?"

"I don't remember the last time we won," he said. "That's why I called for you."

Emily shook her head. "That's not what I asked. When was the last time you had a *good game?*"

The glow of the fairy lights reflected in Fennoc's eyes like sparks of fire. "Ah. Quite a long, long while, then. Many of our players have long since lost the love of the game, if they ever had it at all."

Emily nodded. "You guys and I are in the same place right now. We've both gotten so caught up in winning and losing that we've forgotten what baseball *is*. We just came at it from opposite ends. Baseball is grit and determination. It's a lot of hard work and long hours. But it's also exhilaration and opportunity and freedom, because baseball is *fun*. You can't win if you forget that part. Fennoc, if you're willing to work at it, we can help them see that. I believe it."

And she did believe it. Truly. A power was here, right now, in her and around her and thrumming through the ball Fennoc still clutched. Baseball itself. Not the need to win. Not the fear of losing.

It was *almost* enough to make her understand her mom's idea of baseball magic all over again.

Fennoc met her eyes unflinchingly. "I'm more than willing, lass."

Emily stood, brushed the dirt from her uniform pants, picked up her batting helmet, and held her hand out to him. "Good. Do you have a spare Small Folk team uniform in my size?"

Fennoc gave a click. "The brownies have one set aside for you already."

"Good," she said. "It needs to be number 11."

"As I have it on the roster."

"All right," Emily said, holding her hand out for the ball Fennoc still held. "Let's get to work."

CHAPTER EIGHT

Callie McMasters felt strange standing on the mound at Unicorn Field now.

Holding the ball in her mitt, she adjusted the bill of her cap, then rubbed her free hand down the thigh of her uniform pants. It was just past three o'clock in the afternoon. The sky was partly cloudy, and the temperature was great for a ballgame. The stands, usually almost empty at Unicorn Field, were over half full. The weather and the fact that the Unicorns had pulled off that surprise win last game had apparently brought people to watch.

Usually that would bring Callie's competitive nature to the forefront.

Nothing was better than beating a team in front of all their fans.

But something was different now.

Two days had passed since she entered her clandestine pact with the Unicorns, and now they were ready to play the second game in their series. She had spent those two days with those same Unicorn players running various trials meant to find fairy magic around the field — most of which made her feel stupid. She had, for example, followed Patsy around the whole of yesterday afternoon as the Unicorns first baseperson attempted to dowse the field.

"I'd shut your trap if I were you," Patsy had snapped at her when Callie made fun of her. "I'm an empath. Very sensitive to the world around me. I've dowsed for lots of things. Call it my superpower. Found my dad's lost car keys under the garbage can once."

Callie managed to bite her lip and follow her the rest of the day, but nothing came of it, which she admitted was disappointing, especially when Patsy brought her dowsing rods to home plate. She still didn't believe in the whole fairy realm thing, to be honest. But if they were going to find something magical about Unicorn Field, Callie felt certain it would have to be home plate — because, of course, that was where DeWitt had disappeared from.

They'd done a Drano test, too, which was something stupid that one of the Unicorns had found on the Internet. They poured a whole bottle of Drano around home plate, then put baking powder over it and got bupkis other than a horribly stinky mess.

While some of the kids were trying to pool their money to buy a used radar detector off the Internet, nothing had come from it to date.

Despite these failures, Callie agreed she couldn't explain why a digital thermometer Jake Nesbitt had brought showed a sudden drop of five degrees at several spots around the field. And then there was Jamal, who she and Benji had met with last midnight hour to help "record the field," which meant they covered the field in a search pattern, phones out and recording both audio and video. A glance at both Unicorns showed that they were probably as tired this afternoon as she was after the late night out. She'd barely gotten any sleep after sneaking back into her bedroom so early in the morning. Benji had stayed up all night, though, running their recordings backward and forward, looking for something they called "spurious events," and a few minutes ago, as Callie had been warming up nearby, she caught Benji's fabulously purple-lined gaze, and they nodded back to her.

"Something weird here, but I can't tell what," Benji said quickly.

The news made her heart leap.

"Talk later?" Benji asked with a tone of anticipation.

"Sure," she said.

Now, standing on the mound and waiting for the umpire to wave Jamal, the Unicorns leadoff hitter, to the plate, the hair on her arms rose. The air felt sharp now, filled with a faintly astringent scent that seemed at once as clean as it was edgy.

She began to fidget even more.

Her dad had been pretty jazzed when he'd learned his daughter's biggest competition had left the field, as it were. His company sponsored her Marion High School club. With DeWitt out of the picture, Callie was certain to carry the McMasters' Ball and Glove name to even greater success. But all these weirdnesses with Unicorn Field added to the fact that, to Callie, DeWitt's absence left a gaping hole in her gut. She wanted to win, yes, but winning didn't mean anything if it wasn't against the best competition. The Unicorns' best player was annoying at times, but her absence made Callie understand just how good Emily DeWitt was. She wanted her back.

For totally selfish reasons, she thought. Two days spent with Pattersonville West's players had brought her to realize just how worried these Unicorn players were, and how much they missed their teammate.

Well, so what if they cared?

All their friendship circles and daisy chains had gotten them exactly nowhere so far. So, it was Callie's turn to try and figure this place out, and she was going to do it the only way she knew how: by playing a damn solid game of baseball and letting the straws fall where they would.

"Let's go," the umpire said.

Jamal, a thin kid who could run like a deer, took his stance.

Callie took her place on the pitching rubber and peered into the plate. For just an instant, she thought Jamal's bat looked so much like a crooked tree limb she stepped back and looked again. But no, it was just a Louisville Slugger, built of composite material rather than pure lumber. She shook her head.

"Get a grip, McMasters," she said, then took her position again.

Fastball, the sign came.

She wound up and delivered, grunting with the effort. Jamal swung at the pitch, which was a strike, but managed only a weak foul ball.

There was a flash, though.

As the ball glanced off Jamal Douglass's bat, Callie was certain she'd seen a spark. A flare. A glint of golden-silver light clear and bright enough she brought her glove hand up to protect herself. But nothing seemed to come from it, and no one else seemed to see it.

She frowned.

Waiting for her catcher to throw the ball back, Callie ran a hand over the back of her neck.

Had she imagined it again?

She threw another pitch. Wide this time. No flash came.

The count was a ball and a strike, but Callie found she didn't really care about that. Her brow furrowed as she considered the situation. *Hit the bat,* she thought. *Let's see what happens.*

The catcher called for a fastball, but Callie shook him off. *Change-up,* she thought. Something Jamal could see more easily. The catcher called the change, and Callie went into her windup, throwing a fat one straight down the middle of the plate.

Jamal's bat whipped around, and the crack of the ball rang out over the park.

Line drive to left field. Base hit. Jamal rounded first base, but then stayed put.

Callie's teammates shouted encouragement at her to shake it off as she got the ball back, but she wasn't listening. She'd felt it this time more than seen it. A spike of power just as the ball crossed the plate to impact the bat. A wild, hornlike sound had come to her. Clearing dirt from the rubber with her spike while Patsy — the next hitter — took her place, Callie glanced around to note that, again, no one else seemed to have seen or heard anything.

Jamal danced around, taking a lead at first base.

Enough experimentation for now.

Jamal was fast. She had to concentrate to keep him from stealing second.

She threw over once, then again.

Fans on the Unicorn side of the stands booed her, but she didn't care.

Her next pitch was a hard fastball that Patsy hit into the ground, straight at the second baseperson. Perfect for a double play, which her teammates promptly turned, second base to shortstop to first base. Pretty as a picture. There was something pristine about the timing of a routine double play. The sound of a ball hitting a mitt, the arc of a relay throw, and the leverage of a clean pivot at second base. A double play was a thing to behold. Like watching a clock churn, the second hand ticking like a metronome. As the ball disappeared into her glove, Callie McMasters screamed a cheer to her teammates, and felt that thrill of perfection run up her spine.

Nothing magical this time, though. No fairy woo-woo. Simply baseball.

She'd always disparaged superstition in baseball, even from Coach Jameson, who was currently going through his finger-snapping, bat-tapping routine in the dugout, probably trying to ensure she didn't load the bases again.

Wasn't he the quaint one?

She gritted her teeth, trying to ignore him, then grinned, realizing that with the bases cleared, she could maybe experiment again.

As she climbed back to the top of the mound, a scent of oak leaves and a rustle of long grass came to her. Not from here. It couldn't have been, because while Unicorn Field was quaint, the trees across the way were too far out to carry such a strong odor, and the grass was well mowed.

She threw another cheeseball to Jake Nesbitt, and Jake promptly plastered it into right center, good for a double. Her teammates groaned and tried to rally around her, obviously distressed that their leader had given up a pair of hits already.

But Callie Really. Did. Not. Care, though. Not At All. Because when Jake's bat made its nearly perfect impact on the baseball, Callie had felt a thrill of energy run through her body that was unlike anything she'd ever felt, and she'd seen a brilliant silver arc of light following the ball that she couldn't possibly describe.

There was something going on.

"It's all right, Callie!" her catcher called to her. "Just bear down! Get this guy and we'll be fine!"

But Callie needed to see something.

Another pitch — a slow curve that barely curved at all — brought another solid hit, and more important, another flash of light, complete with a tone of a horn.

Nesbitt scored from second. The Unicorns led 1-0.

Her teammates, clearly confused, still cheered for her, exhorting her on.

The next batter struck out.

Striding off the field and into the Bulldog dugout, Callie shook her head in a motion that her teammates and coach interpreted as annoyance with herself, but which was really disgust at the hitter. She'd thrown three pitches straight down the middle. *You've got to be able to hit those*, she thought. *How am I going to learn more about this place if you can't put your bat on a ball that's thrown that easy?*

AN HOUR LATER, Callie McMasters sat on a bench in the visiting team's changing rooms, feeling her teammates glances.

"What happened, Callie?" Coach Jameson said, voicing the concern that was on everyone's mind. "Are you okay?"

They'd lost by a score of 10-2, the two Bulldog runs coming when Callie hit a ball that may well still be orbiting the planet. Well, technically, it had come down somewhere in the copse of trees growing far beyond the left field fence, but after a bunch of kids had gone looking no one could find it. So, yeah, still in orbit.

Callie wondered, though.

The swing had been perfect. The impact, equally so.

There had been no explosion of light, though. Nothing special about it beyond that outer orbit bit, which she already knew she could do.

"I'm fine," she said. "Just one of those days, I guess. They were better than me."

The coach stared at her and opened his mouth as if he was going to say something else, but then thought better of it. Callie understood that dynamic. She wasn't fooling anyone, leastwise herself. If she'd been anyone else, Coach J would have read her the riot act and sent her back out to run laps for her lack of concentration. Or, if nothing else, given his propensity for using stupid superstitions to break a mood, have her spin around three times or throw salt over her shoulder, or *something*. But she was Callie McMasters, the best player on the team and a top college prospect. The one he'd never tried to offer his lucky mitt to, or suggested she not change her socks for two weeks. She got a pass. The first time, anyway.

She totally understood the whole thing.

Her teammates knew she'd let up. Her coach knew she'd let up.

She couldn't blame them for being upset.

But sitting on the bench and reflecting on the events of the game, Callie knew she'd done the right thing. A chill of fear threaded through her mental replays of each pitch, each catch, each at bat.

She would never feel good about beating a team without their best player, but now things were deeper than before.

For the first time, she was actually worried about DeWitt.

Fairies or not, something was going on here at Unicorn Field. Callie felt that now so deeply the certainty might well be infused in her bones. Emily DeWitt had not run off, as Callie had first thought.

Nor was she hidden away in some stupid publicity stunt being run to attract attention from the scouts.

Callie didn't know what to do next, but in her mind the game itself had changed.

Unless she and the rest of the Unicorns could break this mystery, Emily DeWitt wasn't coming back at all.

CHAPTER NINE

Emily stood in the sawgrass behind second base, watching her team practice for the first time since she had arrived in Fairyland. They weren't on the Other Field, where she'd come into this Narnia-made-real. That place, Fennoc had told her, was only where the official games were played. Instead, they were using one of the practice fields that were tucked amid the glades surrounding the Other Field. This field was much smaller, merely an open expanse in the forest, with a meadow of lumpy grasslands kept grazed by a few wild deer. Thickets of wild brush grew at the base of the wall of tall birch trees that warded the area.

Given it was springtime, leaves were coming in, but the growth was still thin enough that Emily could make out a large number of straw-lined nests built into the nooks of branches, reminders of the hooting owls she often heard in the evening, and the rustle of hawk wings that soared on occasion overhead.

At a weed-choked home plate, Fennoc tossed a ball up to himself, then swung a thick log to hit practice grounders around the infield. Delananey, the thin elf who played second base for Emily's Small Folk, scooped up the ball and whipped it over towards Maddoc, who stood at first base. The ball flew wide and high, disappearing into the bramble that ringed the ruggedly maintained practice field.

"That's okay, Delananey," Emily called out, hesitating a heartbeat to let her initial reaction fade. "It just shows you've got a really strong arm."

She hadn't ever really thought about things from Coach Amabe's viewpoint before. But watching this team she'd decided to train up play gave her new appreciation for the man's patience. Coach A was a saint.

Still, as bumbling as Emily realized her Unicorn teammates were, they were a billion times better than the Small Folk, who seemed to simply be in the moment at all times. The next grounder Fennoc hit, for example, slipped past Shady Marie at shortstop because, rather than even looking at the ball, she was bent over, blowing into a dandelion so she could watch the little clouds of fluff mix in with the fairy lights that were loitering over the outfield grass.

"Shady!" Emily yelled. "Look sharp!"

The dryad stood up and faced Fennoc, as if he was just now going to hit it to her. From behind, Jessebel, the pixie sister to Mellica who was practicing left field, picked up the grounder and proceeded to throw it in, calling to herself "hit the cutoff fairy!" just like Emily had taught her. The ball flew through the air and beaned Shady Marie.

"Ow!" the dryad called, turning to face Jessebel. "Why did you do that?"

"Because Miss Em said that's how you play baseball!" Jessebel beamed back. "This is fun!"

Emily groaned.

She had learned this much about baseball in Fairy World.

With only six clubs in the Fairyland League, seasons were both short and intense: Two games against each team in what Emily considered the regular season, then a postseason series to award the Web Gem, in which only the top four were able to participate. The first round was a one-game elimination, but the final series was a five-game set, with the first to win three taking the championship.

The Fairyland teams played a cycle of four seasons a year, crowning a winner for each — a champion who then controlled the Web Gem until the next season was complete.

At this rate it didn't matter, though.

At this rate the Small Folk were going to continue their string of never making it to the Fairy Series.

"All right!" she called out, having seen enough already. "Everyone come here and let's have a talk."

The team gathered around and listened up. Even the little brownie leaning out of Greeven's shirt pocket shut up for a bit, which alone helped the decibel level immensely. The brownie was an enthusiastic chatterbox on the field, and her voice — though tiny — was piercing.

"Look," Emily said, leveling her gaze at the whole team. "We're never going to get better if I'm not honest. And the fact of the matter is that, well, you all could use some intensive training. So, this is what we're going to do today. I want everyone to line up, and one-by-one I'm going to work with you alone. While I'm focused with one of you, the rest can play catch or pepper, all right? Focus on throwing and catching."

The Small Folk looked to Fennoc, and Emily realized she might be stepping out of bounds. This might be Emily's team now, but the faun was their manager. She was usurping his position.

Fennoc's jaw churned as he chewed his blade of grass.

A gleam came to his eye as he glanced at Emily. "You heard Miss Em," he said. "Time to line up!"

The team did so quickly.

Emily sighed in relief. "Count off," she said when they were finished. "And remember your number so you know when it's your turn."

"One!" Greeven called.

"Two!" pierced the brownie from the edge of Greeven's pocket.

Emily chuckled, then bent closer. "What's your name, little one?"

The brownie's tiny cheeks gave a rosy flush. "No one outside the Small Folk ever asked my name before," she replied.

"Well, don't give me your true name, of course. But what should I call you?"

"I'm Essie!" the brownie said, throwing her arms wide over her head, tiny fingers spread wide.

"Well, Essie. I think we should definitely have an individual training session at the end of practice, but right now I want to focus on the players who will be in the field, all right?"

"Oh. Well," the brownie was embarrassed now. "That's okay."

" I'm serious," Emily said. "You're a great cheerleader and mascot, and those are really important to get right."

Essie perked up. "I agree!"

Emily stood upright, and looked at Maddoc, who stood behind Greeven.

"Two!" Maddoc called.

"Three!" said Shady Marie.

In a moment, every Small Folk had a number, and Emily got to work.

Hours later, after Emily had been through the entire team, and after a sprightly conversation with little Essie, Emily took a seat against a tree behind home plate of the (finally) quiet practice field, elbows resting on her pulled up knees, fingers dangling downward.

"It's not safe out at night, lassie," Fennoc had said as practice closed. "You need to come with us."

Despite Fennoc's concern, she needed this moment.

"Don't worry," she'd said. "I need to be alone for a moment. I'll just be a minute."

She laid her head back against the rough bark of the birch tree that soared straight up into what was now a slate-gray sky above.

A moment later, she closed her eyes to rest them.

Physically, she was drained, but the bulk of her fatigue was between her ears.

Focusing that hard for that long gave her a headache, and sitting here with only the cool breeze and the rattling of dry branches for company gave her a chance to let herself relax.

"That was a long day," she said to herself.

But it had been a good one, she knew.

Every player she'd worked with had gotten noticeably better during their workouts. Greeven's elven litheness gave him an athletic grace at third, and by the time they were done, he was catching everything hit his way. Same for Shady Marie at shortstop. And it turned out the dryad had almost perfect muscle memory. Once she understood the mechanics of throwing, Shady Marie almost never failed. In the outfield, the pixies realized they could let their concentration go between innings, but that if they could keep the fairy lights from being diversions while on the field, they could catch just fine. That, and their combination of lanky legs and double wings gave them great range. By the time Mellica and Jessebel were finished, Emily was beginning to wonder if anything beyond the sharpest hit line drive would ever fall onto the grass with them in right and left.

And Izusa in center field was amazing.

It took Emily a while to get comfortable with the twisty somersaults and cartwheels that were the male pixie's standard method of ambulation, but the fact was there wasn't another Small Folk who had more fun playing the game than Izusa, and no other Small Folk outfielder who had better range.

Even the backup players had improved today.

It made her wish she'd tried something like this earlier with her Unicorn teammates.

A crackle of snapping wood out in the forest broke her moment of quiet reflection, and she sat bolt upright, her heart suddenly pounding and her memory ringing with Fennoc's parting words to get in early.

The evening was noticeably darker now. The wind whistled sharper.

Had she fallen asleep?

Bracing herself, she looked across the field to where the crackling had been, hoping she wouldn't see anything resembling the Wild Huntmaster or his minions.

Instead, through the darkness, Emily saw another form.

She couldn't make out much detail due to the way the shadows clung to the figure, but she saw enough.

A masculine shape. A tattered, out-of-style baseball uniform.

Human.

Recognition made her stomach clench. It was the Designated Hitter. The Unseelie Court's best player.

"Get out of here!" she screamed, standing up. "Don't you dare spy on our practice!"

She took a step toward the almost spectral form.

A moment later, the shadowy form disappeared into the darkness and, if it weren't for the pattern of cleat prints left behind, Emily might have doubted that the spy had ever been there. It was that pattern — which left behind a big platter of flattened thistle brush — that let her know the Unseelie spy had been there the whole time.

Damn it, she thought, clenching her fists into balls.

The idea of being spied on burned in her gut.

She should have known better. The reigning champions and their evil queen would never lie back and let the Small Folk rise above their station without some interference.

But the joke was on them, because underhanded moves like that always got Emily's blood pumping. It was the same when Callie McMaster's dad openly sponsored the Bulldogs, getting his daughter's team the best equipment money could buy. The idea bugged her now as it had then. McMasters Ball and Glove. What kind of overly-fancy name was that for a company? Pretentious, anyone? Couldn't it just be a good-old sporting goods store and be done with it?

Whatever.

The game that had followed the sponsorship had been the closest Emily had ever come to beating Callie during their high school years. The closest until the one that had landed her here, that was.

Back then, she'd been trying to carry the whole team all by herself, and it hadn't been about having fun anymore.

It had been about winning. And she'd lost.

A gust of wind blew, and the crescent moon rose over the tree line. She glanced over her shoulder and into the deep forest, convincing herself that she was truly alone now.

The shadow-cloaked Designated Hitter was really gone.

Time to go, she thought. It was getting dark.

Fennoc would kill her if she got lost.

CHAPTER TEN

Despite Emily's newfound drive and equally fresh sense of cohesion with her team, she was finding their next game even harder to adjust to than the one they'd played against the River Kin.

Their opponents this time were the Hag Sisters of the Wood, a team that fully encompassed the spectrum of "witchy." The field was swarming with black-clad women, from slinky shadow-draped seductresses to back-bent crones who cradled baseballs as if they were poisoned apples, and all of them were throwing what Fennoc and the team called "minor magics" around like buckets of Halloween candy in the posh neighborhoods of Marion. Feathery wings sprouted from a few, especially those playing the outfield. Their infield chatter was loud and screechy.

The stands were full once again, but the upper spot with the thrones remained empty of all but shadows. Even the Web Gem itself was gone, taken away by its current owner.

Apparently, this game amongst the lower peoples of the Realm wasn't worth the Unseelie Queen's time. But Emily was glad of it, to be honest. Without the burning stare of the Queen to distract her or the whispering lure of the trophy they sought throwing her off balance, she could focus on the baseball itself.

They were entering the bottom of the first inning now, having managed to keep the Hags from scoring somehow, despite all that witchy magic their opponents were freely working.

Emily watched from the dugout as Shady Marie walked nervously up to the plate as their first hitter. She'd given the dryad a firm clap on the shoulder and a "you got this" when Fennoc had read out the lineup, and had gotten a shy smile in return. Practice the last few days had gone well, and Shady Marie in particular had really improved her control over where the ball went after she hit it.

But when the first pitch came and Shady Marie started a promising swing, the Hag Sister in left field gave a harpy scream that caused the line drive off the bat to dip down and go foul.

"That's totally cheating!" Emily shouted, jumping up from her spot on the bench to point at the offending player. "Come on, umpire! Are you blind?"

"It's not cheating," said Maddoc. "Not here."

"What do you mean, not here? You can't do that kind of thing and get away with it. That was going to be a sure double." A double would have been such a great start, something the whole team could rally around.

"Oh, don't get me wrong, Miss Em. The Hags will cheat at the drop of a hat, but using your innate abilities isn't cheating in the Fairy Series. You are who you are."

Emily glared out over the field, seeing the way the Hag Sisters took their positions as Nash went to the plate next. Being gnome-short and possessing a fair eye, Nash should be a natural to lead the Fairy Leagues in walks if he could just keep from getting too excited about swinging. Emily had been working with him on keeping a squat stance, which limited his strike zone even further.

The first pitch was a ball.

"Innate abilities," Emily said. "What innate abilities do we have?"

"I can disappear into my tree," said Shady Marie, as she returned to the bench. At least she didn't look too bummed about the lost hit.

"I love a good practical joke," Maddoc said, guffawing at whatever had run through his mind at the moment. He was sitting with a rounded cord of wood in his hand, swinging it a few times in preparation to go up to hit next.

"If only you were any good at them," Fennoc said with a sniff of disdain as he riffled through the papers on his slab of bark.

"Like you're any better."

"A far sight quicker with the sleight of hand than you are, brother."

"Harumpf."

"Enough," Emily said. "No more bickering between you two or I'll have to send you to bed without your suppers," she *tsk-tsk*ed to good laughter from the team. "All right," she said. "What else?"

"We sing," said Shayla and Twy, the two nymph sisters who filled out the team as bench players.

"Nash digs tunnels quite... *enthusiastically*," Fennoc added, pointing to the gnome at bat, who had just taken a fourth straight ball and was waddling toward first base.

Maddoc stood and went to the plate.

"I like to dance," Izusa said. He did a plié, and then a full turn on one toe before finishing with something that Emily thought might be *the hustle*. His wings glistened pleasingly throughout, never throwing blinding dazzles at his viewers.

Emily sighed. "Not a lot to work with."

"It makes me feel good," Izusa said, defensively. "And people like it."

"It's true. Izusa is always a big draw at the Winter Festival."

"And the sisters rule the Spring Rites, too, Master Fennoc," Izusa added. "Don't you forget it. Their voices are magical all by themselves!"

The crack of lumber on ball rang out over the Other Field as Maddoc got hold of one. He pulled it foul, though. The ball disappeared into the woods, only to be retrieved by an elven sylph. "Found it!" She returned the ball to the Hag Sister pitcher, who proceeded to screech and rub it up, an action Emily understood was the application of magic to the ball.

Emily sighed and grabbed a bat. She would hit next.

The next pitch was a strike, the second on Maddoc. One more and he would be out.

"Come on, Mads. It's no better than a spitball," she said under her breath.

She stopped then.

The Hag Sister's screech still rang in her ears, turning her stomach to acid. But she'd been struck with an idea.

The screech was sound. Mr. Donaldson's science class had said sound was a wave. She hadn't really paid attention to a lot of that class, but that part had settled into her because she liked to imagine the sounds of the crowd rising and falling like ocean tides.

Waves could cancel out, though. That much she remembered.

She turned to the sisters.

"You sing?"

"Of course, silly," Shayla answered.

"Come here. Both of you."

On the field, the ball had been returned to the pitcher. Shayla and Twy floated over to stand next to Emily.

"No time to dilly-dally," she said. "When the pitcher bends to do her screeching, I want you to sing a tone that cancels out the Hag's screech. Can you do that?"

Twy started to answer, but the pitcher was already bringing the ball to her mouth.

"Now!" Emily said.

The sisters sang, but their pitch was high. The song rolled over the field and crashed into the screech to create a tonal mess that made Emily's stomach roll.

The Hag Sister turned her gaze to the Small Folk's dugout so abruptly the brim of her black cap twisted in the breeze. Her glowing green eyes flared with astonishment.

But she shook it off quickly and held the ball up once more to receive another screech.

"Again!" Emily said.

The nymphs sang again, this time more boldly, coming to understand their role.

The pitcher put her head back and screamed. "The little fools cheat!"

The umpire put his monocle to his one eye, then pulled out his tattered rule book — a tome of arcane mysteries if Emily had ever seen one.

"Innate magic," the cyclops said, running a finger along the page. "I can't see anything that says the nymphs can't use their magic to block other magic. I say play on."

The Hag screamed again.

"We're playing under protest!"

"Understood and registered," the umpire said. "So play on."

Maddoc took his position in the box and waggled his log of a bat. The pitch came in, and he plastered a rocket into left field that moved Nash to second base.

Emily pumped her fist in the air as all the Small Folk cheered. "Yes, Maddoc! Go, Nash!"

She turned to the nymphs, her cheeks aching from smiling so wide. "Every pitch," she said. "You got that? We don't have much to help us, but if we work on it, maybe we can at least make this game a fair fight and a *good game*. Let the best *baseball* team win!"

Shayla gave a sharp little nod, and Twy followed up.

Emily pounded her bat against her palm as she approached the plate. As she adjusted her new uniform across her shoulders, the pitcher began her screech. But the Small Folk's counter weapon crashed her party.

The first pitch was probably supposed to have been a curveball, but it didn't curve, and Emily got good wood on it. The ball skipped down the third base line, past the defender and into the corner.

"Run!" she called to Nash, whose little legs were churning as hard as he could churn them. His cap flew off his head as he rounded third and raced for home.

The ball came in, the throw closer than it probably should have been — but Nash dove headfirst into the dark dirt at home plate and slid his chest across before the catcher could apply the tag.

Nash gave himself a pumped-up "safe" signal just as the umpire was doing the same. He popped up, shirt filled with dirt and a beaming smile across his wide lips.

"Yeah!" he called, fists in the air.

Maddoc had made it to third on the throw.

Emily, too caught up in the moment, had stayed too close to first base, so didn't advance. But she wasn't even bothered about it. She was having *fun* for the first time since Mom had gotten sick.

She called out to her teammate. "Great job, Nash! Beautiful slide!"

The gnome beamed even more brightly.

After things settled, Emily took a careful lead at first base. Now that things were moving, she didn't want to get picked off.

Eager Greeven stepped up to bat, but this time the pitcher didn't even try to screech her spitball magic.

ONCE THE HAG Sisters understood that their magic wasn't going to get them as far as it normally did, they knuckled down. They weren't a horrible baseball team, just not a great one. And, yes, they still managed to pull a few fast ones, enchanting their gloves between innings to catch anything the Small Folk hit once, and later using a magicked apple to convince the Cyclops that a fair ball was foul. Emily successfully argued that that one really was cheating, and the guilty player was kicked out of the game. The Hags scored the tying run in the third inning, and after the Small Folk got a run on a sacrifice bunt and an error an inning later (true small ball for the win, Emily thought), the Hags' cleanup hitter got to Emily for a homer in the fifth.

After nine innings, the game was tied up again.

Two and a half extra innings later, nothing had changed.

When Emily returned to the dugout, she saw the team's fatigue in the way everyone's energy had flagged. It worried her. To be so close and then fall would be devastating. But the truth was the truth. Nash, the catcher, could barely drag himself to the dugout, and Shady Marie was walking the whole way back in from the outfield, stiffening up as if she were already back in her tree. The sister's voices were growing ragged.

They needed a boost, Emily realized.

And this was her team.

"We're doing great, everyone. That's not a bad team over there, you know?" she said, pointing to the opponents' bench. "I'm soooooo proud of us. That was a great double play Delananey! And the way you backed up Nash's bad throw to first saved us a run. We're really working together. This is so much fun to watch!"

"I think we're still going to lose, though," Shayla said, her voice cracking. "I don't think we can last much longer."

"So what if we lose, right?" Emily said, barely believing the words coming from her mouth until she heard them. Those words were right, though. "This is our team. And our team is going to be about reclaiming the fun of baseball. Win or lose, this has been a great game to play in. It's one we can tell people great stories from."

"Just think of the epic tale we can get from little Greeven actually getting his bat on a ball for once!" Fennoc interrupted, giving a soft, almost fatherly chuckle. "Who among us has ever seen an elf split his pants running to get on base before?"

"The tale would be even better if I'd been safe," Greeven grumbled as he plucked at said pants.

"That's in the next chapter!" Emily said.

The rest of the team seemed to brighten.

"Seriously, guys. This has been a really fun game, so let's not spoil it by worrying about losing. Stay together, I say. Let's have fun. If we play well enough, we'll win. Otherwise, we'll get 'em next game."

"I like it, Miss Em," Nash said, sitting a little taller. "This *is* fun."

"Everyone gather around me," Emily said, putting her hand out like Coach A used to do. "Gather around and put your hand on mine." After a moment, everyone did, the pixies fluttering their gossamer wings and creating a kaleidoscope of a cover. "One, two, three, team, right?" she said. "Everyone ready?"

Emily waited a beat. Then:

"One, two, three ... team!"

Emily raised her hand into the air and the whole team followed, yelling at the same time and drawing stares from the Hags and from the crowd that remained to watch.

Emily went to Shayla. "Make sure you and Twy stay hydrated, all right?"

Emily was up first, and she drilled a single to left.

Delananey struck out, but Izusa followed up with a lucky bloop to right field that the Hag Sister botched, putting Emily on third base and Izusa at first.

Emily watched the pitcher glance for the fourth or fifth time at the nymph sisters as they prepared to sing their counter spell.

There was something to the pitcher's expression, she noticed this time. A sense of longing. A sense of something Emily had seen in the halls in between classes ever since she'd started high school as all the pretty people looked at one another.

"Time out!" she called.

The umpire raised his hand, and Emily jogged to the dugout.

Fennoc emerged to greet her, chewing on his standard blade of grass that sprouted from one side of his mouth.

"I want you to put a pinch runner in for Izusa," Emily said.

"Pinch runner? Why?"

"The right question isn't why, Fennoc. It's who?"

"All right, I'll bite. Who?"

"Twy."

"Twy? She's a bench player. And Izusa is just as fast as Twy."

"I don't care about her speed."

"I don't understand."

"Trust me," Emily said.

Fennoc started to argue, but then simply rucked up the fur at the neckline of his pristine uniform and turned to the bench.

"Twy," he said. "Get in there and run."

As Fennoc reported the substitution to the umpire, Emily walked the surprised Twy to her position at first base.

"Don't get too far off," she whispered. "But focus on the pitcher. And this time, when you sing, sing something about pure longing."

"I don't understand, Miss Em."

Emily put her arm around Twy's thin waist and suppressed a twinge of envy. The nymph was amazingly beautiful, as were so many creatures in Fairy World. It was enough to depress her if she let her mind run. Being so close to such otherworldly perfection made it more than obvious that, even if she could be "cute" on her best day, Emily would never be model material.

"If you were sirens, you and your sister would draw ships from the seven seas," she said to Twy. "But now I just need you to distract the pitcher. She's been looking at you differently ever since the first inning, and I totally understand why."

Twy blushed.

"Innate ability," Emily said. "You are who you are, right? Stand on first, sing, and attract attention."

"What are you going to do?"

Emily gave a smile so mischievous it would have done Fennoc proud. "I'm going to steal home."

A MINUTE LATER, it all played out.

Twy stood on first as siren-like as if she truly were on a desolate island. As the pitcher took her stretch, Twy's song rose, and her aura glowed so warmly it smelled of a summer day. The pitcher glanced over once, then a second, longer time.

When the Hag's glance became a mesmerized gaze, Emily broke for home.

The wind rustled around her helmet.

The ground flew under her feet, and she heard chanting and music as the dancing lights of Fairyland dipped and dived. Air filled her lungs. The rise of voices came like a roaring wave. From the corner of her eye, Emily saw the pitcher break her trance.

The Hag threw toward home, but Emily could already feel her own success.

The plate glittered with golden rays of pure magic. Pure baseball.

She slid, feet first like her mom had taught her.

A cloud of soily dust rose.

Her foot crossed the plate as, a moment later, the ball arrived — too late.

"Safe!" the umpire called, his arms outstretched wide.

Emily yelled in triumph, and before she knew it, her teammates had thrown themselves over her, celebrating so hard she almost couldn't breathe.

It was okay, though.

They had won.

Playing together, her team had won.

And they'd had so much fun doing it.

CHAPTER

ELEVEN

The next morning, Emily woke with anticipation thrumming through her. It was a rainy day, the first she'd experienced here in Fairyland. The drops came down with a soft, musical cadence, sending a cool scent wafting through the air. Usually, rain made her sleepy and lethargic. Now it woke her fully, leaving her invigorated for a great day of baseball.

But instead of putting on her Small Folk uniform and heading out to play a game or even practice with her team, she selected a pretty green dress Mellica and Jessebel had made for her by magicking some leaves together. The end result wasn't "wild girl of the forest" so much as "cute strappy sundress, perfect for going to a baseball game."

Back home, she wouldn't have been brave enough to wear anything like it. But here she was focusing on enjoying baseball. Why shouldn't that include looking pretty while attending a game? She shoved the remembered snickers to the back of her mind as she put it on.

She was going to be up in the stands today, one of the spectators of these strange fairy matches for the first time. She'd skipped previous games played by other teams in favor of running extra practices with the then-floundering Small Folk, helping them improve their skills to something they could be proud of.

And all that extra work had paid off. She still got a thrill when she thought back on yesterday's game. Yesterday's *victory,* she amended. The Small Folk, and she, had earned a day off.

She was looking forward to seeing what the experience was like from inside those fancy covered benches. She was especially looking forward to getting her first glimpse of how the Unseelie Court played.

They were up against the Hag Sisters today. After the challenge the Sisters had put up yesterday, Emily expected it would be a fantastic game.

But when she headed for the Other Field, Fennoc stopped her.

"Nay, Miss Em. The Unseelie Court never plays off their own turf. Today we make for Unseelie Pitch."

He looked wary and nervous as he said it, twirling his large mushroom-shaped umbrella so raindrops flew off the edges.

Emily frowned. None of the other teams had played anywhere besides the Other Field. It wasn't the Small Folk's home field, or anything. She'd thought it was simply the field of the entire Fairy Realm. "That's unfair."

"May as well complain about the rain," he said, lifting one hand in a disgruntled shrug, looking as if he would, in fact, like to complain about the current drizzle. He chewed his ever-present grass blade more vigorously than usual. "The Queen got it that way using one of her many boons from the Web Gem. No turning back now."

Emily's mood threatened to turn as gray and dreary as the weather, but she shoved the inner rain clouds away. Who cared if the Unseelie Court had even more advantages than she'd previously thought? Today was a good chance to do some counter-reconnaissance as well as enjoy a game. Surely the Unseelie Court wouldn't ruin the game day experience for their spectators.

And so she found herself marching through the rain alongside the rest of her team, heading through the dark woods she'd run into during her first day here. At first, it wasn't so bad. The forest was damp and muddy, and the wet leaves slick on the ground, but Nash and Shady Marie worked a spell in tandem that helped lay a smoother path.

But then Shady Marie split off from the group with a jaw-cracking yawn. "I'm so tired from last night's party. If I don't get some rest I'll just stiffen up, and you'll have a tree sitting next to you on the bench. People will complain I'm blocking the view."

But Emily detected a hint of evasion in the dryad's too-casual manner of calling off. Greeven had also begged off after breakfast, claiming a headache after so much concentration on hitting the ball yesterday.

Put together, these nervous behaviors painted an ominous picture. What, exactly, was she about to experience in the Unseelie Court? At least she wasn't going alone. Most of the team was still with her, and if not overly enthusiastic, still suitably excited for the day. Really, whatever the situation, it couldn't be so bad.

As they continued deeper into the forest, the darkness thickened, and the smells of damp and decay got stronger. An acrid tang like old blood wove its way in as they passed a twiggy bramble, making Emily wrinkle her nose.

"I see the Wild Hunt has been through here," grumbled Maddoc. "They always leave such a mess."

Emily carefully averted her eyes from whatever mangled remains lay in the thicket.

The trees grew gnarled and twisted here, their bare branches grasping like greedy talons. Dark shapes flitted through the skeletal canopy, deadly on silent wings. Here and there in the murk, tiny red lights blinked in and out of existence, less like the charming fairy lights she was used to and more like some hungry wild thing looking for its next meal.

And from somewhere just behind them, something let out a

shrill cackle. But when Emily whipped around to see what was about to attack, she found absolutely nothing.

By the time she and the Small Folk reached Unseelie Pitch, her hackles were thoroughly raised. And once she entered the stands she fully understood why Shady Marie and Greeven had called off. She wondered that so many of her teammates had agreed to come at all.

Unseelie Pitch was monstrous in multiple senses of the word.

Larger even than a major league field, it made players entering it feel meek and insignificant, hardly a good setup for stellar play. The grass was neatly kept, but of an unsettling purple color, and it undulated without the aid of any breeze. The dirt of the infield was straight black, making the baselines, which were laid with something that looked like seaweed, glow like eerie ghost light.

The bases, which were stony blocks at the Other Field, appeared to be more like those in the world Emily had grown up in, formed of white canvas or other cloth. But they writhed and bubbled now and again, making Emily ponder what might be trapped inside.

Home plate looked like it would be better used as a gravestone.

The dugouts were built like mausoleums, complete with carved gargoyles in various poses of agony and fury.

On the field, a quintet of musicians played a pregame dirge.

And when Emily went to settle into her seat on the long, marble benches for spectators, her hand met with a patch of unidentifiable black slime. As she tried to scrape it off on the edge of her seat, it started to put out little amoeba-like pseudopods.

"Eugh," she said, scraping harder.

The shrill cackle she'd heard in the forest rang out again, and a pair of griffon-like creatures soared out of the black storm clouds gathered overhead. They bore intricate wooden boxes in their sharp talons. As they swooped down over the gathering crowd, screaming, the smell that leaked from those boxes made Emily gag.

Having carefully selected a seat on the bench behind her, Fennoc folded his umbrella and placed it neatly below his feet. "I'd suggest avoiding the snack vendors if I were you. Not only does the food of the Unseelie Court have a habit of trapping mortal souls here, it tastes bad, too."

"*That,*" Emily said, still holding her nose, "is way worse than *bad.* But thanks for the warning."

Nash came to sit on Emily's left, and Mellica flitted into the seat at her right, both looking a bit like hunted animals. Granted, the Wild Hunt was here in the stands, too, a few sections over from the one the Small Folk had chosen. The hunters kept leering over, showing flashes of teeth and throwing their heads back to add their own howls and yips to the dark cacophony of the denizens of the Unseelie Court.

"They look like they're having a good time, anyway," Emily muttered. She watched as the hunt leader waved down one of the snack-bearing griffons.

Even here, other members of the Small Folk worked as servants, though they trembled with fear as they adjusted seats and picked up refuse. One poor gnome shivered and cried while mopping up a spill, the Unseelie spectator who'd dropped his foul drink shouting curses at her all the while.

Emily ground her teeth and looked away, feeling powerless, but also smaller for her own lack of response.

Essie, bereft of her usual spot in Greeven's pocket, climbed up onto Emily's off shoulder and tangled her tiny fingers into her hair for stability. "I hope it will be a close game today," she squeaked, sounding uncertain. "The Unseelie Court rarely loses."

"The Hag Sisters are good, too," Emily replied as the Unseelie players emerged from their crypt-like dugout. "I'm sure it will be a good game."

As she watched the players take their positions, though, she became less sure.

The top fairy team looked very good as they threw the ball around the infield. They were all big and all athletic. Muscle-bound trolls with glowing coals for eyes. Rabid werewolves easily sliding between their man-shapes and animal-shapes, slavering and growling all the while. Even a long-nailed, sharp-hooved, ram-horned satyr, the terrifying cousin to Fennoc and Maddoc's more gentle race. Emily shuddered to imagine how her entry to this world would have gone had *that* creature been the one to call her across. In the outfield, shadowy entities with limbs that were entirely too long loped like gazelles.

The roster of monsters was clearly a well-oiled machine. The players' movements seemed almost choreographed, they were so precise. No one dropped a ball. Every toss hit the receiver's mitt with an uncanny aura of perfection, the balls leaving waves of scintillating magic in their wakes. The navy-and-silver-toned uniforms flashed with magical trim, the numbers pulsing and seemingly riding on their jerseys rather than having been sewn on.

And in the home team dugout sat the Unseelie Queen, running her fingers lightly over the Web Gem, which was positioned beside her, sending a rainbow of colors running through it. Then she smirked over at a deeper darkness further inside the dugout.

The Designated Hitter.

The mortal. The player that everyone said had put the Unseelie team into Yankee territory — if not quite unbeatable, at least the club that everyone loved to hate. The problem, of course, was that hate them or love them, the Yankees *always* had the best players, and they were *always* good.

An uncomfortable pang crossed Emily's conscience.

He'd spied on her practice sessions with the Small Folk. He was the enemy. But the Designated Hitter seemed lonely, sitting there while his supposed teammates were out being monstrous on the field.

"Does he have a name?" Emily said.

"Designated Hitter," Nash replied.

"I mean, does he have a name other than his position?"

"I'm sure he does, Miss Em," Mellica added. "But you remember about true names, right? The only one who knows his true name is the Queen, and she guards the secret jealously."

Emily grimaced. She'd kind of forgotten, having gotten used to going by "Miss Em" rather than her real name. But knowing someone's true name gave you power over that person here in Fairyland.

She looked at the Designated Hitter again and felt that same sad despair. What would it be like to only ever hear your name spoken by your captor? To have everyone else refer to you only as your compelled role? Of course, exactly how different was her own situation? A glance down the row at her teammates answered that question to a greater degree, but the fact remained that, despite their brighter, cheerier demeanors compared to the Unseelie Courters, the Small Folk had brought her here without her consent. And as she watched the Designated Hitter stretch in preparation for the game, a sense of the confinement he must feel settled over her like a shroud.

Neither one of them could go home.

Still, feeling guilty for her own much better luck, she again scanned her teammates, who were busy chattering and watching the field as the umpire appeared.

The umpire who was accompanied by a cloud of black fog, a rattling of wagon wheels, and a bone-chilling whinny from what could only be described as a demon horse. The crack of a whip ricocheted across the field and through the stands, and a thready heartbeat later, the umpire stepped down from her terrifying carriage.

Her garb was dark and bloodstained, with a cloak of black whipping around in the wailing breeze that accompanied her arrival. A heavy gauntlet covered one hand, but the other hand was uncovered, revealing that it was fine and bony, but wretchedly long and oddly grotesque, tipped in black nails that were dripping with an unidentified ichor.

Within that hand she carried her own severed head, her fingers wrapped in corded bolts of writhing hair.

"Are you freaking serious right now?" Emily said. "And I thought a cyclops was pushing it."

"'Tis home field advantage to choose the umpire," said Nash forlornly.

Mellica shuddered, sending a shower of pixie dust over the bench. “I wish they hadn’t chosen a Dullahan, though. They’re so creepy!”

Emily whole-heartedly agreed. As the Unseelie Queen glided over to take the pitcher’s mound, the umpire lifted that one delicate, corpse-like hand and held forth her head. Her disembodied voice hissed directly into Emily’s ear. “*Plaaay baaall.*”

From the way everyone around her hunched their shoulders around their ears, the same thing was happening to them, too.

For better or for worse, the game was underway.

At least the rain had stopped.

THE SCORE ENDED UP 13-1, the Unseelies the obvious victors.

Their Queen was a devastating pitcher, made even more so without the burden of having to devote any time to improving her batting. The Hags hadn’t managed even a single hit — scoring their run on a walk, an error, and a sacrifice fly.

The Designated Hitter, meanwhile, hit two balls out of the park, and drove another line drive so hard it put a hole in the wooden fence in center field. Magic had flowed like water, but it was clear that the Unseelies didn’t really need it. The Hags had been done even before they stepped on the field.

“After all that, I can’t see us beating them,” said Izusa, his pixie wings drooping as if he felt he’d never dance again. His skin tone had darkened to purple.

Essie, who’d been crying into Emily’s hair, lifted her head with a tearful sniff. “We barely took the win from the Hags yesterday, and what the Unseelies just did to them...” she wailed, then buried her head back into her shoulder to cry again. At least the little brownie’s tears were only teeny drops rather than a messy torrent.

Emily pulled the brownie off her shoulder and cupped her in her hand.

She felt her teammates' despondency inside her own veins, too. The Unseelie display had been terrifyingly, paralyzingly impressive. They'd dominated in all aspects of the game and had barely gotten their uniforms mussed. But looking at her teammates' drawn faces — including Fennoc's — sent a flare of anger up her spine.

"We can't let this get us down," she said as they were preparing for the long trek back to their home woods. "I'm serious," she added when everyone stopped to look at her. They needed this, she realized. After a massacre like the one they'd just witnessed, they needed someone to tell them everything was going to be all right.

They'd called for her specifically so they could have a chance against these dominating monsters.

And, despite the unilateral nature of the Small Folk's initial actions, she'd agreed to join them now. She had donned the Small Folk's uniform of her own free will.

With her, they'd got more than a shackled Designated Hitter. She was their leader now. It was up to her.

"We're going to beat these guys. I know we are. Because when we face the Unseelie Court ourselves, we are gonna play the best game of baseball this creepy pitch has ever seen."

She looked around the horrifying expanse of Unseelie Pitch.

"This place got to the Hags, you know? But we've scoped them out now. We know what to expect. Their scare tactics won't work on us."

The team's gaze followed her motion as she waved her free arm around, still cupping Essie in her other hand.

"It *is* a very big park," Nash said. "Not to mention the unpleasant color of the dirt and grass."

"And the trek through the court looms cold," Izusa added, shivering and rubbing his long fingers over his graceful arms.

"But we've just proved we can deal with it, right?" Emily said.

Maddoc brayed a positive bleat. "That we have," he said.

"See what I mean?" Emily responded. "We just have to focus. The Unseelie players are good, of course, but they don't have to even try if we're just going to collapse because of this place." She gazed over the field again. "We have to remember all this spooky stuff is nothing more than set dressing. Underneath, it's just a baseball field. And it should be fun to be on a baseball field, not intimidating."

"I like that, Miss Em," Fennoc said.

"I like that a lot," added Maddoc.

Emily grinned. "We've got a game tomorrow against the Wild Hunt, but we can use the trip back home now to get ourselves used to this Unseelie Court pitch. We'll be back, after all. I know we will. We're going to play baseball, and win or lose, we're going to have so much fun. So, I say we practice feeling like ourselves now."

Essie gave a shrill cheer. "One, two, three, team!" she called, both arms lifted into the air.

The team laughed, a sound of relief. Izusa even did a pirouette to lighten the mood further.

As they filed out, Emily took a deep breath to try to relax.

She knew her advice had been great. Now she hoped she would be able to follow it.

CHAPTER TWELVE

The Unicorns were in the middle of practice when Callie McMasters arrived.

She could barely believe she was here in broad daylight. Anyone could see her, and even boiling alive in her nondescript brown leather jacket to mask her shape and hiding her face with a sweat-soaked White Sox hat pulled down low over her eyes, she was sure she was still easily identifiable as The Enemy. It would be okay, she thought. As long as nothing got back to her Marion teammates, everything would be fine. But the magic she'd felt while playing on their field three days ago hadn't stopped sparking in her brain. Ideas had sprouted one after another, until the inner workings of her mind resembled an autumn corn maze. A corn maze full of fairies, of all things.

The recurrence of these visions annoyed her at first.

Made her think she was going crazy. Fairies? Really, Callie? *Fairies?*

She had never really bought into the Unicorn kid's fervor for the idea, but after the game the flashes grew stronger every moment, and pretty soon it was clear that something was going on. Something real.

The sensations grew from brief instants of scintillating insights to deeper moments where the images came accompanied with sounds and smells, and a sensation she could only describe as wild. As these flashes came they gave her a sense of excitement. A sense of freedom, maybe. A feeling that there were things she didn't understand about how the world worked, and that these things were worth understanding. The flashes, complete with wide and open aromas that might be clean air or might be touched with cinnamon or spice, well, they made her curious. And they made her feel more alive than ever.

Under all that, Callie McMasters felt a power as strong as baseball.

Through that power, she felt Emily DeWitt.

The feeling was enough that she'd actually gone to the library to do some research.

Research that had been very much like doing book reports, only without the need to do the report-writing part—which she found was interesting. Without the need to write a stupid report looming over her head like a guillotine, she found the process almost fun. Learning about fairy lore would have been fascinating if it wasn't for the circumstance. She spent hours digging through "nonfiction" tomes and other fairy tales. She found herself so engrossed in a book about Tam Lin that she had to put it aside to read later so she could focus on her real work.

Through it all, she laid her new learning over the sensations she'd gotten during the game.

And she believed now.

Not only did fairies exist, but they'd somehow turned this joke of a high school baseball team's field into a portal and used it to kidnap the best ball player that field had seen in probably decades.

Fairies seemed kind of romantic almost.

Kind of sexy, if she let herself go that far. The ideas in these books were oddly attractive in ways she didn't really understand. All her friends were talking about guys and girls and hooking up. Maybe that's how they felt. Or maybe that was why they felt like they felt. Fairy culture seemed quite bold. The idea of wanting things so publicly made her almost jealous.

Last night, she'd followed her intuition, gotten in the Audi that she knew her dad had gifted her as much so that she could drive herself to her own games as because it "promoted the aura of success around the McMasters name," and driven through DeWitt's neighborhood.

She'd slowed as she turned the corner onto the right street then idled at the curb beside her rival's driveway. She'd watched through a bay window, completely unnoticed, as Mr. DeWitt had made himself a microwave dinner, moving like a zombie, running his hand through his short hair and breathing in ragged deep breaths that Callie could see held a deepening sadness.

Police efforts to find Emily had cooled down, but Callie still saw DeWitt's dad on advertisements and on various sites she followed. Three times he'd refreshed the reward fliers he'd posted around town and at the schools.

She watched him sit at the kitchen table and eat the meal while shuffling through papers — obviously more police reports.

She sat there long enough for the sun to fully go down and the streetlamps to flicker on as if each light held a savage little fairy of its own. When she'd pulled away, her jaw ached from clenching.

Her own dad wouldn't even notice when she came home late.

Well, those fairies better get their twee little twinkles all in a row, she thought now as she approached Unicorn Field and loitered at the fence line, waiting impatiently for the Pattersonville West team's practice to wrap up. Callie McMasters was coming to take her best rival back.

She'd learned plenty during the game she'd deliberately thrown, enough to start putting pieces together. Not that she was naïve enough now to think all the fairies were of the Tinkerbell variety.

Even before all that research, she'd peeked into a Grimm's Fairytales tome once or twice as an impressionable kid. Still, she liked to keep a certain haughty frame of mind when preparing to face someone she had a personal grudge against.

She also liked the idea of taking advantage of the element of surprise.

Which was why she was here, on an unseasonably hot day in April, watching the Unicorns practice from her place tucked into the shadows.

As she watched, her enthusiasm to share her idea soured into dread for all the work that lay ahead. Watching proved beyond doubt that, without DeWitt, the Unicorns were a hapless bunch. No wonder her Bulldog teammates had picked up that she'd not even been trying last game. There was no way this pack of baby giraffes could have beaten the Bulldogs otherwise.

Patsy Pell was the first to notice Callie, a grimace making the goth girl's nose wrinkle under her cap's bill.

Callie gave a two-fingered wave and leaned against the brick of the concessions stand, trying to shift deeper into the sliver of shade to stay out of the sun.

Finally, the coach called an end, and the practice broke up.

Most of the Unicorns followed their coach into the lockers, but Patsy came striding purposely towards Callie. Jake followed her, pulling his catcher's mask off his face and making his hair stand in spikes that dripped a trail of sweat behind him.

Up close, Patsy's glare looked strange without her eyeliner. "What are you doing here? I thought we agreed that you could help, but we didn't want anyone linking us to a Bulldog."

A thousand snarky replies ran through Callie's head, but the image of Emily's father poring over police documentation wouldn't leave her mind's eye, and she discarded them all.

"Don't get your cleats all twisted up, Patsy. We've got too much work to do to waste our energy flapping our jaws," Callie said instead.

"Work?" Patsy challenged.

Callie sighed a breath, tried to look casually over toward left field, then turned back to gaze first at Jake, then Patsy.

"I think I know how to open the fairy ring," she said.

That shut them up, at least.

"I'd like to talk to the team," she said, motioning with her gaze to where Coach Amabe was collecting up equipment. "Alone."

It took a half hour before Coach Amabe left the field.

While they waited, the small group of Unicorns Callie had been working with draped themselves over the bleachers, casually hanging out as the afternoon burned on, eating power bars and laughing as if they weren't preparing to attempt something like magic.

Callie waited underneath the stands, soaking up as much dark shade as she could, glaring up through the slats whenever power bar crumbs rained down on her.

The moment their coach left, she clambered up top and ditched the jacket.

"Okay, listen up," she said, rubbing her hands against her jeans to get the sweat off them. "That last game our teams played against each other was hugely helpful."

"Hey, we're happy to cream your team any time you need," Jamal said. He held both hands up for Patsy and Benji to high five.

Callie was not amused. "Dude. I was grooving every pitch and you still struggled to win. And I've been watching you practice. You guys are horrible. All of you."

"I thought you were here to help find Emily," Patsy said. "Not insult us."

"That's the problem," Callie snapped back. "I'm sure we can get DeWitt back, but it's going to require as many of you as possible to get good at connecting with at least the easy lobs I *gave* you throughout that whole game. We can't pretend you're good at baseball when you're not."

She glared around the group, keeping the pressure up until even Patsy looked abashed.

"All right," Benji said, smoothing their pleated skirt over their knees. "How do we open the gate, and what, specifically, do you need from us?"

Callie made herself speak slowly and calmly. "It's simple, really. Each time I got one of you Unicorns to actually hit the ball, I felt the magic flare. When it was a better hit, I could see the power like a burst of light. So, I did some research," she said, looking directly at Benji now. "You are right. It's here. The gate to another field. I can see it and feel it now. It's real, just like you said. I think it's something that's always been happening, and now that it's been pointed out, I can't keep from seeing it."

"Where are you going with this, McMasters?" Patsy said.

"DeWitt disappeared after hitting her homer. But when I knocked Jammy's fastball into freaking orbit, I didn't feel a thing."

Jamal hunched in on himself like a turtle withdrawing into its shell.

"So?" Patsy prodded again.

Callie took a breath. Steady. Calm. She needed these kids on her side, not hating her guts even more than they already did. "So, what I need — what *we* need — is for a Unicorn player to hit a home run. That's it. I'm not sure how many we'll need, but it seems obvious that, at least sometimes, when a Unicorn homers, the gate opens. So, we make that happen, and — since we'll be ready for it — rather than get lost in the fairy realm, whoever hits it digs DeWitt out of the pit, then comes back."

She sat back and waited as the Unicorns digested this information. Would they put together the piece she'd worked out?

Surprisingly — and Callie knew it was mean of her to think so — Jake was the first one to get it.

"Um," he said, plucking absently at the sleeve of his Adventure

Time T-shirt. "I don't think anyone other than Emily has hit a home run here at Unicorn Field since, like, a really long time ago?"

Patsy made a disgusted noise in her throat. "Not a Unicorn player, that's for sure. Because we do suck without Emily."

"Maybe we'll need only one, then," Callie said.

Jamal shifted uncomfortably on the bleacher bench. "So, it's like that book they made us read in Sophomore English, *25 Catches* or something. Man, I was so excited when I thought we were gonna read about baseball."

"*Catch-22*," said Jake. "Unless one of us can hit a home run, we need Emily here in order to be able to save her, but if she were here, she wouldn't need saving in the first place."

Really, Callie was going to have to reassess her opinion of him as a big dumb teenage boy.

The dejection settling over the Unicorns was palpable.

But Callie wasn't going to let them give up that easily. "Right, it's a Catch-22. But, kiddos, you are in luck. Because you've got something better than DeWitt on your side."

"Yeah?" Patsy said. Even without eyeliner, her glare could cut glass. "What's that?"

Callie spread her arms wide and hoped her bravado was strong enough to cover the way her fingers were trembling. Highschool players looking to get scouted tended to frown upon self-sabotage. This moment right here could ruin her career single-handedly if any of her Bulldogs teammates ever heard about it.

"Me. I am going to train your lot up so good you won't be capable of letting anything past you. And then, since we play again in two weeks' time, I'm going to make sure at least one of you gets a chance to hit that home run."

The Unicorns furrowed their brows and glanced back and forth at one another.

"You're going to coach us?" Jamal said.

"In the flesh."

"We already have a coach." It was Patsy this time, arms crossed.

"And I'm sure he's a fine fellow. A real topflight human being. But he's a small ball guy, right? He's telling you to make contact, which you suck at, rather than coaching how to hit homers, which you need. Obviously."

The awkward, drawn-out moment of silence felt like it might never end.

But soon enough, all eyes fell on Patsy.

"All right," she said. "What do we have to lose?"

Callie breathed a sigh of relief.

"Grab your bats and gloves," she said, standing with new authority, trying to match the sense of leadership Coach Jameson always exhibited. "And text your parents. You're gonna be late for dinner these next few nights."

As the gang got itself prepared, Callie chewed her lip.

Two weeks, she thought.

Two weeks until she could stop working with the Unicorns. Two weeks until she could get DeWitt back, two weeks before she could face her true rival on the pitch and feel the rush of real baseball again.

Two weeks until she could put the image of Mr. DeWitt in his glowing kitchen window out of her head.

CHAPTER THIRTEEN

After the trip to Unseelie Pitch, the Other Field felt downright mundane.

The game against the Wild Hunt, however, was anything but. The players of the hunt were a growling, snarling gang. They were aggressive, too. Gristly and grimy. Odiferous to a member. Their uniforms were a mishmash of ill-fitting pelts and animal skins matted and clotted with grease and flora.

Thick chested Centaurs played the outfield.

Wiry, goblin-like Red Caps scurried around the infield, screeching and howling as they chased grounders with a rabid passion that made Emily's stomach feel weird. A satyr took the mound, pawing at it with cloven hooves, and peering into the batter's box with his golden-tinged eyes, grimacing in such a way as to show his tangled, snaggle-toothed fangs with every fastball.

Which was all he threw, really.

It was, however, a very good fastball.

From that same mound, Emily had confronted each Wild Hunt hitter in order and, as each arrived with thick clubs in hand, she recalled the sense of danger that had flooded over her that dark night when the leader of the Hunt had attempted to finagle her onto his roster.

"They seem pretty fanatical," she said to Fennoc after she had gotten out of the first inning.

"Indeed, they are, lassie," Fennoc replied. "They play like the future relies on it because that's what they believe."

She stared a question at him. "What do you mean?"

"So ye don't know Hunt lore, eh, Miss Em?" Nash said, throwing his little body onto the bench beside her with a solid *thunk* and kicking off his catcher's shin guards so he would be ready to hit if his turn came up.

"I guess I don't."

"They think that a Wild Hunt championship will portend success in the whole of the Fairy Realm," Nash said.

"Meaning, " Fennoc added, "that if the Wild Hunt were ever to wield the power of the Web Gem, they believe they could begin an assault on the very realm we live in."

"War?"

"That's what they say," Fennoc added.

"That seems a bit extreme, doesn't it?"

"Not to them."

"I mean, it's just a game."

Fennoc gave Emily a baleful stare. "Is it, now?" he said.

Emily started to respond, then stopped to think about what Fennoc and Nash were saying. There was more here than met the eye. That much she finally understood.

"Why do they think that?"

"The game is the only thing that's kept the Fairy Realm as it is," Nash replied. "In the old days things were quite bloody. Fairies of all types died in masses."

"Then the game came along," Fennoc said. "Now we meet on the field of battle this way."

Emily blinked in amazement.

"To the winner goes the spoils."

"The Web Gem," Emily said, suddenly putting the pieces together. "Fairyland uses the Web Gem to manage the peace."

"As it is," Fennoc said with a shrug.

"I think I need to hear more," Emily said.

"Maybe next inning, lassie," Fennoc replied, motioning Emily toward the field when she began to argue. "It is your turn to take the bat."

Emily set her jaw and grabbed her bat. Three pitches later, she connected to drive a grounder through the hole at second base and arrived at first safely.

"That was a fine hit," said the leader of the Wild Hunt, who played first base, with a wolfish grin. "More proof that you would be a good addition to our team."

Emily crinkled her nose, taking in the odor of something she thought might be old, clotted blood. She examined how the Huntsman's uniform was tight against his muscles, which was counter to the first time they had spoken. The image of loose robes billowing around him despite the dearth of woodland breeze filled her memory.

"Thank you," she said, not wanting to have her sporting nature questioned.

She took her lead as Maddoc stepped into the box.

The pitcher glanced her way, then threw over to first base. It wasn't a good move. She made it back so easily she didn't have to dive. Regardless, the Huntsman slapped the ball hard against her thigh.

"You didn't have to do that," she snapped.

The leader's smile was carnivorous as he tossed the ball back to the pitcher.

"We ponder if you would be open to a negotiation, little Miss Em," the leader said.

Emily ignored him and took her position off the base, only to step back when the pitcher, again, threw to first. The huntsman again slapped the ball against her thigh.

"Stop it," Emily protested.

She wondered if she was going to get a bruise.

"You realize your contract allows you the opportunity to request a trade, right?" the first baseman said, his voice growly despite the tone being a low whisper that got lost in the dancing lights around them. "For the first season, anyway. After that you're stuck with the Small Folk."

"Why would I want a trade?"

Emily felt defensive because, to be honest, since she didn't think she had much of a choice in the matter, she hadn't even read the contract. *Bad player*, she thought. *Always read the contract.*

"Because you want to win, and you know the Small Folk can't do that."

"We beat the Hag Sisters."

The Huntsman yipped a cough of laughter, and the pitcher tossed to first base again.

This time Emily swatted the leader's glove away before it could impact her thigh.

The leader held the ball for a moment, then leveled his tawny-hued gaze directly at hers. For a moment, she felt a mesmerizing pull that might have been gravity. There was an animalistic draw to the leader. A sense of purpose that suddenly seemed to radiate from somewhere deep inside him. She felt hair raise on her arms, bending toward the lanky leader. His gaze slivered, then. His pupils drew to tight points.

"Join us, and we'll see that, when we win, you'll receive a position of no little power. Overall baseball coordinator, maybe?"

Emily's vision wavered, and she swallowed. What he was offering sounded like becoming commissioner of baseball.

A deep breath brought fresh air into her lungs, though, and her thoughts cleared. From the far dugout, Emily was sure she heard strains of a melody from Shayla and Twy. A fresh sense of power came to her.

She blinked away the last of her brain fog.

"You're not talking about winning the game, are you?"

"Your wisdom proves again that we would be an indomitable match."

Emily ground her teeth, still standing on first base as the pitcher took his position again. She looked at the leader, then at the pitcher — who threw back to first base, even though she was still standing safely on it.

Understanding dawned.

"Aren't *you* supposed to be pitching?" she said. Instantly she understood what was going on, completely. The leader pitched for the Wild Hunt most of the time. But now he stood at first base. "You had the satyr pitch just because you wanted to talk to me alone."

"A pact between us could be very powerful, Miss Em. Don't deny it. Together we could rule all the Fairy Realm. The power of our Hunt commingled with your baseball magic would be impossible to defeat."

"You might as well go back and pitch, Dogface" she said. "There's no way I'm requesting a trade to the Hunt. I'm Small Folk."

It was hard to see, but the first baseman's shoulders slumped in defeat. "We sense your resolve," he said.

"And don't try throwing over to first again," she said. "Or I'll bean you next time you come to the plate."

THE SCORE WAS 2-2 in the bottom half of the ninth inning, with two outs and no one on base, so it was looking like it would be extra innings again when Maddoc managed to get hold of a mistake pitch and drove the ball deep into the gloaming fairy sky to plate the winning run.

They had done it.

Two wins against one defeat. Perhaps this amazing thing could happen. Maybe the Small Folk could make it into the final stages of this year's Fairy Series tournament. As Maddoc crossed the plate, his teammates — Emily included — mobbed him, smiles and grins everywhere. Izusa pirouetted back to the dugout. Greeven did a graceful elvish slide in Izusa's wake, holding Essie in his hand, the little lady's squeaky voice piercing with delight as Greeven gave her the roller coaster ride of her life.

"We've never won two games in a row!" Shady Marie said, accepting cheers from her dryad followers who had come out to see the game.

That was something Emily noted, too.

A new energy seemed to be building around the team. The harder they practiced, the better they did, and the better they did, the more friends and family came out to watch the games, not just those who had to work the game as servants, and even those displayed a streak of growing confidence as they turned away from their drudge work to cheer their team on. Earlier, for example, a group of gnomes had sung a beery tavern-song dedicated to Nash and the Small Folk baseball club. The next time up, Nash had driven a double, beaming when the song came again.

The celebrations were fun in one way, but Emily stepped away from the gathering, feeling empty.

She didn't have anyone to celebrate with.

Besides her teammates, anyway. While team bonding was great, when she left the Other Field, even as she'd bunked in a spare room in Fennoc's place, she always felt alone.

She missed her dad. Missed Coach Amabe. Missed her friends at school, some of whom were also teammates, of course, but not all of them. She never thought she would miss going to classes. But there it was. She missed sitting in a row of desks and having other kids comment about a game.

So, she stepped away from the celebration, into the edge of the woods behind the stands where it was quiet, and where the sounds of the stadium were muted in the damp air. The crunch of brush under her cleats was harsh in comparison. She pulled the cap off her head and ran her hand through the shank of her hair, then reseated the cap, looking up into the darkening Fairyland sky above.

The image of her trophy shelf flashed across her mind. This time she didn't think about the missing holes, though. This time she smiled with the recollection of the participation trophies she had received in the process of learning about baseball, and the memory of several of the kids she'd played with.

Those had been fun times.

A voice split the moment.

"You need to be careful."

Emily gasped and brought her hand up to her lips, whirling to face the intruder.

A dark, masculine figure stood in the midst of the trees, tall and lanky, draped in shadows that moved like living things. He wore an old-style baseball jersey that, as her eyes adjusted to the shifting shadows, Emily saw carried the logo of the Unseelie Court and the number 13.

The Designated Hitter.

Emily's fists curled of their own volition as she remembered his earlier espionage during her practices with the Small Folk. If he'd come to work some dark magic over her while she was unprotected, he was about to learn a nasty lesson.

But then he stepped forward, and the shadows dispersed enough to give Emily her first sort of decent look at him.

She'd expected him to be older, some major league professional made entirely of salt and experience. But he was only a boy, a kid about her age.

"I'm sorry to startle you," the boy said.

Uncertain, Emily squinted at him, as if she could discern more details if she looked hard enough. The shadows were still thick enough she couldn't fully make out the expression on his face, and youthful appearances could be deceiving. "You're the queen's Designated Hitter."

His thin lips curled upward wryly. "Yes. And I hear they call you

Miss Em." He tipped his Unseelie cap and gave a proper bow that seemed awkward between two human kids.

When he rose, light filtering through the leaves fell on his face. For the first time, she took him in fully.

"Do I know you?" she said.

"I don't think so," the Designated Hitter replied.

She peered more closely. "You look really familia—"

Emily nearly gasped again. Yes. She *did* know this kid. Or, rather, she knew *of* him.

"You're Adrien Th—"

The boy rushed forward and clasped his hand over her mouth before she could finish. His hand pressed hard against her flesh, and his wide eyes reflected silver fairy magic from the emerging stars.

"No true names," he said.

Emily collected herself, eyes wide, nodding her understanding.

He slowly removed his hand and stepped back again, though not as far as he'd been before.

But she was right. She knew she was. She had seen his picture in Pattersonville West's sparsely filled trophy cabinet. She had read all the news reports about him.

This was Adrien Thorn, the Unicorn player who had disappeared a hundred years earlier after hitting the game winning — championship winning — home run and crossing home plate. Apparently, he'd been whisked away to Fairyland.

Just like she'd done.

Residual heat radiated from where his hand had been, making the cool air sting even more than normal. In the distance, an owl called.

The Designated Hitter was taller, standing this close. His hand had been firm. A shock of dark hair fell over one green eye. He smelled of the woods, and when he smiled at her, though it was a sad, lonely smile, she admitted it was hard not to look at him. She'd always loved the way older-style baseball uniforms looked, even one as tattered as his.

"I've been watching you," he said. "You're a very good player. Probably good enough to eventually help the Small Folk overcome the Unseelie Queen's team. But you need to be careful."

"What?"

"The Queen will never allow you to win."

"Even if we beat her fair and square?"

His smile grew whimsical. "You won't ever beat her fair and square. And I can tell you flat-out that if someone pulls some hanky panky to steal even one game from her ... well ... she can be harsh in her vengefulness. You will not like the result of a single win, better yet an effort to actually take the Web Gem."

"I'm not afraid of a loser's temper tantrum. Especially one who can't even bat her own spot in the lineup."

The Designated Hitter laughed then, and the lilt of his voice seemed to light the fairy dust in the air around them. He gave a furtive glance over his shoulder and shuffled his feet.

"I need to leave now, Miss Em." He put his hand over her shoulder and gave it a squeeze. "But heed my warning seriously. If the Small Folk want to play with the Unseelie Queen's toys, you'll have to play by your own rules again." A half grin later, he was gone, slipping silently through the wooded land and leaving Emily as if she had always been alone.

She hadn't been alone, though.

Her shoulder still tingled where his hand had been, and while her upper lip probably wouldn't bruise due to his first contact, the warmth of flesh remained. The sound of his laughter, too. The tone of his voice.

Adrien Thorn.

Once star of the Unicorns.

Her mother's particular favorite legend about her favorite team.

The Designated Hitter.

She'd thought he was a spy before, and a willing participant in the Unseelie Queen's roster. But his coming here changed things. He was just a kid, like her, displaced from where and even *when* he was meant to be.

He'd been alone here far longer than she had.

Had he truly been spying that day when she'd spotted him lurking on the fringes of the practice fields, or simply coming to get a glimpse of another human being for the first time in a hundred years?

The thought made something in her chest clench hard.

She wasn't certain what to make of his advice. Play by her own rules? Could she even do that here in Fairyland, where she'd been signed on without a chance at negotiating her contract?

Ideas spun in her head, thin, filmy things that, for now, lacked substance.

The sounds of her teammates' celebration over at the Other Field faded, and suddenly Emily felt absolutely sure of one thing.

She was going to do everything in her power to ensure neither of them felt alone here any longer.

CHAPTER

FOURTEEN

Time passed.

Oddly, of course, because this was Fairyland. But however long it truly had been, Emily had been here long enough now to develop a better understanding of what this world was, and how baseball had shaped itself to fit the seasons.

Perhaps the odd passing of time was being affected, too, because something was changing.

It was traditional that the Small Folk's club was among the first eliminated before the postseason tournament, but this year things had been different. The club had practiced hard, and it showed. The Small Folk won their second game against the River Kin, and again — handily — against the Wild Hunt. Then, unsurprisingly, they lost their next game to the Unseelie Court, but the score was close. Or at least close-ish. They lost their second game to the Unseelies in extra innings.

Both games had felt strange to Emily, and not just because of Unseelie Pitch's horrifying build. Facing off against the Designated Hitter, a boy who embodied the oddness of time here in Fairyland, left her with an ache in her chest she couldn't easily explain. She couldn't help thinking, as he plastered her best pitches far over the dark walls of the macabre pitch and ran the bases around her like it was second nature, that he would have been her teammate in another life.

In a way, he was anyway. Like a second cousin a few thrices removed, or whatever.

He'd caught her eye after the final inning of that second game — right before his Queen had whisked him away in a cloud of shadows. He'd touched the bill of his cap with his index finger pointed to the sky: the Unicorn Salute.

So maybe he felt it, too.

The Small Folk lost, too, to the Seelie Court — a team her Small Folk teammates considered the second-best team in the league. But they beat the Seelies in their final game before the tournament.

Which was where time was now.

Postseason.

Days before the Spring Festival.

Having actually beaten the Seelie Court once, the Small Folk had finished with a record of six wins against four losses, good enough to come third — behind both the Unseelie and Seelie Courts, stronger than the River Kin, the Hags, or even the Wild Hunt. They therefore qualified for the tournament. Also, being third meant they would be facing the Seelie Court while the Wild Hunt had to go up against the Unseelies in a game played, of course, at Unseelie Pitch.

Small wonders.

A fresh buzz seemed to hover over and around the team, now, and that buzz itself made time seem to be moving with either lightning quickness or an excruciatingly slothful lack of speed.

She'd been hoping to have some time during the break to focus on figuring out how she wanted to "play by her own rules," as Adrien had suggested. But the demands of the season — the natural season, not only baseball — ate up most of her time.

In tandem with all that, the team was getting distracted, too.

This season would end at the spring equinox and be escorted out with a party the likes of which Emily wasn't sure she wanted to see. The Small Folk had been talking about it for what felt like forever. They were excited to attend after having won something — rather than as the ones expected to do all the work — and enthusiastically talked about gorging themselves on delicacies that ranged from stuffed mushrooms to delectable meats and fanciful pastries.

"And that doesn't even account for the honey mead!" Greeven had said, placing the back of his hand over his forehead and swooning. "I love honey mead!"

Emily just pursed her lips.

She always avoided big parties at school. She hated all the snickered whispers when she didn't have a date for the junior prom, or the odd glances she got on the rare occasions when she wore a dress instead of her Unicorns jersey. The social circles at school put her off that kind of thing.

She wasn't sure how well she could avoid them now, though.

For one, Mellica and Twy had taken a special interest in helping her, making sure she had a steady flow of daring fashion to try out, working to coif her hair in new and surprisingly pleasant ways. Twy added a golden tone and curls that Emily liked so much it made her rethink herself.

She'd considered streaking her hair before but had been too self-conscious to actually do it. What would everyone think? How would Dad react? It had been easier to simply avoid the issue and cut it short so it fit under the brim of a baseball cap.

Here, though, she gazed into Mellica's engraved silver mirror and liked what she saw. The golden highlights brought out her eyes, and her cheeks for that matter.

And when Mellica suggested a yellow-gold sundress with a gauzy green shoulder wrap for an outing to attend a pre-festival carnival, she decided to go with it, and enjoyed the result quite well. She was never going to be a girly girl. She knew that better than anyone. But it was fun to try new things on, and she was surprised to admit that, despite her trepidations, she looked good. Like she almost belonged here with all these beautiful, dangerous folk.

Emily found Mellica's breathless pampering and attention to detail made her feel something she was almost afraid to call "happy."

Whatever happened in the final series, it was a given that the summer season would start on Beltane—May Day—and end at the Solstice.

Then would come a mid-summer Festival, followed by the Fall Festival, and finally the Dark Night Season, which would start with Samhain and run through the winter solstice, and which would be celebrated with what Emily understood would be the biggest party of the year.

All of Fairyland's power gathered around these four points in a big, endless cycle.

That meant that, if she couldn't find a way home, Emily had not just one final senior year season, but those four seasons of baseball every year to help bring her team to victory, for the rest of her unnatural life.

She could live forever saturated in baseball.

Sometimes, in the dead periods that happened between games and festivals and dances, she envisioned herself staying here, winning tournament after tournament with her Small Folk team.

Maybe, she thought one random time, if she won the Web Gem, Emily could make the Unseelie Queen trade the Designated Hitter to the Small Folk as her boon.

CHAPTER FIFTEEN

It had been a long two weeks, but finally the Bulldogs' next game with the Unicorns was ready to start. It was a warm day again. The gray clouds from earlier in the day had burned off, and the air blew in sweet, grass-flavored gusts. Not a big wind, but blustery at times.

Callie McMasters stood on the mound at Unicorn Field and took in the opposing dugout as she considered her need to give them a home run.

One should do it. Just one.

Groove the right pitch, get ready to retrieve DeWitt, then go on to win the game.

That was the plan.

Jammy Douglass would be the first hitter. That was good because she knew Jammy couldn't hit a homer if he had the ball teed up for him, and that meant she could go ahead and strike Douglass out, thereby avoiding raised eyebrows too early. Her teammates' anxiety with her had been as thick as the lunchroom's tapioca pudding all the way through the trip here and hadn't gotten any less obvious during warmups. Last time they were here at Unicorn Field it was almost like she had lost on purpose, and, though none of them voiced the accusation, she felt it. Probably because she felt guilty of it.

Good cause or not, she hated letting her teammates down.

Loosen up, she thought to herself. *You don't have to lose today — just give up the homer and get ready.*

Bottom line, though, Callie figured she'd get only one chance. If she wanted to get DeWitt back, she needed to be in the right place when the gate opened. If she was right, the magic would summon DeWitt to be nearby. Watching the Unicorns get ready to bat, Callie realized that the timing of it all was the thing she was most worried about.

Be quick, she thought, *but don't hurry.*

She shook the worry off.

The hitter after Jammy was one of their best bets — Jake Nesbitt. He was a big kid who had some athletic talent. Patsy Pell might be able to pull it off, if the wind happened to be blowing out, anyway.

Benji Amberman could do it, too.

Actually, her money was on Benji.

Here at Unicorn field, the Amberman kid gave off a glow that never really seemed to fade. There was something about Benji and this field that just clicked. If Callie hadn't been doing her studies, she would have simply pooh-poohed the idea, but she was sure now. She wondered if Amberman, so lithe of frame and with that amazing sense of art they brought to the act of living, might truly have some kind of connection to the Fairy world.

The rest of the team, she wasn't confident of at all.

Or, rather, she was 100% confident that none of them would ever hit a homerun.

They had worked hard. Harder than she'd expected they would, really. And they were all considerably better baseball players now. That's what happens when real interest meets good coaching. But there was only so much that two weeks of training could accomplish.

"Play ball!" the umpire called, adjusting his mask as he took his place behind the catcher.

Callie leaned in to get the sign, bearing down and feeling the tip of her tongue lick the corner of her lips like she often did when she was tense.

Her windup helped her relax. The fastball was the right call to start with. Pure heat, as hard as she could throw it. The seams felt great against her fingertips as she let loose. Jamal swung and missed.

"Strike one!" the umpire called.

Two pitches later, Jammy was out.

Jake stepped into the box next.

Callie caught his eye. Jake's return nod was nearly imperceptible, but Callie saw it.

The catcher called for a slider.

Too hard, Callie thought. She didn't want to throw anything that moved. She shook her head until the catcher called for the changeup, which she knew Jake would be looking for. She took her windup, reared back, and threw a slow, straight one right down the middle of the plate.

Jake swung hard.

And missed.

She did it again, and this time Jake popped it up. Two out.

Her teammates called out encouragement, but Callie stewed. She was making it so easy, but even with her expert coaching the Unicorns weren't making the magic happen in a game.

Benji came up next. She settled herself. One chance at a time.

She checked through the signs again.

Changeup.

Right down the middle.

Crack!

The ball rose into the air. Unicorn fans cheered as the ball flew higher, deeper, and farther, landing behind the fence with enough get up and go that it only had to bounce once before disappearing into the woods beyond center field.

The stands erupted. The second Unicorns homer of the season — the first by someone other than star player Emily DeWitt.

Benji pumped a fist, and almost danced with joy as they rounded the bases.

A golden hue hovered around Benji's shoulders, though Callie knew she — and maybe her co-conspirators — was the only one who saw it.

Callie, heart pounding, ignored Benji's jogging, and the Unicorn cheers, and the way her teammates' faces drew darker, and instead stepped toward the plate. To fish DeWitt out of Fairyland, she needed to be there as the Unicorn crossed it.

"What are you doing?" the umpire said. "You need to stay on the mound."

"Just coming to get the next ball," Callie replied, brushing him off.

"I'll throw it to you when the runner crosses the plate."

Benji was nearing third. Callie hesitated.

"Just saving you a throw," she said, delaying further.

"Go back to the mound," the umpire repeated sternly as Benji rounded the base. The ump was clearly concerned that Callie might do something unsporting because she'd given up the homer. He wasn't *totally* wrong in his assessment. She was getting more nervous every second. If Benji Amberman didn't start running more quickly, she might well punch the kid right in the nose.

"No problem," Callie said, raising her hands in surrender, but still not moving. "I totally understand."

"Then get back there."

Callie took a tentative step back. Benji was close enough now that she could hear cleats hitting the basepath. She hunched down like a track star waiting for the starter's gun. She timed Benji's approach. The gate would open when their foot hit the plate. That's what must have happened with DeWitt, anyway.

Two steps away.

One.

Callie leapt forward with perfect timing. The rim around home plate seemed to flare with purple and gold power. She reached her arm toward it, pushing for the gate just as Benji's foot hit the plate...

And crashed hard into Benji's back.

She fell hard to the ground, her tailbone crunching painfully into the surface of home plate. She sat there in the dust, stunned. Benji, too, was on the ground, their pants and jersey now caked with infield dirt. She boggled, trying to get a grip on what had happened. Or, more appropriately, what hadn't happened.

Even with Benji Amberman's glow, the gate to Fairyland had not opened.

"I told you to get back to the mound!" the umpire called out. "I'm going to throw you—"

"It's all right," Benji said, holding Callie upright and coming to her aid. "No reason to throw her out of the game. I'm sure she didn't mean anything by it."

A subtle flare of power accompanied their soothing words.

The umpire paused.

Benji shook Callie's hand. "No harm, no foul, right Callie?"

"Um," Callie finally gathered herself enough to talk. "Right. Terribly sorry. That was a good hit. You really rocketed it out of here." She shook Benji's hand harder, not fully sure what she was doing.

"All right," the umpire replied. He handed her another baseball. "Get back out there, though."

"Thank you," Callie mumbled, trying hard to take everything in as she walked to the mound again.

Nothing had happened. She'd given the Unicorns a home run, and the gate hadn't opened.

She wasn't sure what to do next.

It was possible she needed to give up more homers, but that didn't feel right now. She had felt magic at Benji's hit, after all. That was for sure. It had followed Benji on the path around the bases, and it had come to their call in the confrontation with the umpire.

But she had been wrong.
Something was missing.
She just didn't know what it was.

CHAPTER SIXTEEN

Having finished warming up, Emily stood in the bullpen and watched her teammates prance around over the Other Field. They were excited, and for good reason. They had never been in a game that mattered like this before.

She hadn't, either, Emily realized. Not since little league, anyway.

This was her team. She should be more excited. The fact that she wasn't made her discomfort that much more worrisome.

"Are you feeling all together, Miss Em?" Nash said as he drew near.

"I'm fine," she replied, hoping her guilty posture wasn't too obvious. "Just getting my game face on."

"I see, Miss."

His tone of voice said he didn't really see. He was her catcher, too. She was pretty sure he'd noticed a bit of a zing missing from her warmup tosses.

"I'll be fine," she said, waving a dismissive hand.

Truth was, Emily was feeling odd. Out of sorts. Like different parts of her were being pulled in different ways. Especially as she stood in the infield. Her attention was dancing all over the place. Her balance was off, almost like the field itself was shifting under her feet. There was something going on, she thought. Something she didn't understand and something she couldn't control.

For an instant, she'd actually caught a sense of being back home at Unicorn Field.

Every now and then, as the breeze ebbed and flowed, she thought she could smell popcorn — which was not something prevalent in Fairyland.

It made her yearn for a rainbow slushie.

Maybe it was the time of year — drawing close to the equinox — which everyone told her was such a powerful time here, and which was why the Fairyland seasons lasted only a month before culminating in the coronation of a champion.

Maybe that was what had gotten into her?

Or maybe it was the uncomfortable amount of time she'd been spending daydreaming of staying here rather than trying to get back home. She got such a headache, sometimes, trying to figure out if she liked the person she was while she was here in Wonderland better than the one she was back home. And when she let herself think of the Designated Hitter, she got even more confused. One moment, she was making plans to help the two of them escape, and the next, she felt herself plotting ways to tie him to her own team's roster as if she were trying to replace the Unseelie Queen as top villain.

All in all, it was enough to have her smelling popcorn that didn't exist.

"Well, game face or not, it's time to go," Nash said, breaking another bout of malaise.

Teenage mayonnaise, her dad's voice floated up from her memories. She had a lot more to feel *mayonnaise*-y about these days, anyway.

Emily shifted her cap on her head, and trotted onto the field, feeling determined. Whatever was going on around her or in her head could wait. She had a game to pitch, and her team needed her.

She picked up the ball and felt the seams at her fingertips.

Looking at the first hitter of the Seelie Court's lineup, Emily knew she was ready.

CHAPTER SEVENTEEN

Callie went to the plate, fuming.

She had quit trying to figure anything out after the home run. It seemed she'd been wrong, and the chances of anyone else hitting a home run to test the theory again was slim to none. Besides, the umpire wouldn't let her near home again, anyway. So now she had no idea how to trip the gate and rescue Emily DeWitt. That's all that really mattered. The thing that bothered her now was that even after she'd spent so much time with the Unicorns, when Benji hit that home run, they all acted like she hadn't just handed them the lead on a platter.

They *were* better, of course. Actually, they were a lot better. Though few of them had developed any real power stroke, they were able to hit much harder than they had been earlier.

It annoyed her that they didn't seem to understand that was her doing.

To be honest, it annoyed her, too, to hear the Unicorn players chattering amongst themselves that they had decided to keep up the regimen after Callie was finished. If they did that, Pattersonville

West's baseball team had enough real talent that it might actually become decent enough to win some games.

Talk about the last straw.

It was time to show them who was boss, Callie decided.

It was time to win, and win big.

She took her stance in the batter's box and whipped her bat in a couple brief practice swings, feeling an odd sense of power with each. It was her lightsaber, she thought. The bat hummed with energy, and a thick scent of what might have been sugar came over her. Yes, sugar. Warmed. Browned. It left a sweet, caramelized taste on the roof of her mouth.

Baseball magic.

Hearing Jake Nesbitt moving behind her, Callie focused. Then she sent Jammy's first pitch rocketing off the fence in left field, good for a triple.

A hitter later, Callie scored the tying run.

"Get prepared to lose by a million," she snapped at Jake as she crossed home plate.

In the third inning, Callie drilled another Jammy Douglass pitch hard, this time down the right field line. The ball skittered around long enough that Callie made it all the way to third base with another triple standing up.

She clapped her hands as she adjusted her helmet and cheered herself.

"Not bad for a pitcher," Benji Amberman, who was playing third base, said as they stepped closer. "Another couple centimeters and that one would have made it out of the park."

"There's always next time," Callie replied, trying to be intimidating. She was going to say more, but she caught another whiff of warm caramelized sugar as Benji stood nearby.

She took a lead.

Her triple had scored another run. The Bulldogs were ahead four to one now. When Jammy's next pitch got past Jake at catcher, she scampered home with the Bulldog's fifth run.

Yes, Callie McMasters thought as she returned to the Bulldog dugout.

Five to one.

Things were back to the way they should be.

She may not have been able to get Emily DeWitt back, but at least she could feel good that she tried.

Still, as she sat on the dugout bench, she couldn't shake the wild, expansive aroma of sugar that was building around her, or the sudden, low peal of a distant horn that had seemed to moan from somewhere over home plate as she'd scored that last run.

The horn was new, she thought before heading back out to pitch again.

CHAPTER

EIGHTEEN

Emily watched the first Seelie Court hitter apply maple resin to his bat before striding to the plate in a uniform that was both brilliant and perfectly creased, pure white with thin streaks of gold trim threaded through it. The hitter's helmet glowed with its own luminescence. The team's logo — crossed bats of gold flanked by winged fairies — pulsed from high on the uniform's right side of their chest, the numbers lower on the left.

All part of the brand.

The Seelie Court team was everything the Unseelies were not. As a front, anyway.

Where the Unseelie team was known to use magic to sway games or umpires at any moment, the Seelies were adherents for the rules of the game — both written and unwritten — though the ways they interpreted those rules seemed to sway depending on what the team needed from moment to moment.

Where the Unseelies seemed always draped in shadow, the Seelie Court came doused in such bright light they could be hard to look at.

Rather than the Unseelie Queen, the Seelies were led by their King.

Emily twitched her lips as the first hitter approached the batter's box.

If the Unseelie Court were the Yankees, she thought, the Seelie Court were the Dodgers. Both considered themselves gifts to the baseball world. Both could stand being taken down a notch.

A moment later, the hitter was ready, and Emily peered into Nash to get the sign for the first pitch.

A wind-up later, the score was 1-0, as the Seelie leadoff hitter drove the ball over the wall.

Emily retired the rest of the Seelie hitters in short order, though, so she was surprised to return to the dugout to find Fennoc sitting there with a dejected countenance, the droop of his ever-present blade of grass deeper than usual.

Fennoc's uniform was still resplendent, but even his fastidious nature couldn't hide his mood. He gave a brayful sigh as Emily took a seat beside him.

"What's the matter?" she said.

"Rumor says the Unseelie Court has knocked out the Wild Hunt," Fennoc replied.

"So? One of them had to go." And given the fact the Unseelie Court had won every game during the season, this result was hardly surprising.

"Well, we've done good numbers against the Wild Hunt, while against the Unseelie Court..." He shrugged, a rather despondent motion that spoke of resignation. "It was a fanciful wish, that's all."

"I see." That made sense. But inside, Emily was glad. She was starting to see the flow of power in this world, and the same competitive fire that usually only flared in her for Callie McMasters was flaring for the Unseelie Queen.

She'd been pulled in a hundred different directions lately, unsure if she ought to lean into the wild and dangerous nature of Fairyland or reach back to who she was back in Pattersonville. But if Emily wanted to take the latter path, to continue calling herself a star player, she had to go up against the queen. And she had to win.

Even if it meant, as the Designated Hitter had advised, playing by her own rules.

"Well," Emily said, staring out over the field where the Seelie team was leading the Small Folk by a run. "One problem at a time. We need to score, or it doesn't matter who won that game."

"That we do, lassie. That we do."

Alas, the rest of the game was a defensive battle — a true pitcher's duel, with Emily allowing only a single base hit, and walking only two in the next seven innings. Her opposite, the King of the Seelie Court, had done her one better, allowing no hits, only one walk, and a single runner on base on an error.

Entering the ninth inning, the Seelies still led by that one to zero count — a gap that the Small Folk's demeanors showed they thought was insurmountable as they tumbled back into the dugout for their last time at bat. They looked worn out. Drained. As if the adrenaline they'd been riding during warmups had long ago drained to zilch.

Shady Marie sat stiffly against the far wall, gazing forlornly at the woods.

Greeven sat with his head back against the wall, Essie poking out from a pocket, her own dour expression speaking volumes.

A blanket of fatigue draped over Emily, too.

The season had felt long, and the emptiness she felt now was even more hollow for the excitement that had preceded it.

"It was a good run, though," Maddoc said, clopping his cloven hooves on the dugout dirt. "We'll get them next season."

For a moment, Emily let that lethargy drape over her, too, it was a force of its own, as if the Fairy Realm itself was putting its pressure on them to return to their proper places and resume their designated roles. Don't rise above your station. You can try again later.

Maybe it was the fresh scent of popcorn she picked up at that very moment, or simply the fire of competitive drive that always seemed to hit her when she needed it. But a spike of anger ran through Emily to break her defeatist mood.

Maybe the denizens of this world had infinite seasons to try. But Emily did not. She was human, and mortal.

"Enough!" she said so firmly that every eye in the dugout turned to her. "*This* is our season, and this game isn't over. Not by a long shot."

The team looked at her fully, shuffling their feet.

In that moment, with her blood up and her passion running freely, she felt Mom again, the same way she always did when she pitched her best on Unicorn Field.

"Baseball is supposed to be fun. Remember that? It's supposed to bring us joy and freedom. It's not supposed to be this..." *this cage the entirety of Wonderland can keep you in*, she thought, taking in their forlorn gazes. "Look at us," she said, sweeping her arms wide to encompass the whole dugout. "We're the Small Folk. And this is the first time we've been here, at the playoffs, in how long?"

"Well," Fennoc said, standing taller. "Many cycles."

"Not since I was born," the brownie squeaked. "It's really very exciting when I think of it again."

"And we got here by doing things our way, playing to our strengths, and having fun doing it. I don't see a reason to stop any of that now. So, to heck with all this dour and sour attitude. The game's not over. Let's have fun now, playing for something that matters."

Izusa gave a laugh. "She's right, you know."

Greeven stood up brightly. "Indeed, she is!"

From the other side of the dugout, Shayla and Twy gave a harmonic tone that danced with fairy light.

"'Tis another fanciful wish you speak of, I think, lass," Fennoc said, stepping up toward the field and tipping his cap to Emily. "Let's make this one come true."

WITH ONE OUT, Emily scratched out her team's first base hit, a dribbler past third base that made the entire Small Folk bench leap for joy. When she stole second base, then scored on another Izusa single, she returned to such a wall of cheering teammates and pats on the back that she thought she might lose her breath.

The game was tied!

Nash walked next, moving Izusa to second base.

But Delananey struck out to bring light-hitting Greeven to the plate.

There were two outs. One more and their chance at winning outright would be lost.

Twice the lithe elf swung his thin bat, and twice he missed by a mile.

Emily watched from her seat beside Fennoc.

The faun seemed anxious, the tip of his blade of grass churning in tight circles.

"It'll be fine," she said. Like the rest of her team, Greeven was dialed in. She felt it.

The elf stepped out of the batter's box and whipped his little bat back and forth savagely, a frown of deep concentration furrowing his beautiful little forehead. He glanced nervously into the Small Folk dugout.

"It's all right!" she yelled at Greeven over the sound of the crowd. Even if Greeven struck out, which Emily realized really was the most likely outcome, it would be fine.

"Have fun!" Essie's piercing voice screamed. The brownie was standing on the bench stump where Greeven had left her, shaking her tiny, clenched fists above her head in mock victory.

The cheer brought a sudden bright smile to the elf's face.

Greeven's body language relaxed, and his expression turned sly.

A moment later, the Seelie King wound up to throw. Both Izusa and Nash were off with the pitch, and, as the ball came toward the plate, the little elf squared around.

The ball hit the bat and dribbled down the third base line.

Bunt!

A total surprise, to the Seelie players, anyway. Emily merely pumped her fist in satisfaction.

With two strikes, the winged Seelie at third base had been playing deep. She swooped in as Greeven dropped the bat and dug toward first base.

"Run like the wind!" Greeven's little brownie companion screeched from the dugout.

The Seelie fielded the ball with one bare hand and tossed it toward first.

Greeven beat the throw, though, and better still, the ball skipped before arriving. It bounced off the first base mitt, careening wildly into the outfield.

Izusa, who was still running, rounded third and headed home!

The entire crowd and Small Folk bench both erupted at the same time as the pixie did a triple cartwheel to score the team's second run.

"Izusa scored!" Shady Marie screamed, suddenly jumping like a sapling. "Izusa scored!"

For the first time, the Small Folk were ahead.

From his place at first base, Greeven smiled so hard he started glowing as brightly as Emily remembered Benji Amberman once did.

CHAPTER NINETEEN

"Knock three times," Coach Jameson said as he returned from the scorer's table after making the substitution.

Callie grimaced.

It was bad enough that the coach was taking her out of the game for the last inning. He didn't have to make it worse by pretending there was some kind of method behind his madness, or by falling back on more of his stupid superstitions. Coach was taking it easy on the Unicorns. That was all there was to it. Removing her from the game now that it was beyond reach. It wasn't even that she minded sitting out. In fact, it was clear that the Unicorns couldn't score now if the replacement pitcher tossed them the ball underhanded. But enough was enough.

The coach's *knock three times* to ensure his move worked was just annoying.

Sure, baseball had a randomness to it that some might consider "luck," but she didn't believe in that the way Coach J was using it. Superstition was silly. A ball gets hit, and maybe it's in the fielder's reach or maybe it's not. Sometimes the difference between a hit and an out was a meter — sometimes less than a hair's breadth. That wasn't luck, though. That was physics.

Still, she watched her coach go through the motions he always went through when he returned to the dugout. He stepped carefully, making sure his feet avoided cracks in the concrete, then adjusted his cap again, and spit to his right.

He followed it up with a final trio of knocks.

She was on the verge of actually shouting at him to stop, when something about the hollow ring of his knuckles on wood nudged at Callie's mind.

Her time in the library filled her brain.

Three, she said to herself. *Three.*

It was a powerful number in Fairy. Yes. She was certain she remembered that.

Three had power in baseball, too.

Three strikes and you're out. Three outs and the inning is over.

None of that was luck. Not even in Fairy.

If anything, as Callie had read more and come to understand it, in Fairy, magic *was* science. Or at least it was more like science than anything else — playing by a set of rules that one magical creature might be able to warp, but only at the cost of something elsewhere.

Three.

As the idea settled in her mind, she smelled another blast of wild sugar.

The deep tone of the horn blew again in the distance.

Emily DeWitt, she thought, sitting bolt upright. Callie felt her nearby, so close she thought she could touch her, and suddenly, Callie McMasters understood what she'd gotten wrong.

Three.

The home run DeWitt hit had been the third time she scored.

That was the magic. She felt it in her bones as sure as she'd ever felt anything. She'd even read something like it in a book of old stories at the library: *Strike thrice upon the bone-white plate. Call to home some bloodthirsty fate.*

Yes.

She was certain.

And as certain as she was about the legend, she was certain of something else, too. Unlike every other player on Unicorn Field today, and specifically unlike any Unicorn, Callie had already scored twice.

It had to be her.

She had to hit the home run. But she also had to be a Unicorn.

She felt sure of that, too.

Without fully realizing what she was doing, Callie slipped out of the dugout, pulling a nondescript jacket over her Bulldog uniform as she made her way under the Pattersonville High grandstands to sneak to the Unicorn dugout.

Where she finally caught Patsy Pell's eye and motioned her closer.

Patsy's gaze hardened to cold dots from under her charcoaled lids.

"What do you want," Patsy huffed when she came close enough.

"I understand why you're mad," Callie said, "but I need your help."

"Fat chance."

"DeWitt needs your help," Callie said, pleading now.

Patsy stared at her impassively.

"*Emily,*" Callie said. "Emily needs your help. I was wrong earlier. Or, really I was right, but not right enough. We need a Unicorn to hit that enchanted home run to open the gate, but it has to be one that scores her *third* run."

"Third run?"

"Three, right?" Callie said. "It's a power number. *Emily* scored three times against us when she disappeared."

"Crap, McMasters. You've gone full crazy now."

"I'm serious, Patsy. I mean it. If I can get a third run, I can get DeW— *Emily* back. I know I can."

Patsy's brow furrowed and Callie could see she was thinking.

"You're up in two batters," Callie said quickly. "I can help."

"I don't need any more coaching."

"No, not that. Of course, not that. You haven't scored any runs yet, so even if you hit a home run it won't matter."

Patsy gave a double clutch. "You mean...?" she said.

"Yes, I mean ... let me hit for you."

The silence that hung in the air grew thick.

"Swap uniforms with me," Callie said, breaking it with a sense of desperation. They were running out of time. "And maybe take a fast shot at your gothy makeup. It doesn't have to be great."

"You've got to be kidding me."

"I most definitely am not kidding you. Do this and I think I can grab your best player back."

Patsy pressed her lips together. Sounds of the game filtered through the background.

"If this doesn't work, I'm going to kill you."

CHAPTER TWENTY

As much as Emily tried to model the confidence her Small Folk teammates needed to see, nerves still prickled her skin as she went to the mound for the last inning.

The sky was darkening, and the air carried that crisp late-spring tang that she loved so much.

Out past the fences, fairy lights danced at the edges of the shadow-lined forests, the trees gnarled and twisted together even tighter, and the air filled with dark forms of creatures gliding in its currents. The smell of grasslands came thick from around her, riding under the heavy aroma of the black mix of clay and soil that comprised the infield dirt at Unseelie Pitch. The excited buzz of the crowd rose and fell in waves, making her flash on Mr. Donaldson's science class. The clinking clatter of goblets and mugs being drained was almost a steady percussion. Under it all, flames crackled low and melodic from the lighting lamps that illuminated the sky as it fought a losing battle against the fairy twilight.

That was something she admired about Fairyland. Everything about it was so intense.

The whole place was amazing, and as unsettled as Emily was

feeling about the world around her, she couldn't deny that everyone in the stadium felt history in the making.

The score stood Small Folk two, Seelie Court one.

If Emily could only get them out of this inning, the rag-tag bunch that made up the Small Folk baseball club would play in the final Fairyland Series for the first time in as long as anyone could remember.

Emily breathed deeply in a vain attempt to calm her nerves.

She picked up the baseball, hitched up her trousers, then ran her hand down the brown number eleven that was stitched on the front of her jersey.

She wished her mom was here.

Her dad, too, of course. But right then she missed her mom more.

Before her, the first Seelie Court hitter stepped into the box, tipping his cap to her with a charming nod and a dimpled grin, as all of the Seelie hitters did. At least all of them with dimples.

So proper, the Seelies.

His uniform was freshly cleaned with the King's magic, as they all were each half-inning. Its sharp creases flashed brilliant white in the late gloaming.

Emily's first pitch was a ball, but she got herself together and struck him out on the next three pitches.

The crowd rumbled as the next hitter blooped one over Greeven at shortstop, though.

One out, but a runner was on base.

"Have fun, right?" Nash called to her, probably noting the way her brow had furrowed as she took in the next hitter. It was a young, limber fairy with smooth, and (of course) beautiful features. She was the Seelie's best batter.

Emily smiled at her catcher. "Thanks," she said.

A ball and a strike later, Emily pulled the string on what she hoped was her best curveball and got the Seelie Court hitter to tap a ground ball to Greeven at shortstop. The toss to Delananey got the force out at second, but the throw to first was too late to get the fleet-footed fairy.

She was pleased to get at least one out, but the distraction made her let up. She walked the next Seelie.

And the next.

Two outs. Bases loaded.

The Seelie King stepped up to bat, his gloriously smooth face glowing with smug pleasure.

"No place to put me, little Miss Em," the King said, licking his lips with the tip of his blood red tongue. "What are you going to do?"

Emily put everything she had into her first pitch, a fastball that rose like a mirage and induced the King to swing and miss.

"Fine effort, lassie," he called. "Let's see you do that twice more."

Her next pitch, a tired slider, was way outside.

Her fastball missed, too. The King swung at a changeup, and barely managed to foul it off.

Two balls, two strikes. Bases loaded. Two outs.

Emily rubbed the ball in her hands, feeling the field around her like it was part of her body. This was it, she thought. This was the pitch that would decide it all. *Curveball*, she thought, waiting for Nash to signal it. If she threw him a curveball here, low and away, the King would chase it.

She leaned in to get the sign, blinking at the sensation of her vision wavering — ignoring for a moment the way she thought she saw Patsy Pell standing at the plate at Unicorn Field. She brushed the vision away. There would be time for feeling homesick later. Now there was a baseball game to win.

For an instant, she wondered if her vision might have been planted by the Seelies, though that kind of foul play wasn't supposed to be their thing.

Someone else, maybe?

Were the Unseelies afraid of the Small Folk? Could they be cheating to make the Small Folk lose?

A moment later, Nash dropped two little fingers, and Emily, getting her thoughts together, nodded.

Standing, she went into her stretch, then checked the runners to keep them close.

A moment later, she stepped toward home and unleashed her pitch.

"PATSY!" Coach Amabe called down to the dark corner of the dugout.

"How do I look?" Callie whispered.

"Better than me," Patsy said, her voice almost wistful. She was wearing Callie's Bulldog uniform, cringing with distaste.

"Not a chance," Callie said. "You always look great."

Patsy rolled her eyes. "Whatever. You'll do fine. Just keep your cap pulled down so your hair doesn't come out."

"All right."

"You're up, Patsy! Get going!" Coach A called again. Getting antsy.

Callie stood up, pulling Patsy's blue and teal uniform around her to make it fit more comfortably. She wanted to be able to look at herself in a mirror, but there was neither time nor a mirror available, so she had to trust that Patsy had done the job right. If so, she would pass — or at least no one would mistake her for Callie McMasters because Callie was, in general, about as far from Goth as it was possible to get.

She grabbed a bat on the way to the plate, swinging it a few times to get her nerves under control, and pulling the Unicorn batting helmet down further.

She admitted she liked the little horn logo someone had painted on it.

Very magical.

She kept her head down to protect herself from being recognized as she stepped to the plate, then peered out at the pitcher she had faced almost every day in practice.

She knew what he threw. She knew how to hit it.

Heat rose from home plate as she neared, radiating upward as she ground her back foot into the box like Patsy always did. Electricity snapped along the plate this time, and a glow she knew no one else around her could see came up golden and silver. It gave her a warm sensation. *I'm right*, she thought. *I know I am*. She didn't want to know how disappointed she'd be if she wasn't.

A chant echoed inside the ear holes of her helmet, thin and cackling, almost more like a set of ancient branches clattering together than a string of syllables, but still they came to her in words.

Strike thrice upon the bone-white plate.

They gave her resolve.

She wanted to beat the best. This was how she was going to do it.

For just an instant, she thought she saw Emily DeWitt on the pitching mound itself, peering in to get a sign, wearing an odd brown and green uniform with words she couldn't read stitched into them. Then DeWitt was gone, replaced by the Bulldog Callie knew so well.

The pitcher wound up. The ball came in. Callie gripped the bat and swung.

The sound was lightning on wood.

The ball rose high and far. Callie didn't watch at all though. She dropped her bat and ran as fast as she could, crossing first before the ball landed, and already nearing third by the time it disappeared with another crackle of lightning into the darkening woods.

By the time Callie rounded third, she had blocked out the rest of the world until there was only the third base chalk line, leading onward to home plate, which lay before her, scintillating with silver flares laced with golden spikes.

Three steps away. Two steps.

One.

The pitch dipped. The King swung his bat.

Though the hit was just a little nubber out in front of the plate, the sound of contact was like a cannon blast to Emily's ears.

Nearly stumbling with the follow-through of her pitch, Emily raced toward the ball.

It was hers to play, but Nash, too, raced for it.

"No!" she called, realizing he would be out of position when she grabbed it.

Her admonition was too late, though, and even if it hadn't been, her voice was drowned out by the roar of the crowd. The runners were all on the move, the Seelie Courter on third heading home, the King racing to first. The ball still dribbled toward Emily as she raced forward. No way could she field it and throw to first for that last out.

And with Nash away from the plate, there was only one play to try.

In one motion and in full stride, she scooped the ball with her mitt and took off toward the plate. She was closer than the runner coming from third, but the Seelie had a full head of steam now and she was just getting going.

Her heart pounded like taut drums.

Her legs burned as they pumped.

She smelled wildfire and forest spice. Ahead of her, home plate crackled with golden lightning.

The runner was a step away.

She dove headfirst, pressing the ball in the web of her glove toward home plate as the impact of her dive drove all the breath out of her lungs.

The umpire bent close.

"Out!" he called as Emily's mitt hit home a fraction before the runner's cleat slid in.

The crowd roared.

In the distance, Emily heard her teammates yelling and screaming, little Essie's piercing cheer slicing through them all, and for an instant Emily flashed on the pure joy that would be on the little brownie's face, her tiny arms raised in glory.

Then home plate pulsed with an intense flash of light that blinded her.

A pressure came at the back of her neck. A hand, grasping the collar of her uniform, she realized.

"Come on, DeWitt," a voice growled at her. "Let's get out of here."

The force yanked Emily up to her feet, and a hand pulled her around to face her manhandler. Blobs of light still danced in her vision from home plate's flare, but Emily could swear it was...

"Callie?" Emily said anyway. "Callie McMasters?"

That made no sense. Callie would never wear a Unicorn jersey.

"No time to thank me now," Callie said.

She put her arms around Emily, and, with no warning, literally body slammed her back down to home plate.

Heat flared. Light blasted.

The roar of a crowd harmonized with the call of a hawk at night.

A wrenching, tearing pain rippled from deep inside her, scrubbing down to the very cells that made up her blood.

Then it was over, and all Emily could see was a darkening sky over the dirt of the batter's box at Unicorn Field.

CHAPTER
TWENTY-ONE

Having been slammed to the dirt, Emily struggled to draw a first, ragged breath.

Her head spun in a rush, and colors all around her merged into a pool. She clawed air desperately, though, in, then out, then in again.

She felt even more out of sorts than she had when she'd first stepped into Fairyland.

The first step is Adoo Zee, she remembered Fennoc telling her in his gentle, soothing voice. There was no gentle or soothing voice this time. Instead, there was only the crushing weight of Callie McMasters pressing her into the dirt, then becoming a grasping tangle of hands that yanked her to her feet with a grunted "get up, DeWitt."

Emily remained in a daze of pain and confusion as things continued to happen around her.

"Come on!" McMasters' voice sounded desperate now. Her arm around the small of Emily's waist pulled her around, fighting to move her, pulling like a fish on a line.

Everything was moving so fast.

"Stop!" Emily called, but nothing stopped.

Her unsteadiness bled into a cacophony of players shouting, spectators screaming, and adult men yelling, until all she could do was cover her ears and huddle in on herself. Something felt wrong, even then. A pressure twisted in her heart. She felt people in the stands gasping, and the opposing Bulldogs coming forward as if they were compelled.

But her friends surrounded her — the Unicorns, as if knowing that's what she needed — making a barrier of themselves to buffer her from all that noise and energy.

A soft glow of magic rose from one of them — Benji. Each time someone tried to get too close Benji got in the way, and Emily clung to that like a lifeline.

Then there was a huge push, and Emily almost fell through the crowd.

"Get out of the way!" Callie McMasters' voice echoed in the warped space around her.

Then she was away from home plate, away from Unicorn Field, in the parking lot, her Small Folk cleats clattering and clicking over the lined black asphalt.

A car door opened, and Callie shoved her into the passenger seat. Hot, stuffy air enveloped her like a smothering blanket. The lifeline that had been Benji was gone, but still she felt a tether pulling at something inside her. She had nothing to ground herself with as she found herself in the inconceivable situation of having Callie McMasters, who had slipped into the seat opposite her, driving her away.

"Callie McMasters?" Emily said, still dazed.

Yes. It was her. Wearing a Unicorns jersey.

Emily blinked. Trying to breathe. Trying to focus.

"Y'okay, Emily?" Callie said as she inched forward at a stoplight, her voice strangely soft.

Emily flinched so hard she cracked her knee against the fancy wood paneling of the glove compartment. "No true names!"

Embarrassment instantly washed over her. What kind of response was that?

But instead of the biting remark she expected from Callie McMasters, long-time rival and all-around snotty rich girl, all she got was a single nod and a softly spoken "that's right, I read about that."

The rest of the drive passed in silence, but Emily's brain was still spinning at full throttle.

"Wha' happen'd?" she said, her tongue feeling thicker than normal.

The Unseelie Court, she thought? Some dark magic to stop the Small Folk from even entering the final series? Or something else gone horribly wrong?

The pain in her chest got worse the farther away from Unicorn Field she got.

At times she had to concentrate to breathe.

It was getting so bad, in fact, that she was on the brink of telling Callie to turn around and take her back when it suddenly became obvious where McMasters was taking her.

Then the front wheels bumped over the curb of her own driveway, and the front door of the house she'd grown up in slammed open so hard it knocked the porch siding loose.

Dad.

Barreling down the drive and yanking at the car door handle before Callie had even come to a full stop, his fingers slipping the first time, but scrabbling again and pulling the door open.

"Emily," he sobbed, throwing himself half into the car to hug her to him. "Emily, Emily, Emily." Awkwardly, the hug never breaking, she slipped out of the car. He crushed her so hard the internal pain faded to nothing, and Emily found herself sobbing right back at him. She didn't know how long they kept on like that, but when they finally separated enough for her to turn and thank Callie, they found she'd already driven away, as if she'd never been there in the first place.

"Daddy," she choked out, then. "I'm so sorry. I missed you."

The only reply she got was another, even tighter bearhug and another breathless "*Emily.*"

It was enough.

CHAPTER TWENTY-TWO

"They aren't going to let me play?" Emily, standing in the doorway that led to Dad's office, nearly wailed. "That's not right."

It was two days later.

Dad sat at the computer screen, his body turned toward her — the screen glowing with the official letterhead of the Pattersonville West principal's office.

"You've missed four months," Dad said.

"So?" she replied. "It's not my fault."

Emily fought the urge to argue further. The flow of time here, though rigid, passed almost as oddly as it did in Fairyland. She was trying to let one day flow into the next, the way it had in Fairyland and the way it had *seemed* to flow in the "real world" before, but each day took so much concentration — or seemed to grind along so slowly — that by nighttime she found herself worn out and crashing, sleeping late the next morning.

She'd crossed into Fairyland back at the start of the high school season. But though she'd felt like only a single month had passed while she was on the other side, she found herself now in the growing heat of May leading toward June.

Which meant the state tournament.

And graduation.

Emily had missed not only four months of games, but four months of classes and homework and tests. Now that she was back everything was different.

First, she was now Officially-A-Local-Celebrity.

Her disappearance and subsequent reappearance had journalists and TV news anchors from all over the tri-county area shoving microphones into her face and asking invasive questions about her home life, her childhood playing baseball, and even her mom's death. They wouldn't take no for an answer — or even "I don't know" when they asked what had happened. She kind of understood that, but she wasn't about to open her mouth and tell them the truth. If she said she'd spent one-to-four months in Narnia-slash-Wonderland, which by the way definitely existed somewhere underneath Pattersonville, the men in the white coats would take her away next.

And she was pretty sure that facility didn't have any baseball teams.

So, other than Dad, she didn't tell anyone anything, and even he got only a superficial retelling. Fairy Narnia Land. Perpetual baseball. Weird, dreamland players. Nothing about Wild Huntmasters, evil Unseelie Queens, or lifetime contracts.

Her story to everyone else was only that everything went gray.

Callie McMasters told reporters she was in the dark, too, that she simply ran into Emily at home plate — which no one could deny, since things had happened so quickly. That helped make the story settle down, at least among the locals. They stopped openly asking questions whenever Emily dared to appear in town, anyway.

The reporters didn't stop there, of course. They asked whether she intended to rejoin her team as they made their drive for the Regional semi-finals, and, without giving her a chance to answer that, barreled on to ask what her strategy was for carrying the Unicorns to their first State championship in exactly one hundred years.

At least they'd stopped when she finally responded by bursting into tears.

The paranormal zealots were worse, though. They kept showing up at her doorstep, snapping pictures and scurrying away talking about golden auras, or simply trying to touch her. Then there were conspiracy theory kooks who kept bothering her.

Now there was the school's eligibility requirements to deal with.

Emily's gaze went to the screen, reading again the words that doomed her.

"It's not fair," she cried.

"I don't think they'll let you graduate this semester either, sweetie," Dad said.

Tears welled up and Emily's vision blurred. She gripped the doorway and tried to ignore the cold pull she could still feel deep inside her chest, tried to pretend it didn't exist — tried to imagine that she'd been here in Pattersonville the whole spring, sleeping each night in her bed rather than the hard cot in one of Fennoc's spare rooms.

It's not fair, she whispered again.

It was gone, she thought. Her senior year. State finals. The chance to catch the eyes of the college scouts.

Everything she'd wanted.

Gone.

Benji came to her house later that evening, dressed in charcoal sweats and a simple T-shirt which, since Emily had never seen Benji condescend to be seen in such casual attire while cavorting in general public, she knew had been chosen specifically to make her feel more comfortable.

Dad served lemonade and store-bought oatmeal cookies, then left them alone in the living room.

"Are you okay?" Benji said from the padded chair.

"No," Emily surprised herself by admitting. Things were going to crap. Might as well admit it. But there was more to it, too.

Despite everything, she couldn't stop thinking of Unicorn Field.

Everyone seemed to be treating the place differently now. Her dad, for example, had barred her from going back to the ballpark *just until we can find out what happened*. It was annoying, even if she understood why he was so shaken up. Part of her even agreed with him. Now that she knew how dangerous the world on the other side of that portal was, how could she risk accidentally going back? And yet, she *needed* to go to the field. The place pulled at her with a growing strength every time things got quiet. Lying in bed, she heard voices: chattering fairies, chuckling fauns, singing nymphs. When she closed her eyes to try to sleep, she saw dancing lights like pixie glow on the back of her eyelids, and once she was certain she heard the piercing cheers of a little brownie.

Even now, sitting here with Benji, she nearly choked on the well of power that tugged through her torso to clot in her throat.

But as she glanced at Benji, the sensation she'd felt when they shielded her from the rest of the world came back to her. Her gaze narrowed, but in a soft way. "You feel it, don't you?"

One corner of Benji's lips tweaked upward.

"What does it mean?" Emily asked.

"I'm not entirely certain. My family has always known Unicorn Field houses a fairy ring. Passing through the ring is sure to leave a mark," Benji said, crumbling a cookie into bite-sized chunks idly. "But I think what you've got going on is bigger than that."

Benji explained what her teammates had done to search for her — themself, Patsy, Jake, and Jamal, anyway. And Callie McMasters, too.

"That explains the Unicorn uniform," Emily said. "What do you mean by *bigger,* though?"

"Maybe the field is the only crossover point, or maybe not, but if all my Amberman family stories are right, the Fairy Realm has a lot of ties into the city. We go back generations, and we're not the only family who does. There are several others, even if they don't know it. But that doesn't necessarily mean we're tethered to the world on the other side. More like ... there's a standing invitation?"

"An invitation?"

"Yeah. You know, like," Benji's voice twisted around. "A *Great-Ma will be delighted if you show up for Hanukkah dinner* kind of thing." Benji chewed a cookie and cocked their head, and one eye seemed to get bigger as they examined her. "You feel more like you're being guilt-tripped into doing the dishes, though, and woe befall you should you try to ditch out and watch the game, instead."

"I can see that," Emily said, nodding slowly. "Kind of."

At first, she was going to argue over the idea that Benji could decline their Great-Ma's invitation, but then realized that was parsing things too finely. She sipped her now-lukewarm lemonade, swishing the tart flavor around her mouth as she let the idea settle over her. "Yeah, I think that's right. Somehow."

Benji tilted their head to the other side this time. "Do you want to talk about it?"

She drew a deep breath, considering. She wanted to release some of the internal pressure, and she knew it would help if she told someone the full story, even if it was just a little bit. But when she tried to think of where to even start, everything jumbled together into one humongous tangle.

The Small Folk. The Web Gem. The Unseelie Queen and the Wild Hunt and the Hag Sisters of the Wood throwing magic around the field and the way it was all intertwined with the very fabric of Fairyland society. Adrien Thorn. It was too much.

"Maybe later," Emily said as she slouched back and gave a deep sigh. "For now, I'm just glad I'm not going insane."

Benji gave a big, toothy grin. "I think you're fine."

Emily scoffed, thinking about the school's memo. "Well, then I'm just sorry I can't play for the team during the Regionals."

"Me, too," Benji said. "We might actually win something this year."

Emily gave them the slant eye.

"Callie McMasters coached us for awhile. And we've been working with her drills ever since. We're actually not terrible anymore. Our last regular season game is tomorrow. If we win it, we get a bye in the first round."

"Wow," Emily said. She gasped as the power inside her jolted again, hard enough this time that stars flared in her vision, forcing her to see a strong connection between her two teams. Both had worked harder than ever before. And just as the Small Folk had been winning their way into the Fairy Series, the Unicorns were about to earn their ticket into the semi-finals.

Benji raised an arm to shield their gaze after the flare.

"You saw that?" Emily said.

"Hard not to. But don't worry. We'll help you work though this, I promise."

Emily smiled, glad to have a friend, at least.

Later, after Benji had helped her clean up the cookies and lemonade and left, after she had said good night to Dad, and after she heard him give up his own efforts and retire to his room, Emily flicked on the lights.

She stared at the empty side of her personal trophy shelf and felt the burn of desire.

After all this time, she was free of the Fairy World, just as she'd wanted to be.

But she wasn't truly free, was she? Not really.

She couldn't play baseball now. And she wasn't graduating.

In the quiet of the night, lying in her bed, Emily's stomach flip flopped with discomfort. The tie to Unicorn Field twisted in her mind — and her tie to the Other Field, too. Making it worse, she saw clearly that she'd left two teams in a lurch. The authorities wouldn't let her play for Pattersonville West, and she hadn't even gotten to try to wrest the Web Gem from the Unseelie Queen's dark talons, either.

The sensation of Limbo was excruciating.

"I'm sorry, Mom," she said to the empty night. "I wish I knew what to do."

She'd left her closet door open and, in the dim light of her bed stand, she made out the brown threads of her Small Folk uniform hanging in the dark back corner where she'd numbly placed it beside her Unicorns jersey. She gazed also at the rows of plain shirts and pants filling out the rest of the space and recoiled as she felt the bars of her own familiar cage closing in around her.

She felt too, the pressing memory of Adrien Thorn. The Queen's Designated Hitter, who she now understood better than anyone else ever had. She felt her own freedom — having been returned to her own world — and she reflected it back against Adrien's continued imprisonment. He probably would have given a lot to be where she was now, even as muddled up as she felt.

Her chest throbbed with something she might have once considered acid reflux from tonight's lemonade, but that she now understood better.

"Are you there, Mom?" she whispered.

Emily didn't feel anything in response, though. Nothing but the pull of Unicorn Field, which had always been the place where Mom had talked to her strongest.

A fresh wave of resolve crashed over her.

She slid her legs over the edge of the bed and gave a nervous gaze toward the hallway. She waited, motionless for several minutes, until the snort of her dad's snoring became steady.

Then she stood up and pulled sweatpants and a practice sweatshirt on, adjusting the tails to line up the Pattersonville West Baseball logo.

Emily may not know what to do, but she knew where she needed to be.

Jake Nesbitt, arriving early for practice the next day, found Emily kneeling on the mound and crying as she cradled her aching arm.

"What are you doing here?" Jake said, bending over her. "Are you okay?"

No. I'm not okay, she thought, rubbing at her shoulder. *Maybe I should go to the hospital.*

But she already knew that what ailed her wasn't anything a doctor could help alleviate.

Though Jake tried his best to console her with a few poignant Taylor Swift lyrics while helping her ice up in the dugout, she couldn't articulate that the pain in her arm wasn't what had turned her into a wreck.

It was frustration and disorientation.

It was being different from who she'd been before. It was being alone and unable to do anything right. It was that she had been here all night, throwing baseballs at full power, listening to them rattle hard against the chain link fence behind home plate, but no matter how hard she threw, the pain that had jangled through her blood at the moment Callie McMasters had dragged her back to the real world would not dissipate, and that its constant throbbing and spiking interfered with her ability to concentrate. It was that her arm, without the magic of the Fairy Realm to protect it, burned from hours of overwork.

And it was that now even standing on the field wasn't enough to hear her Mom anymore.

"How long have you been here?" Jake asked, taking in the scattering of baseballs all around home plate as he finished affixing the ice packs.

She checked her phone on automatic pilot and saw a string of texts and calls from her dad, the strings growing increasingly scared as time ticked by without response.

She'd been standing on that mound, throwing pitches since approximately 3:30 AM. It was past ten in the morning now.

She felt horrible.

She called him immediately and then remained on the phone with him for most of the next hour, even as the rest of the Unicorns arrived, and practice got underway. By the time she hung up her ice had become a bag of lukewarm water, and the Unicorns were nearing the end of a tight, well-utilized practice. She spent the last of it just watching them, half zoning out due to fatigue, lack of sleep, and the occasional flash she could swear she saw of the Other Field.

The way the Unicorns played was so strange, now.

Nobody sang songs of magic or did cartwheels in the outfield. No one tried to make the ball levitate straight into their gloves or practiced maneuvers to evade black magic. She didn't feel the need to keep an eye out for the nasty tricks of the Wild Hunt.

It was just normal, clean baseball. And she couldn't wrap her head around it anymore.

All she could do was sit, and watch, and try not to focus on the way the dull pain dragged itself across every nerve of her arm.

What did help, just a little, was the way Patsy, Jake, Jammy, and Benji took turns to come to sit on the bench beside her, all of them radiating calm.

"Take your time," Benji said. "We're just happy you're here."

Emily thanked them from the bottom of her heart.

She just wished she felt the same.

CHAPTER
TWENTY-THREE

Later that night, Emily woke up, drenched in sweat and tangled up in her thin sheets, moaning out Adrien Thorn's name. Pale silver moonlight spilled from her window, setting the foot of her bed glowing like fairy fire. Her lungs heaved as if she'd been running hard to avoid a tag out, which she had, except the tagger was the Unseelie Queen, and the ball she held was made of soul-sucking black magic.

Calming down but still panting, Emily pulled her hair from her face.

The illuminated numbers on her alarm clock ticked over another minute.

The dream was similar, if not the exact same as the dream she'd had the first night she'd been home.

She stared at the clock and just breathed for another two minutes, deliberately counting the seconds. It was a trick she'd discovered that helped anchor her when she was feeling particularly adrift. When she hit one hundred and twenty seconds, she let her mind return to the dream, and to the pull she could no longer pretend wasn't driving her mad, the pull she'd felt every night since returning, the one that had her crawling out of bed in the wee hours of the morning to return to Unicorn Field and hurl balls until her rotator cuff threatened to tear.

Emily rolled her shoulder, still feeling the dead throb of pain.

Her gaze went to her closet, where moonlit motes of dust were still dancing in the open air. Tonight's dream lay fresh on her mind and the motes felt mystical, levitating there, almost singing in their silence. She felt the presence of the Small Folk uniform boldly then. Smelled pine scent and dry timber.

The vision of the Designated Hitter came to her. The moment he had stood before her in the woods behind the Other Field. It was a stolen moment for him, she realized. A risk he'd taken to deliver his warning.

Play by your own rules again, he'd told her.

Like that made sense?

When had she ever played by her own rules before?

Never. That's when. She had never bent the rules. Ever.

She'd grown up following her mom's coaching, then being the best little player in Tee Ball and on to Little League, where her coaches had commended her for never playing anything but clean ball.

She'd even refrained from stealing bases until Mom, covering her mouth with the back of her hand and giggling lightly as only she could, explained how that part of the rule book worked.

But the Designated Hitter's words came clearly to her in the dream.

If the Small Folk want to play with the Unseelie Queen's toys, you'll have to play by your own rules again.

The moonlight motes danced then, and as they danced, she heard the darker curl to his words.

The Small Folk, he'd said.

Not her.

He'd been talking to Emily as if she were a member of that team.

A new understanding sliced brilliantly through the whole of her existence, and for a moment she thought she might not ever be able to breathe again. But she drew a breath, and when she did it felt clean and bright. Sharp. Understanding struck with a sudden rush that made her sit bolt upright and stare even deeper into her closet space, searching for that uniform, unsatisfied magic humming in her blood.

They hadn't told her the whole truth.

Fennoc and the team.

The Small Folk had done something underhanded to get access to her.

Moving like a shadow herself, she untangled the sheets from around her legs and, hoping not to wake Dad, stepped silently over to her closet.

She didn't need the benefit of a light to find her Small Folk uniform where it hung beside her other clothes. Her fingers slipped into the pocket of the trousers and, as she knew they would, brushed up against a papery edge. It tingled against her skin as she drew it into the moonlight.

Her contract.

Handed over in the aftermath of that initial encounter with the Wild Hunt. Shoved into her pocket unread. Forgotten about completely.

Until now.

The paper rustled like dry leaves as she unfolded it.

Emily DeWitt shall henceforth play on the roster of the Small Folk in the position of pitcher until such a time as said team wins possession of the Web Gem.

By the authority of the Other Field, and with the blessing of the Web Gem.

Witnessed by Fennoc, leader of the Small Folk.

. . .

THERE IT WAS. Her true name.

Rage flowed through her in such a torrent it held her completely immobile. If her dad had stepped in and seen her at that moment, he'd have thought nothing was wrong in the slightest. Unless he caught the hard glint of her eyes.

They'd used her true name.

They'd compelled her, just as surely as the Unseelie Queen had compelled Adrien Thorn.

Standing in the moonlight, Emily realized something else, too.

Something that made her feel embarrassed. Ashamed.

Stupid.

She'd never questioned the spell they'd used to bring her across. Had never thought to wonder how, after all the years since the Other Field had let another player through the portal, they'd managed to do it. She'd never questioned how the Small Folk, the weakest of all the people of fairy, had done this amazing, awesome thing. Instead, she'd simply shrugged and bought their story that they had simply wanted a better player and she happened to be handy.

But now she understood something deep and powerful, understood with a strength that made her connection to the Fairy Realm burn even if she didn't know what to do with it.

The Small Folk had controlled the Web Gem.

Somehow, they'd used its power to trap her.

Magic fire burned through her.

She returned the contract to her Small Folk uniform and pulled on a pair of pants and a t-shirt. Then she swept her glove and cleats up from the floor of the closet.

It was time for another midnight pitching session.

EVEN THOUGH SHE could not play, the next day Emily donned her Unicorn uniform and went to watch her teammates. Since she wasn't attending classes, she wasn't allowed in the dugout, but she grabbed a rainbow slushie, took a seat nearby, and cheered.

It was late May. Quite warm despite the overcast that threatened rain.

One more win and they would advance out of Regionals and into the state tournament.

"Come on, Patsy!" she called when her friend strode to the plate with a runner on in the first inning. "It's all right," she clapped when Patsy struck out.

Even if Emily weren't feeling the unbearable need to get onto the field, the Unicorns were a hard team to watch right now. They *were* better than they had been when she was on the team. That much was sure. For her faults, Callie McMasters was apparently a pretty decent teacher. They'd also gotten a burst of enthusiasm from successfully rescuing her, and (Emily wondered with a certain sense of dread) maybe even a touch of the power of Fairyland.

They had a chance to actually win now.

Not a great one. But a chance. Even without Emily playing.

Maybe that idea should have bothered her, but for whatever reason it didn't. No matter how tattered she felt about herself, she couldn't make herself feel bad about her friends winning.

Every run they left behind was valuable, though, because while the Unicorns were *better*, they were not yet really *good*.

Apparently other students felt the same way. Success breeds excitement, and today the stands were relatively packed with kids and adults — though most of the adults were teachers. "Good to see you back, Emily," Ms. Pitcairne, an English Literature teacher said when she approached between innings. "We were all so worried for you."

"Thank you," Emily said, feeling awkward.

It was an intimate moment, really. Just the teacher and her. So different to the pressures that came from other directions — including the reporters here to cover the game that had tried to corner her earlier. Ms. Pitcairne accentuated it by lightly laying the fingers of one hand on Emily's elbow.

"Hope we have a good game," the teacher said.

"Yes."

"And the silver lining is that maybe we'll have you back next year?"

Emily nodded, swallowing hard and trying not to cry at the reminder.

"Yes," she finally said. "Maybe I'll be back next year."

But she wouldn't. Emily felt that deeply in her bones, and as Ms. Pitcairne made her way back to her own seat, that feeling flowed all the way through her. It wasn't so much that she wouldn't be back, Emily realized. It was that she didn't belong.

Not here, anyway.

Sitting at Unicorn Field, speaking to everyday, normal people, made her disorientated.

Disjointed.

And that was it. She wasn't supposed to be here.

Her memory burned with the letters and words of her contract. The contract that she had not yet fulfilled. *That's what's pulling at me*, she thought. *The contract.*

As she thought it, power rose to burn in her throat.

The very fact that she'd been "rescued" had left her essentially only half of herself. The other half was still tied up in her contract with the Small Folk.

She didn't belong here because she wasn't a Unicorn.

She was Small Folk.

No wonder she couldn't hear Mom's voice anymore.

And, as much as the idea scared her, that meant she had to get back. If only she had the slightest idea of how to do that.

Callie McMasters knows how.

Her Bulldog nemesis had somehow made the gate open once. She could do it again.

The first coming of the idea was escorted by an ember of anger —

the first such Emily had felt about Callie since coming back home. How dare she do whatever magic she'd done to bring Emily back here, and then leave her so mixed up she couldn't even tell what time of day it was, let alone what day of the week. But that ember faded soon.

She had wanted to talk to Callie.

With everything else going on there hadn't been time, but now, feeling a bigger truth to the world around her, Emily needed to talk to Callie McMasters more than she ever had.

And Emily knew where to find her, too.

Resolved, Emily bolted her whole slushie at once, suffering the cold headache that came with it, then set herself to cheering full bore.

SEVEN INNINGS LATER, the Unicorns had, after Benji Amberman had made a miraculous, game saving catch, gained victory.

For the first time since the days of Adrien Thorn, they were going to the state tournament.

While her former teammates celebrated their victory, Emily went home.

Dad made lasagna for dinner. Neither of them mentioned the dish's former role as "victory lasagna."

It hadn't been that since Little League.

But Emily didn't mind.

After they ate, and after Emily helped Dad clean up, she picked up her phone and tapped out a text.

Tomorrow, she sent. And she gave a location.

CHAPTER TWENTY-FOUR

The start of summer break meant the library was basically dead, which made it an ideal place for two students from opposing schools to meet up. It was also far enough away from Unicorn Field that Emily hoped the constant pull she felt toward it would be less distracting.

Emily sat outside the front door, on one of the wood-and-wrought-iron benches placed in the shade of a huge oak tree to the left of the main entrance. It was warm now, but a morning rain had left behind quiet little pools on the plaza in front of the building, each reflecting the now-blue sky. The sound of tires on concrete came from the distance. Her brown paper bag stayed perched on her lap, though she hadn't touched either the ham sandwich or the pear slices inside it yet. It was mostly a prop, anyway, alongside the stack of schoolbooks that said she was working diligently to get a head start on the remedial coursework she was now required to complete due to her absence.

She was not even remotely working on any such thing. But she'd thought the impression would help keep people from approaching her while she waited for Callie McMasters to show.

Turned out she didn't have to worry: the library was even more dead than she'd imagined it would be.

She tipped her head up to look up into the branches of the oak and began picking out which boughs she thought would make good perches for the pixies she'd thought were her friends. In mid-count, the crunch of sneakers on grass finally announced her wait was over.

With zero fanfare, Callie settled on the empty side of the bench and tipped her head back, too.

A quick glance showed Emily that her rival's eyes were closed, which surprised her.

Callie looked weird. Rather than pinned up or deliberately styled, her hair, while not totally unkempt, was down and untended. Her slack expression seemed almost relieved, but also almost as unmoored as Emily had felt these past two weeks. She wore no hint of makeup, which Emily thought unusual for the rich girl from Marion. She'd never seen Callie McMasters away from the field without at least a touch of help. That was one of a hundred things that separated the two, Emily thought. Callie McMasters could be popular even if she wasn't a contender for best athlete in the tri-county area.

There was a loose, boneless look to the way she held herself, now, too. As if, after keeping her muscles in prime shape for her entire life, she'd suddenly decided to let it all go.

She didn't have a single stitch of Bulldogs apparel on, either. Or anything with even one of her dad's company's logos. Staring at Callie through a haze of confusion, Emily realized that the person who sat on that bench beside her *wasn't* a contender for best athlete in the tri-county area.

She was just a teenager who'd been through something.

Emily had never found Callie McMasters this relatable before.

She unrolled the top of the paper bag on her lap and fished out a couple of pear slices before silently offering one to Callie. Callie took it with a grunt of thanks and ate it in two bites.

Emily didn't eat hers. Instead, she toyed with it, turning it over in her hand as she struggled with what to say. She'd planned it all out when she sent the text asking to meet her, but now the words jumbled in the same tangled mess as when she'd tried to tell Benji about her experiences.

"It's funny, isn't it?" Callie said.

Emily jumped, almost dropping her pear slice. "What's that?"

"Everyone around us." Callie lifted a hand and motioned so Emily knew she was indicating not the library, but the whole of Pattersonville. "They're just going about their days the same as always, even though we know the truth about this place."

"Yeah," Emily said. "It's weird."

The exasperation oozing out of Callie's very posture made that tangle inside Emily loosen.

"Every time one of those stupid reporters gets in my face about it, the only thing I want to do is throw my head back and laugh until I cry. But they still wouldn't get it, would they?"

"I did cry once," Emily said, laughing. "That kept them away for a while."

She lifted the pear slice and finally took a bite. The soft tang sent a burst of energy through her.

When she spoke, her words surprised her.

"I can't thank you enough for what you did for me, Callie. It must have taken a lot to put yourself in that position. If our places had been reversed, I hope I would do the same for you, but I don't know. So, thank you."

Callie smirked, a hint of her usual fire returning to her eyes. "I could say you owe me, DeWitt."

"You could." Emily nodded. "And I do. But I'm afraid I'm going to have to keep adding to my tab."

"Why is that?"

"Because I need your help again."

Callie twisted her lips. "How's that?"

"The thing is, I can't *be* here, Callie. I have to go back and finish what I started. Or rather, what was started for me."

"I don't understand."

Emily sat back, suddenly completely sensitive to the rustle of summer breeze filtering through the leaves above them, and the smell of the asphalt and brick around them.

It was strange, she thought, how the things she'd found impossible to say to either her dad, who would have been loving and supportive, or to Benji, who was a friend and almost certainly did have family connections to the magic of Fairyland, came so easily when she told her story to her bitterest rival. But they'd shared something in that single moment over home plate, straddling two worlds together for a split second. In this way, no one else in the world understood Emily better than Callie McMasters.

Emily told her about her arrival in Fairyland, about the existence of baseball over there, and of the Web Gem which fueled the whole cycle of seasons. She told her about the six teams and about what was at stake if the Unseelie Queen kept hold of the Web Gem. She told her about the taste of honey there, and about the way magic lit up a baseball field to make it come alive. She described the dances and festivals she'd attended as someone more confident in herself than she was here.

And though the words turned sour as she reached the revelation of her contract and how all of the beauty she'd come to see in Wonderland had been tainted by it, they didn't slow or become harder to get out.

"I think it's this contract that's still pulling at me," she said, gasping at the pinch she felt in her chest as she focused on it. "I can feel it all the time, but it's so much worse at the ballpark. That's why I can't be here, you see?"

"You think you need to go back?"

Emily put her lips together, and simply nodded her head.

"The Small Folk used you," Callie said, the set of her jaw and the anger in her voice lending Emily support.

"They're no better than the Unseelie Queen," Emily said through her own tightening jaw. "Though I guess I should be grateful they didn't make me a Designated Hitter like the Queen did to poor Adrien."

Callie quirked an eyebrow upward. She took a bite from the half of the ham sandwich Emily had given her during the tale, then chewed, thinking. She swallowed, then said, "You're talking about Adrien Thorn, right?"

"The very guy," Emily said, only slightly surprised Callie knew of him. She'd been working with the Unicorns heavily, after all. It made sense that she'd picked up some Unicorn lore. "He's another reason I have to go back. Even if I didn't have this bad contract tethering me to Fairyland, I couldn't just leave him behind to keep playing magic baseball for all eternity."

"DH until the heat death of the universe." Callie shuddered. "What a waste of a star athlete."

"Right?" Emily said. "I don't know how things will go rejoining the Small Folk after what they've done to me, but I've got to find a way to power through it somehow, for him and for me."

"I see," Callie replied.

"So, will you help me?"

Callie looked at her for a long moment. The door of the library swung open, and a lone guy came out carrying a pair of books. He glanced at the two of them, gave a surprised little jump, and pulled his phone out as he scurried away, probably already sharing his brush with the local celebs on social media.

Emily rolled her eyes. Callie was right. They just didn't get it.

Callie gave a sharp nod, her examination of Emily apparently complete.

"I've got two things to address before I can agree to help you."

"Okay," Emily said.

"One, don't be so hasty to judge the Small Folk. What they did was messed up, but I guarantee you they did not get something for nothing. If my reading is even half right, opening that portal is no joke. Whatever they did to get a mortal player — to get *you,* the best player Pattersonville has seen in a goddamned century — it cost them something big."

Anger tightened Callie's face.

Despite herself, for just a moment, Emily felt a jolt of something that might have been joy, or pleasure, or amazement. To hear her bitter rival call her the best player in Pattersonville was something close to stunning. Then guilt twisted Emily's gut. She looked at Callie and saw exactly how, for all their differences, they were so similar. And she saw something else, too.

"What did getting me out cost you, Callie?"

Callie laughed, a hollow sound.

"At first I thought it didn't cost me anything. I just figured it, you know? Three runs and a homer, and let the Fairy Ring do the rest."

"But that's not how it works, right?"

"No. That's not how it works."

Emily waited.

"They kicked me off the team."

"Oh, Callie," Emily said.

"They said I was cheating."

"That's not fair."

Callie shrugged. "It could have been worse."

"How?"

"Did you know they almost decided the Unicorns couldn't continue in the tournament at all? But I told them it was all me, trying to sabotage the team from inside."

"Talk about a real monkey's paw situation," Emily said, still trying to take it all in. It was too much.

"I'll probably never play baseball again."

"Oh, *Callie,*" Emily said again.

But Callie shook her head. "It's not so bad, actually. Don't feel bad for me."

"Bullshit. This is horrible."

"Nah."

Emily waited, knowing now that something else was happening.

"Thing is, my dad is so pissed, but not because I was cheating. He thinks since I hit the homer, I should stand my ground. He's mad that I 'agreed' to let them bar me from playing, as if I could do anything about it." Callie stopped there, and Emily saw she was fighting tears. Callie took a breath and steeled herself. "But he can't have a top-tier baseball player for a daughter if she's not playing, right? He thinks it's fine and good, actually, to sabotage your competition. He..."

Callie did choke now, but she covered it with a cough.

"It's all right," Emily said to fill the moment.

"When you disappeared, he kept telling me how *great* this was, how much of an *opportunity* your absence gave me. Without you here, I had no competition for the top spot. It was like you weren't even a person, like you weren't a teenage girl who's someone's daughter, just like I am. But then, if our situations had been reversed, I don't know if *he* would have been poring through police reports at all hours searching for me like your dad did."

She sniffed and scraped one wrist under her nose angrily.

"Anyway, Dad's hissy fit about the optics for his company has made me see things more clearly. I used to think baseball was all business, you know? Swing the bat, throw the pitch, get on base, or tag someone out. You win more than you lose, and the ones who lose deserve it because they didn't put in as much work as you. Like they didn't want it as bad. But that's not what baseball is really about, now, is it?"

"No, it isn't," Emily said distantly, feeling a fresh sense of energy roll through her and remembering the pure joy that came with every Small Folk game. She nearly laughed out loud remembering little Essie's cherry-cheeked excitement at key moments.

Callie continued. "Baseball is about truth. It's about being in the moment. The beauty of a perfect play, and those days when the team is grooving so well together."

"Baseball magic," Emily whispered.

"Right. It's about baseball magic. And after everything these last few months, I'm pretty certain I can say that the magic is real as hell."

Emily sat perfectly still, letting Callie's words flow over her. She had chosen this spot for its distance from Unicorn Field, but suddenly she could feel her mom's presence behind her and hear her mom's voice ringing in her head as strongly as if they both of them were standing on the mound, Mom hovering right behind her shoulder, teaching Emily how to throw a good, solid curveball.

Be loose and open, Mom had said one afternoon when Emily was in sixth grade. Right before Mom had gotten sick, when she was still full of vigor and the bright mirth of life. They had been on the mound, early in the day, practicing. *That's when the magic works best. If you let it, baseball magic will take you to the most fantastic places you can dream of.*

Emily had dreamt of college and the big leagues then. Now, though, Emily felt like her Mom had been talking about bigger things.

College wasn't magic. Neither were the institutions that organized professional sports.

Baseball, though she had denied it, baseball *was* magic.

Emily felt the power of her mother's strength burn in her.

The best way to keep loose and open, Mom continued in Emily's memory, *is to always play your best for a team you love.*

The word *always* seemed to pulse in her veins.

Did she love the Unicorns? They were good kids. Good friends. She genuinely liked hanging out with Patsy and Jake and Benji and Jamal and all the rest. But as a team? As *her* team?

No.

The Unicorns were Mom's team.

Or would have been, anyway, if she'd been allowed to play.

But Emily had never felt comfortable enough to blow up at them the way she'd done to the Small Folk after that first disastrous game against the River Kin. She'd never held them accountable to themselves. She'd never felt the drive to work with them and help bring out their best play or revive their love of the game.

The Small Folk may have tied her to their team with that contract, but fact was that they had called *her*. Specifically her. And she'd woven herself into their very fabric, and she'd had fun doing it. More fun than she'd had playing baseball in a long, long time.

Callie was right to ask her to give the Small Folk a chance.

There was something bigger going on than they'd let on. That much was certain.

And she was Small Folk, after all. Maybe had been all along. She needed to give them a full chance to explain what had happened.

What had the Small Folk paid to call her to their team?

She wanted to know.

"You're right, Callie," she said, turning back to her nemesis. "Baseball magic is real. There's stuff out there that would corrupt it, like your dad and his need to be a winner all the time or the Unseelie Queen and her monopolizing of the Web Gem. But it's still there for us to use. And I think it's worth fighting to keep it out of their hands."

Callie nodded. "It is."

"You've already paid a huge price once," Emily said, clasping Callie's hand. "I don't think I can ask you to do it again."

"Don't worry about me. I want to help. Whatever the price, I'll pay it. But we still haven't covered my second point, and it's the one I'm not giving any ground on."

Callie's eyes narrowed, and her glare turned intense. Her grip on Emily's hand grew even more firm.

Emily swallowed. "What is it?"

Callie leaned closer until their foreheads nearly touched. Their gazes locked.

"You cannot, under any circumstances, leave your dad in the lurch. You have to tell him you're going."

CHAPTER TWENTY-FIVE

It was the hardest thing Emily had ever had to do.

When she got home from the library, she came into the living room where Dad was watching the White Sox game and simply sat in the loveseat opposite him, snuggling into the pillows Mom had sewn with her favorite Cubs logo fabric. For a while, there was only the distant crack of the bat and the jabber of the announcers from the TV's speakers, the steady huff of Dad breathing, and the soft brush of Emily's sock feet against the carpet as she kicked idly.

She wished she could keep this moment forever.

But then she noticed that he had Mom's baseball — the one Emily usually kept on her own desk — in his hands. He was running his index fingers over the worn red seams in a repetitive motion, as if soothing himself with it.

He caught her looking when the commercial break came on, and he quirked a smile up at her. "Nice to have us all together like this, don't you think?"

Emily's smile matched Dad's.

"You probably think I'm going crazy saying that kind of thing," he said.

"No, I don't."

"Do you know, I used to think I could hear your Mom's voice when I held this ball real tight?" He squeezed it hard, then gave a little chuckle that revealed more than he probably wanted to reveal.

"Dad," Emily said through a throat thick with sorrow. "I... I have to..."

His eyes turned dark and drawn, and in that moment, she saw that he already knew what she was going to say.

But before she could gather her words and make it real, he visibly forced the darkness aside and clapped one hand on her shoulder. "I was thinking, we should have breakfast for dinner. Blueberry pancakes, bacon, OJ. All right?"

"Dad," Emily tried.

"Sounds good." Dad stood, placed Mom's ball on the coffee table in front of them, and turned towards the kitchen. "You know what I always say. Champions can't win on an empty stomach, and you're a champion no matter if your school says you can't play anymore this year. Just means you've got all this extra time to get a head start on training for next season!"

Emily shot up off the loveseat. "Dad, listen, I—"

But Dad kept chattering, stepping into the kitchen and banging pots and pans together loud enough to drown her soft attempts out.

For a moment, Emily burned with hatred for Callie. She was the one who put her in this position. But her eye fell on the white cover of Mom's ball, and she recalled the feel of those seams against her fingertips, remembering the one stitch that was off-balance, barely, and a sense of calm smoothed that hate over. She picked the ball up and held it in her pitching hand, loose and open. Callie was right to make this a demand. She couldn't argue about that. She carried the ball with her as she came to stand at the kitchen counter where Dad was getting out the pancake mix.

"Dad," she said, still quiet, but firm this time. She put the ball on the counter beside him.

Dad paused, his arm frozen halfway up to the cabinet overhead. He didn't look at her.

After an eternity, he sighed.

"I can't keep you, can I, princess?"

Emily drew in a long breath through her nose, held it until her stomach stopped churning, then let it out again. "I'm sorry, Dad. There are a lot of people counting on me — I played with a team over there, in the place on the other side of Unicorn Field."

"I know you did."

"The people there — including a kid who got pulled across the same way I did, only he's been there so much longer me — they need me in a way the Unicorns never did. They need Mom's baseball magic, and now that I know how to use it, I can't *not*."

"But what about how *I* need you? You're all I—"

He cut himself off with a sharp intake of breath. He was trembling.

"Dad—"

"No. No. I'm sorry." Dad finally turned to face her. "That wasn't fair of me."

"It's all right."

"No. It's not. You're growing up to be so much like your mom."

Emily nodded. She could feel that. Sometimes.

"Ever since you got back, you've been different, though. I've seen the way you're not fully here," he said. "And when you told me the bits you told me I knew this wasn't over. I guess I still hoped you'd get over it, though. Somehow. If I held onto you as tight as I could, I hoped that you'd be my little girl again the same as you were before. But you don't ever get over growing up, do you?"

"I'm sorry, too," Emily said. "I wish I could stay. But I have to go."

"I know you do."

"I have to go tonight, Dad."

Distress twisted in his expression, but he didn't voice a protest.

"Will you..." he started, stopped, blinked hard. "Will you come back?"

Emily laughed through her own welling tears. "Of course, I will. If I can, anyway. And just as soon as I can. It's hard to tell when that will be, though. Time is weird there."

"Time is weird everywhere, princess," Dad said. "Sometimes I'd swear it was just yesterday your Mom was sitting on that loveseat, shouting at the umpires on TV and making a toddler-sized Cubs jersey for you."

Emily smiled at the thought. She picked Mom's ball up from the counter, reached for Dad's hand, and placed the ball there. "You'll take good care of this for me while I'm gone, won't you? I want to be able to put it on my trophy shelf when I get back. I'll have earned it, then."

Dad laughed, sniffed, then pulled Emily into a bone-crushing hug that Emily returned with every last scrap of her strength.

"How about that breakfast, huh?" Dad said, wiping an eye across his shoulder when they separated. "If you're heading off to play baseball in Wonderland or wherever, you're definitely going to need a championship-worthy meal to see you off."

Emily smiled; her heart felt lighter than it had been in weeks. "Thanks, Dad."

EMILY WAITED until dark fell before texting Callie and heading to Unicorn Field.

She was kitted out in her Small Folk uniform. The brown weave still smelled like the forest, like mushrooms and leaves and damp rocks, and the woody scent of the dugout at the Other Field. It was a nice counter to the stench of fresh tarmac from the construction happening on the roads outside Pattersonville West.

She'd had to take the back entrance to the parking lot, but she made it without losing too much time. She parked her beat up Ford next to Callie's sleek Audi. They were the only two cars in the lot this late.

Callie was already on the field, a basket of balls beside her, tossing warmups at the chain link behind home.

"I told him," Emily said by way of greeting.

"And?"

"You were right. Thanks again."

"Duh," Callie said. She hurled another fastball.

Emily snagged a bat from the gear bag she'd brought, then went out to join Callie at the mound. The pull of the field was a deep throb in her chest now, heavy with expectation.

Callie turned to face her. "Nice jersey. Very magical."

"Are you sure you're good to do this?" Emily asked. "I'll understand if you want to back out. The cost might—"

"Oh, shut up, DeWitt. Baseball's worth fighting for. And they've already kicked me off the team. What worse can they do?"

"Maybe you don't want to know."

Callie smirked. "Besides, your Rip Van Winkle boyfriend needs you, remember? I'm a sucker for a good Rom Com."

Emily fought back the urge to stick out her tongue. She was about to use the baseball magic, for real. She couldn't be behaving like a five-year-old.

Instead, she nodded and said, "Fine, then. We're doing this. Tell me what to do."

Callie pointed at the basket of balls beside her. After all her warmups, she had only three balls left.

"I throw three pitches. You hit three home runs. You run the bases each time. Oh, except..." Callie trailed off, her cool demeanor melting into uncertainty.

"Except what?" Emily prompted. The magic was growing more insistent.

"Except I'm worried the hitter needs to be a Unicorn, and you're not really one of them right now, are you?" To Callie's credit, she said it in a softer tone, like she felt bad about that loss.

But Emily felt a twang in the pull of the magic that told her Callie wasn't entirely correct.

"I think it's going to be okay. I'm Small Folk. The fairy ring here makes it their field, too."

The magic would recognize that connection, and it would work for her.

Callie looked at her, then shrugged. "Okay, then. Three home runs for the Small Folk."

Three home runs. Emily rolled her shoulders, shifted her grip on the bat. Yes. That felt right. But there was one more thing.

She held out a hand to Callie for a shake. "Don't throw me gravy. Pitch like it's for real. I don't think it will work otherwise."

Taking Emily's hand in her firm grip, Callie's wolfish grin would have given the leader of the Wild Hunt a run for his money. "As if I'd do anything less."

"All right, then. Throw your best."

Emily tromped over to home plate feeling a thrum of readiness. This was it.

She took her stance and waggled her bat.

Callie stood on the mound, which was somehow illuminated now despite the lack of any official lighting.

The baseball magic is in her, too, Emily thought, looking at Callie as she wound up to deliver the first pitch. Yes, she was right. Magic flared in a silver wave that rolled off Callie McMasters' shoulders.

The pitch came. Fastball, just as Emily had suspected. It came blistering towards her, a burning streak in the night, and when Emily's bat connected with it to send it rocketing upward like a shooting star, the magic inside her twisted deftly.

She ran the bases in elated silence and felt Callie's satisfaction turn about with her.

Back at home plate, she picked up her fallen bat once again.

Callie already had her next ball in hand. The power built around it as she began her pitch.

Emily prepared for a changeup after the fastball, but what came was a slider dripping silver dust in its wake.

They were passing the magic back and forth between them like a pair of weavers working a loom. As the pitch entered the strike zone, Emily plastered it with everything she had. Once again, the ball became a firework of silver sparks overhead, and once again, Emily rounded the bases.

That's two, she thought as she touched home plate. One left.

But as she grabbed her bat again, a voice echoed out of the night.

"Wait!"

Emily turned, her bat drooping. "Dad."

He stepped from behind the backstop, striding towards her at home. He wore a light White Sox jacket with his hands pushed into the pockets. A look of determination made his mouth a black line.

Emily's heart dropped. He'd changed his mind. He wasn't going to let her leave without a fight.

But then he came even with her and paused, hesitating with something that felt like anticipation.

"One more should do it, yeah?" he said.

"Yeah," Emily said.

He pulled something out of his pocket and held it out to her.

Mom's ball.

Emily gaped.

"Better make it one worth knocking out of the park, just like your mom would want."

The tears she'd swallowed down earlier came flooding out now.

Once again, Callie was right. Even with their understanding of the baseball magic, opening the portal would still incur a cost.

Swiping her arm over her eyes, she took the ball from him. "I love you, Dad. And I will come back. I promise."

It was a true promise. With the baseball magic thrumming through her, it couldn't be anything less.

Dad drew her close and pressed a kiss to her forehead. "I love you, too, baseball princess. Do what you need to do. I'll be here, cheering you the whole way."

Callie had come from the mound to stand awkwardly beside them. "Mr. DeWitt," she said with a sharp nod when he looked at her.

Emily held Mom's ball out to her.

When Callie closed her fingers around it, they both jumped. A jolt of power tingled through both of them, and a smell like fresh rain on grass blew across the field. Distantly, the sound of a hunting horn broke the silence of the night, bringing Emily a familiar chill.

Dad climbed up into the stands.

Callie returned to the mound, and Emily took up her bat one final time.

Everything glowed like fairy light.

Callie wound up. The power built.

Mom's ball left Callie's hand like a magic spell. Emily felt a surge of delight at the effortless way Callie had pitched it, watched the sphere spin like it was in slow motion, twisting and tilting, to finally drop as it came to home plate.

Curveball.

Her delight doubled as she caught it with the sweetest part of the bat.

The crack of impact was magic all on its own.

Even without watching, Emily knew it was out of the park, doomed to be lost forever among the trees beyond Unicorn Field.

Dad was right. Mom would have wanted it that way.

She rounded the bases, and as she ran, each step found more pale grass beneath her cleats. Each breath smelled more like cinnamon and spice. She saw fairy lights dancing.

As she started down the third baseline towards home, Callie came down from the mound. She was also heading for home, dashing as if she intended to tag Emily out despite not having a live ball in hand.

"What—?" was all Emily got out.

Callie grinned, looking more like her old self again. "Might as well see if the fairies will let me play ball, too, right?"

Then they were both stepping onto home plate, their cleats clicking against the bone-white stone at exactly the same moment, and Callie's laugh was swallowed up in the flare of the portal opening to admit two mortals onto the Other Field.

CHAPTER TWENTY-SIX

This time it was Emily who prevented a traveler from face planting, catching Callie McMasters by the crook of the arm and keeping her steady.

"You weren't supposed to come along!"

Callie righted herself. "Can't let you have all the fun, now, can I?"

Emily chuffed back a new feeling of dread as the full realization of what had happened fell over her. The Small Folk had called her here at the start of the season, and she'd always presumed the Unseelie Queen had done the same to Adrien Thorn. But Callie McMasters had crossed into this world of her own volition, under her own power. How did that happen? What would Wonderland do with a mortal free agent? She didn't know. Clearing her mind, though, Emily finally took a look around and felt a fresh new layer of the same dread grow over her.

This *was* the Other Field.

But it was empty now. Dark and silent. Not even the tiny fairy lights that usually danced through the outfield were around to greet them. A stale scent hovered over the ground, lingering in the still, dead air. The flowers that made up the baselines looked overgrown and unkempt. A glance at the dusty, abandoned dugouts told Emily they hadn't been used in a while.

Her elation at successfully working the baseball magic quickly twisted into a sick sense of dread.

Beside her, Callie looked around with obvious distaste. "This is the Fairy Realm? I thought it was supposed to be more, y'know, magical."

Emily tried to stifle her panic. "Are we too late?" she said wistfully.

She'd been away from this place for two weeks, real world time. How much time did that translate to here? A month? A year? Had the Unseelie Queen won the Web Gem yet again? Had she used it to do something unspeakable to the Other Field?

Had the Small Folk been punished for daring to reach too high?

Was baseball dead in Fairyland?

But then, from the dark mass of the woods that separated the Other Field and its surrounding Glades from the Unseelie Court, came a nearly inaudible, far-distant crack of a bat.

Though it had been faint, both girls spun to face the sound.

"Someone's playing," Callie said. Her voice tilted with yearning.

Understanding flooded Emily, followed by shaky relief. "I see. The Unseelies never play off their own home turf. The Fairy Series will be happening at their pitch." The Other Field wasn't really abandoned, everyone was just at the queen's terrifying home field, possibly by compulsion. The Small Folk were still safe — as safe as they'd ever been, anyway. At least for the moment. "All we have to do is cross through the forest."

And hope we don't run into the Wild Hunt, she added silently.

Callie clapped her hands together and rubbed them in readiness. "Let's hit the road, then. There is a road, right?"

"Um. Sort of." Emily hoped Shady Marie's and Nash's earlier work was still in effect. Otherwise, she suspected they were in for a rough time.

Luckily the silvery moon was out, and after leading Callie

through the tall grass that surrounded the Other Field, she was able to find the trailhead easily enough, even in the dark. But peering into the deep gloom beyond the first pair of trees, she didn't like the way the creepy factor increased so much sooner than it used to. She remembered the path being flanked with beautiful, silvery birch for a good long stretch before these thick, rank-smelling, hulking monstrous clusters of trees took over. Now they were growing only a few steps along the way. Greenish-black slime dribbled down through the cracks and creases of their gnarled bark, its uneven dripping all that broke the silence.

Then, from deep within, something inhuman screamed.

"Good, great," Callie said, her back straight as a bat, her fists clutching in fear. "I can totally see why you wanted to come back."

Despite the wavering tenor of Callie's voice — or maybe even because of it — Emily felt a fire light inside her. This wasn't her first ball game in Fairyland. She would not be frightened off. Beyond that, Emily felt strength fighting against her own fear. Holding her questions about the Small Folk's motivations at bay, she focused on her desire to be with her teammates. She wanted to play. Win or lose, she wanted to be in the game.

Feeling that need so close to the bone, Emily knew just how to get Callie to feel that fire, too.

She slid a narrow gaze towards her rival. "It's all right if you're too scared to go on... I'm sure the Small Folk don't need you."

"Like hell, I'm too scared. If you're going, I'm going." Callie steeled herself so resolutely that Emily was happy the shadows cloaked her satisfied smile.

So, they went.

But the forest's creepiness did not lessen any due to her fiery determination. As soon as they stepped past the first trees, the darkness closed in around them, stealing all but the slightest sliver of visibility. The path before them became a barely-there depression in the growth. Meanwhile, the silence pressed so heavily even their footsteps crunching through the brush was muted.

Emily was certain something wicked and starving was right behind her, breathing down her neck. But she remembered her previous treks through this forest and held herself in check. Turning to look would only waste time.

She did, however, grope with one hand until she found Callie's sweaty fingers.

Callie tightened their grip wordlessly.

Moments later, Callie tugged on Emily's hand.

"There's a light. Over there."

She pointed, though all Emily could make out was a dim shifting of the shadows. Emily squinted, then saw it. A hollow flicker of warm light, barely more than a candle flame, twinkling serenely in the unknowable distance. It looked so inviting, so full of love and friendship. So full of promise.

Such a light in this darkness, even so minuscule, was balm for the mind.

Emily's heart yearned to move towards it, and she felt Callie's cleated foot rise to move forward and Callie's body posture shift as if she were contemplating dashing off after it.

She yanked back on Callie's hand.

"I don't think we can trust it. It'll lead us into a bog, or worse."

Callie sighed and turned back. "Yeah, I bet you're right. I've read all about fairy tricks. So, okay. Joy. Anywhere but the light."

Emily calmed Callie's sentiments with an invisible shrug. "I know. It sucks."

They pressed on into the darkness. The trail still held, though they had to move slowly and examine the path before them painstakingly to ensure they weren't wandering down a deer trail instead.

All the while, that sensation of something breathing right behind her kept pace.

"Are you sure we shouldn't go back and find that light?" Callie said in a wistful tone.

Emily had to wrestle with her own desire to do exactly that. "We have to keep on the trail. That's the only way we'll make it to the Unseelie Pitch."

The instant the words were out of her mouth, the two had to pull up hard to avoid walking straight into a solid wall of tangled vines. The wall stretched across the path and as far into the woods on either side as they could see. A thin, silvery glow emanated from needle-like thorns that bristled from every inch of its bramble. Beads of a clear, viscous liquid reflected the cold light at the needle tips.

"Time to find another way, then," said Callie through a hiss of pain. The sudden stop had kept them from getting jabbed, but it hadn't been easy on the muscles.

This all felt deliberate, now. Almost personal to Emily. As if these dangers were not simple tricks laid to catch whatever might stumble upon them but were specifically targeted at her. Something was hunting her, herding her where it wanted her to go.

It reeked of the Wild Hunt.

Emily gritted her teeth. "Something is playing tricks. This wasn't here before."

Callie let out a bark of laughter that felt harsh in the intimate, yet oppressive silence of the woods. "Yes, very surprising of the fey folk to have a little joke at our expense. Come on, let's backtrack. Maybe there's a new fork in the road we can follow."

Silently, Emily allowed Callie to lead them back the way they'd come. Their hands were still joined, and Emily focused on that point of contact as a way to block out her growing anger.

"Just don't go back to that light," she said.

"Yeah, yeah."

The faint illumination of the thorns had ruined her night sight, and as the two of them retreated, Emily strained to see in the full darkness once again. After a few steps, she realized it wasn't just her imagination: the trail seemed even thinner and more ragged than it had when they'd passed over it mere moments ago.

Wild Hunt or not, whatever was toying with her wanted Emily

disoriented and lost. It wanted her to run blindly into the darkness. It wanted her alone.

She tightened her grip on Callie's hand. Callie squeezed back.

"I think there's a fork here," Callie said.

Emily saw it. She also saw a shadow within the shadow, moving toward them, not two steps along that false trail.

"Cal—"

The shadow crashed forth in a tumble of brush and coarse fur, snarling and flinging hot threads of saliva before it. Teeth flashed, claws slashed. A scream like the one they'd heard at the trailhead shivered through the close air.

Emily's muscles locked at the sound.

She was dead. Callie was dead.

But Callie dropped Emily's hand and stood her ground, delivering a hard uppercut to the monster's toothy jaw. The punch connected with a crunch that had Emily wincing and hoping Callie didn't now sport a fistful of broken knuckles.

Fractured hand or not, Callie followed with another strike.

But the monster was ready for her this time. Its bared fangs gleamed in the night.

Something whizzed past Emily's ear, ruffled Callie's hair, and a split second later, buried itself in the creature's throat. With a sharp yip that ended in a thick gurgle, the thing died.

A wave of hot breath cascaded down Emily's neck.

"Little hunter has brought a friend, we see," came a familiar gravelly voice.

Unlike the first time they'd met, the leader of the Wild Hunt was not on horseback, nor, as far as Emily could see, was he flanked by any of his hunters. He stood alone among the strapping black trees, his wrappings billowing around him in the still air, an enormous white bow held in both hands.

His golden wolf eyes glowed with intensity as he fixed his gaze on Emily.

Emily glared right back. "So, you've got hold of me after all."

One side of the leader's lips quirked up.

Overhead, something rustled in the branches. Emily and Callie flinched, but the hunter whipped his bow up, pulled an arrow from his quiver, and fired as smoothly as breathing. A screech rang out, and a shadowy, bat-winged creature tumbled out of the tree to land on the path between the three of them with a thump.

"Why are you keeping me from rejoining my team? They're playing, right?"

The leader chuckled. "You misread the tracks, little Miss Em. 'Tis the Unseelie Queen herself who casts her nets about these woods. Your beloved Small Folk have just lost the second game of the Fairy Series," he said, his voice straining, and his eyes narrowing in something Emily felt might be fury. "One more loss, and the Web Gem falls once again to the queen. She knew you had the power to return, and she is uninterested in allowing you to make a triumphant, last-minute reunion with your teammates."

"You're here to help me," Emily said, truth dawning.

"You really must learn to read the trail better, Miss Em," he snarled. "A Small Folk win will not bring about the warfare and bloodshed we lust for."

"Then?"

"We are here only to put our hunting grounds to rights," he snarled. "Not even the Queen can be allowed to taint our lands with such disregard for the nature of things."

"Warfare and bloodshed, huh?" Callie said, massaging her knuckles. "Sounds pretty intense."

"Be silent, mortal."

"But is it more intense than a good game of baseball?" Callie continued, disregarding the leader's warning snarl. "Eh, I'm not so sure."

She said it with exactly the right amount of disdain. Emily

marveled at her daring.

The hunt leader growled low in his throat. "You do not understand what you speak of."

Callie shrugged. "I understand there's a trophy up for grabs. Seems to me you're just bitter your team wasn't good enough to make it to the Series."

Emily elbowed Callie, trying to get her to shut up, but having no more success than the leader did.

"But I guess you hunt-folk must not want your big, bloody dream all that bad, huh? I hear you're not even willing to put in the effort to field a team every season. Not like the Small Folk do, anyway. Now there's a team worth joining."

"What are you doing?" Emily whispered.

The hunt leader was practically vibrating with anger now, his fist white around his bow. He looked about half a second away from snagging another arrow and planting it right in Callie's heart.

But Callie waved Emily away. "Shut up, De— Miss Em. I'm negotiating."

Callie stepped closer to the hunt leader, full of the confidence that came with being a CEO's daughter. "You know these woods, even with the queen's little tricks, right?"

The hunt leader nodded with a gruff growl toward the affirmative, his eyes barely more than slits.

Callie continued. "Here's the offer, then. You take us straight to the Small Folk tonight, avoiding all those nasty traps. Get us there in time to help them win those last three games. In exchange, I will agree to enter into discussions regarding a potential contract between myself and the Wild Hunt's team for next season."

Emily gasped.

It was too much.

Once again, Callie was paying the price for Emily's chance at success.

But Callie's posture oozed with such blatant assumption that she was going to get everything she was asking for that Emily had to admit it was a good play. What did Callie McMasters, currently banned from baseball and estranged from her family, have to keep her from spending a season in Fairyland? If anyone understood Callie's need to play baseball, it would be Emily. And Callie was not only good at the business side of baseball, she was practically born to it.

Emily felt a momentary pang of embarrassment at her own bungled contract.

She hadn't even read hers until far beyond too late to do any negotiating, and here Callie McMasters was, bargaining with even the basic idea of bargaining.

Recognizing the deal being offered him, the leader of the Wild Hunt settled.

With a deft twist of his wrist, he slung the bow across his back, then held one meaty hand to Callie. "We accept your offer. Your name, if you will?"

Callie smirked as she gripped his hand in a shake so firm it might have broken wrists. "Nice try. Not sure what I'll go by with everyone else, but I think *you* can call me Mistress."

Emily hoped it wouldn't come back to bite her, but what was done was done. As the leader brought out his hunting horn to call up his eerie, skeletal horse and the rest of the Wild Hunt with a single sharp blast, she understood that she couldn't spare any further worry on Callie's deal.

It was time to worry, instead, about what she would learn when she finally stood beside the Small Folk and Fennoc once again.

The leader of the Wild Hunt mounted his dark horse and lifted Callie to a position behind him. As Emily, too, clambered onto the horse's back behind Callie, she contemplated the network of deals and contracts that had spun out of control around her.

The Small Folk had paid something at the start of the season.

Callie was on the hook to pay twice now.

When the collector finally came to Emily's doorstep, she wondered now, how steep would she find her own bill?

CHAPTER TWENTY-SEVEN

The second inning of the third game of the Fairy Series had just begun when, like an apparition, the whole of the Hunt appeared at once from behind the center field fence at Unseelie Court's Pitch. The peal of the leader's horn split the air, and the attendees, who had a moment earlier been raucous with song and calls for refreshments, turned as one to take the Hunt in. The Unseelie players, too, playing the field in their navy darks with silver trimmings, stood and gawked as Emily slid off the leader's horse. Her leap over the fence was a beautiful double-handed vault that any Olympic gymnast would weep over.

Behind her, the leader of the Wild Hunt focused on the pitching mound and deliberately caught the Unseelie Queen's gaze with a pointed stare, then gave a sarcastic tip of an invisible baseball cap. A moment later the slavering horde was gone, disappearing into the woods as if they had never been there.

As Emily pelted toward the visiting dugout, she couldn't help but notice the posted score: 1-0 to the Unseelie Court, and the Small Folk had not a single runner on base.

I'll change that, Emily promised.

Little Essie's voice was the first to pierce the night.

"Look, look! It's Miss Em! *It's Miss Em!*" the brownie called.

A confused rumble rolled over the crowd as Callie, too, made it over the fence to race a few steps behind Emily.

A moment later, Emily and Callie arrived.

Their appearance on the pitch had been so sudden, most of the Small Folk hadn't yet stirred from their spots on the bench, where they all sat slumped in utter dejection. They looked like a pack of beaten dogs, complete with purpling bruises and fresh scrapes oozing blood. Even the air near the dugout tasted like defeat, like utter decimation.

But one by one, as Essie's screams of delight sank in and realization dawned, they unfurled themselves in open wonder.

Shady Marie, standing stiffly at the edge of the dugout, put one delicate hand to her mouth, her eyes shining with tears. "Oh, Miss Em..."

Fennoc flung aside the papers he'd been listlessly flipping through and surged up out of the dugout to catch Emily up in his arms.

"Lass, lass! Are you really here?" Fennoc said, his voice quavering and boyish with disbelief and delight. The fleshy flat of his nose seemed to glow in fresh pink tones. The loop of grass spun in tight circles with his rotating jaw, his uniform as clean as ever and pressed perfectly sharp.

"I'm here," Emily said, breathless as Fennoc squeezed her tight.

"We thought you'd left us for good," Nash said, his own beady eyes shimmering as he stumped up beside them.

"We thought you got tired of playing with us," said Mellica. Her pixie wings fluttered at full speed, creating a high-pitched hum of happiness and spreading pixie dust absolutely everywhere.

Emily shook her head emphatically. "Never. I just needed a little help remembering something important. I'm sorry I'm late getting back."

"Who is this?" Maddoc said, joining his brother and pointing to

Callie, who was not-so-subtly inspecting the Small Folk's equipment.

Emily caught Callie's eye. "This is my best rival. And a very good friend. She came to help us."

"I can't believe it!" Shady Marie called from the edge of the dugout. She was working to unstiffen herself, but her knees were still locked. "Two mortal players on our little team? Maybe we *can* turn this around."

On the field, the Unseelie Queen stepped toward the umpire. A darkening cloud of black smoke had built around her, and ominous sparks of electricity flickered within it, a blatant hint at her barely constrained power.

"She can't play," the queen said, pointing into the Small Folk dugout. "She's not on the roster. Neither of them are."

"Oh, yes, I am," Emily said. "By the authority of the Other Field, and with the blessing of the Web Gem."

She reached into her trouser pocket and pulled out the contract.

Its golden glow lit up the darkness of Unseelie Pitch in a momentary flare, and when the light faded to a bearable level, a murmur of disbelief swept through the entire stadium.

The queen's face twisted in a grimace of pure fury. "What nonsense is this? Who would *dare?* Someone will pay for this."

"Someone already has," Emily said through clenched teeth. She glanced at Fennoc to find him trembling beside her, too many emotions flitting through him to read. The set of his face let her know she'd been right to wonder about that payment, and though she wasn't going to reveal her need to the queen, she intended to discover exactly what that cost had been.

The queen's eyes were flashing purple now. "I refuse to allow this! Umpire! Throw this little wretch out of my game."

Fennoc shook himself out of his emotional turmoil. "Oh, no, you don't," he called, his cloven hooves clattering as he ran out to argue his case.

Fennoc inserted himself between the queen and the ump, and as the argument ensued, the crowd began to roar.

Emily turned to Maddoc, though, and stared daggers at him. She was not going to be distracted from her purpose.

"I need to know two things, Maddoc. And I need to know them now."

"Miss Em?" The wiry faun replied.

"Why me?"

"I don't understand."

"Yes, you do. When you called a mortal player, it could have been anyone. Why did you select me?"

"But it couldn't have been just anyone. Ye carry the baseball magic inside. Isn't that obvious, Miss Em? Ye come from a line of players with that power. The connection is quite strong, lassie."

The revelation hit her harder than maybe it should have. Not only was the baseball magic something her mother had believed in enough to try to pass down to Emily, it was also their heritage. Emily put her lips together, feeling that connection back through the ages. If she let herself, she could touch it.

The thought of how much she'd truly missed out on when Mom died sent a wave of grief crashing over her so strong she longed to curl up and sob.

Instead, she pierced Maddoc with a glare so hard he flinched.

"And what did you pay?" she said.

He stammered with a soft, distressed braying sound, and avoided meeting her eyes.

She stared harder.

"*I* didn't pay a thing, Miss Em." Maddoc finally said. His deerlike gaze flitted to where his brother was now going chest to chest with the Queen. Maddoc's lips pursed, then his gaze returned to Emily's.

Another piece of the truth fell to her.

"All right. What did Fennoc pay?"

Maddoc dropped his gaze, then returned it to her.

"My brother was once a great player, he was," he said, as if that was enough.

"I don't understand," Emily said.

"Don't be stupid, De— Miss Em," Callie said, turning now to Maddoc. "The little dude out there gave up his talent to bring her across, didn't he?"

"Aye, Miss Rival. He did."

Emily couldn't believe it. "Why would he do that?"

She took in the gathering of her team, saw Twy and Shayla in the back of the dugout, their faces growing dark with guilt. Delananey holding a bat in readiness to hit but looking sheepish. Mellica turned her gaze away when Emily stared at her. Even Izusa had grown subdued at the conversation.

"It's all my fault!" Essie broke in. She crossed her arms over the fabric edge of Greeven's pocket and buried her face to cry into the crook of one arm.

"What?" Emily said.

"I stole the Web Gem!" Essie wailed softly now, tears running down her little face as she pulled her head up. "I was doing maid work at the Unseelie Castle in the pre-season, and it was just sitting there, all unguarded. I thought... I thought we could try to get a boon! So, I took it. It's all my fault!"

"Now, now, little Essie," Maddoc said, holding his hand out to gently rub the brownie on her tiny little shoulder. "You mustn't blame yourself for taking advantage of an opportunity."

"But it cost—"

"Never mind the cost," Shady Marie said. "It was worth getting the chance to try. Fennoc said so himself."

"What is everyone talking about?" Callie said. "Can we just shut up and play ball?"

The roar of the crowd grew rowdy, and from the corner of her eye Emily saw several Small Folk ducking and dodging, others cowering, as spectators grabbed goblets and plates and the various grotesqueries of Pitch food, some throwing it onto the field in a wicked mockery of pure joy, others stuffing their faces and demanding more.

"I see it now," Emily said under her breath.

"What do you see?" Callie said.

Emily glanced at Essie, who was lost in another bout of distraught tears, then turned to Callie. "Small Folk do all the work here. I knew that already. I thought they were simply trying to get a break. But it's so much more than that, isn't it, Maddoc? The Small Folk have an agenda, too. Like the Hunt. This whole thing is because Small Folk are being oppressed."

Fennoc wouldn't have given up his ability to play for anything less.

Maddoc's chest heaved with a resigned breath.

"You're right, Miss Em. Us small folk are shackled. We do all the hard work throughout the realm. We build and we cook. Harvest. Clean. Repair. We do it all. Always have. Always will. And never a feast nor a festival nor even a 'thank you' do we get in return, unless you count a hard cuff across the face as gratitude. And it's not fair. Every year — even the few times the Unseelies lose control — it's no better."

"It's so hard!" the brownie moaned. "I'm so sorry. I just wanted it to be less hard."

"We want to free the Small Folk from our chains, and controlling the Web Gem is the only way we know to do it. When Essie brought it to us one night, completely unexpectedly, we knew we had to take advantage. We couldn't keep it forever. We had only one night to make some use of its big magic before the Unseelie Queen was sure to notice its absence. So, it was then or never."

Maddoc shook his head, and Emily understood. She felt the same frustration she got when she thought about putting her mom's baseball on her trophy shelf. "You hadn't earned the Web Gem properly. Without winning the right to command it, you couldn't just compel the Unseelies and the rest to let your families and friends be freed."

"We could not," Maddoc said, shaking his head sadly. "Though I wish it were so. We tried asking for that boon directly, but when that didn't work, instead, we decided to try and call a mortal player to the Other Field. And when the cost came due, Fennoc paid it gladly. He told us to think of it as trading up."

Emily felt the truth of it all. She remembered the moment after that first game when she and Fennoc had stood in the little glen, tossing pitches and talking about how baseball magic couldn't exist, because it had let them both down so much.

Fennoc had known better, though.

The sound of hooves against dugout flagstones clopped as Fennoc, still full of the argument, blustered into the dugout. Outside, the fans seemed to have settled, also.

"You can play!" he called jovially, eyes beaming.

Then he saw the expressions throughout the dugout. He stopped and pulled himself more stiffly upright, only his blade of grass drooping. "What is it?"

Emily worked to keep her voice calm. "You lied to me."

Fennoc scanned the team members, and his jubilant expression tightened. "You told her, didn't you?"

No one answered, but Emily knew that now he, too, understood the truth was out there. Or, he thought he did.

She stepped closer to him, her fists balling at her sides. "You told me you didn't believe in the baseball magic when you knew perfectly well it was real. You even knew my mother had it, didn't you? You said she'd have made a good third sacker."

Fennoc held himself on the dugout stairs carefully. "I didn't mean to insult you. I only needed— I simply required—" He cut himself off, glanced over Emily's shoulder at the gathered Small Folk, then let out a sigh that had him practically folding over himself. "I wanted to make you feel like you had an ally here, like there was someone on our team who felt the same as you did, so you would play for us. I was scared that if you found out how the baseball magic worked, you'd become so good at it that you'd be able to break your contract before we won the Web Gem."

Hearing the truth so cleanly from him gave Emily a sense of relief. She was still angry, but it was a low, simmering thing rather than a pot in danger of boiling over.

"The thing is, Fennoc, I understand why you did that," she said. "The Small Folk's freedom is worth playing by your own rules for. But I don't know that I can forgive you. I wish you'd trusted me enough to tell me the truth. You gave up your skills willingly enough, but you had no right to take my mother's gift away from me."

Silence rang in the dugout. Even the crowd, which couldn't possibly be hearing this conversation, seemed keyed-in to the tension.

"I'm sorry," Fennoc said, very quietly.

Out on the field, the Unseelie Queen clapped her hands. "I'll lodge a complaint for delay of game if you lot don't hurry up!"

Fennoc cast a desperate glance at Emily, but didn't say anything.

Emily nodded. Then she turned to the rest of her team.

"Well," she said, "I guess the only thing left to do is to win this thing, right?"

The Small Folk shuffled awkwardly, but relief colored their motions as they moved into batting order.

"I want to play, too," Callie said, running her hand over her hair. "Can I get a uniform?"

Fennoc glanced at Callie first, then to Emily, then back. The things they'd left unsaid would have to remain so for a while longer. "As much as I'd love to have two mortal players, that cannot work out now."

"What do you mean?" Callie said.

"There's a matter of a contract," Fennoc said.

"I'll sign whatever."

"I'm afraid that won't play, now," the faun explained. "The queen informed us that ye've already entered an arrangement with the Hunt."

"I've done no such thing."

"I'm sorry Miss Rival, but an agreement to consider an agreement is still binding till it ain't."

Callie's face fell. She breathed deeply. "You mean, after all this, I can't play?"

"That's correct, Miss Rival. Ye can't play."

Emily put her arm around Callie and felt the raw edge of disappointment that trembled through her. "It's all right," she said. "We'll figure something out. With the baseball magic—"

Callie shrugged the hug off and threw herself onto a dugout bench. She looked out onto the intimidating field full of magic, but her face clouded. "Easy for you to say."

Emily bit her lip to keep from saying something banal back to Callie, and instead followed Callie's gaze out to where Delananey was now trying to get on base against the Unseelies.

Her friend was right.

It was easy for Emily to say because at least she could play baseball again.

Even if, inside, all she wanted to do was cling to the mother she'd long-since lost.

CHAPTER TWENTY-EIGHT

Emily gave up a run that inning. She was, admittedly, nervous, and the moment got to her. She left a changeup too high in the strike zone and the hitter plastered it into Neverland.

She settled down after that, and the game was tight.

Izusa got on base in the fourth inning by bunting and made it to second on a squibbing grounder thanks to Shayla's quick counter-song work against the Unseelie Queen's impromptu magery, which would have had the ball rolling into foul territory if left unchecked. A ground out and sacrifice fly later, the score was at 2-1 for the Unseelies. But Greeven had also gotten on base and even made it all the way to second on that mis-cast grounder, and when Maddoc stepped up with his giant log of a bat, he smashed the queen's next pitch all the way into left field, which let Greeven make it home before Maddoc himself was tagged out, ending the inning with the score evened up.

Which was how it stayed after five innings, then six, then seven.

The crowd was getting tense. With the Unseelies ahead two games to none in the series, everyone knew what these next two innings meant, and when Shady Marie communed with her bat carefully enough, then stroked a clean double off the right field wall, and then Mellica snuck a hot grounder past first base to score her, the attendees got caught up in a quandary. This was, of course, the Unseelie Queen's home field, and the queen was not known to be well pleased with cheering that went against her team. Yet, the Small Folk were the beleaguered under bet. It was hard not to get excited for the novelty of being able to say they were there the night the Unseelie Court lost a Series game to the punching bag of the Fairy Realm.

Emily retired the Unseelies in order in their half of the eighth inning, and then the Small Folk went scoreless in the top of the ninth.

So, the game turned to the bottom of that ninth inning.

Small Folk 3, Unseelie Court 2.

The suspense bordered on exquisite. So rapt was the attention that even the gnome and pixie attendants were chewing at fingernails and running hands through hair so often it shed. When the first Unseelie hitter struck out swinging at a perfect curveball, the spectators groaned, then cheered. Small Folk chanting turned into a song.

The second hitter scorched a liner to center field, and Izusa had to perform an extended somersault to reel it in. It was a spectacular play. Amazing.

Two outs.

Emily watched the next hitter arrive, whipping his bat backward and forward to limber his wrist. The Designated Hitter stood in the on-deck circle.

Get it done now, she said to herself, not wanting to take her chances with him.

She glanced at the dugout and saw Callie there.

"You got this!" Callie called.

Emily pitched. Curveball, with extra spin.

The hitter was ready for it, though. He drove a sharp ground ball down the third base line.

Greeven dove, extended his elven glove as far as his elven glove would extend — but it was just out of reach. The elf flopped to the hard dirt, and the ball skipped past, rolling all the way to the wall, twisting into foul territory — and, as the ball twisted, the field itself shifted, adding land to let the ball roll farther and farther, until finally, Jessebel was able to flag it down and throw it back in.

But by then, the runner was at third base.

Greeven, however, was still writhing on the ground, cradling his wrist.

"What's wrong?" Emily said, rushing over to check on him.

"I jammed it," the elf said, following it up with words in a language Emily was glad she didn't understand.

"Great," she said, turning to Nash, who had joined her, his catcher's mask pushed up on top of his head.

A moment later, Fennoc arrived, too, timid submission evident in the set of his slumped shoulders and averted gaze. He was afraid of her, she realized. Worried after their last exchange.

"We need to replace Greeven," Emily said firmly. There would be time to deal with everything else later.

"No, I can play!" Greeven said even as his wrist was swelling to the size of an orange.

Emily looked at Fennoc. The few bench players they had were all outfielders. An expression of fear crossed his gaze.

"It's you, isn't it?" Emily said. "You're Greeven's backup." It came out sounding like an accusation, and she wasn't entirely certain she didn't mean it as such.

He pursed his lips. "I did play third base before, Miss Em."

"Then grab a glove. You're still on the roster."

"But I can't, Miss Em. My skills are gone. I can't play."

"Bull hockey," Emily said. "I'll do my best to keep the ball from being hit your way. But even if you just block anything that comes at you, you're better for the team than an injured elf."

For an instant Emily felt certain Fennoc was going to cry. Carefully, she made herself take a deep breath. Then she softened her tone and clapped a hand on the faun's shoulder.

"Get a glove and let's have some fun."

Fennoc stiffened for a moment. Then he gave a bray and bucked up. "I swear you'll be the death of me, Miss Em."

The umpire arrived to speed things up, and before Emily could do more than smile, Fennoc announced he was replacing Greeven.

As the official called up the scoring register and made the change, Fennoc fetched his mitt. Greeven walked dejectedly off the field.

In her dugout, the dark queen, who surely understood the situation, gave a wicked slant of a smile.

Fennoc took his position close to third base, looking uncomfortable as a newborn colt trying to stand. His pristine uniform stood out, and he looked strange without the blade of grass poking from his lips.

Emily retook the mound.

As the Designated Hitter dug trenches in the batter's box, Emily tried to ignore the pounding of drums and chanting of spectators.

Instead, she focused on the tingling of the baseball magic as she built up from within herself. She had an idea of how she wanted to use it, too.

She peered in to see Nash give her the signs. At third, the runner took an extra-long lead, daring her to throw the ball to Fennoc, who may or may not be able to catch it. Nash signed curveball.

Emily gave him a wink — throw to third, she was telling him.

The Designated Hitter had owned her all season. She didn't want to give him anything to hit. If they could pick the runner off third, that would finish the game.

The magic she'd gathered pulsed inside her. This was the moment.

She pitched, purposely so far outside that not even Thorn could get his bat on it. Nash grabbed the ball and obediently tossed it to Fennoc at third.

The ball bounced off Fennoc's chest. The runner was easily safe at third.

The faun's cheeks flushed rosy pink under his fur as he picked the ball up. Rather than throw it to Emily, he walked it to her. His discomfort grew more obvious as the jeering of the crowd turned abrasive and personal.

"I don't think I can do this, Miss Em," he said, holding the glove out so she could grab the ball from it. Hurt and embarrassment radiated from him. "I understand that I owe you for lying about the magic before. And you're right, I should have told you about your mother's connection to it. But I wish you'd let me make amends to you some other way."

Emily nodded. In truth, her anger was fading rapidly. How could she hold onto it when the baseball magic was with her now?

She reached out and wrapped her hand over the ball, and then — leaving the sphere in the glove — transferred her hand into her own glove. Her eyes twinkled. "I remember hearing at one time that you're pretty good with a practical joke. Better than your brother, anyway, right?"

He felt the ball in his glove and gave an expression that turned into a sheepish grin.

"Innate ability, right?" Emily said.

"That's right, Miss Em. Innate ability."

"Then let's work some innate ability baseball magic together, eh?"

Emily turned to walk away, grinding her fist into her glove as if she had the ball.

The roar of the crowd rose as she approached the mound, then walked to grab the resin bag. Standing on the pitching rubber without the ball would be a balk, so instead she stalled for a moment, giving Fennoc time to take his defensive position.

And giving time for the runner to take a step of his lead toward home.

Then another step.

And two more.

Emily glanced to third in just enough time to see Fennoc leap from his position, race to the runner and tag him out!

The umpire raised one fist.

At first the entire crowd hung silent, stunned. Then pandemonium broke out.

A hidden ball trick! The game was over! Small Folk three, Unseelie Court two! Miracle! Miracle!

Voices rose so loud that Emily could barely hear the Unseelie Queen's screech.

A hidden ball trick! A hidden ball trick, and now Fennoc was jumping and running and braying, and the Small Folk team was mobbing him, dragging him down into the dirt and mussing his pristine jersey without so much as a complaint from him, and the Small Folk in the stand were cheering and crying and yelling and pounding each other on the back.

A hidden ball trick!

Can you believe it!

Emily, too, cheered. She pulled Fennoc up from his dirt bath and pounded him on the back as he grinned furiously, and she cheered and cheered as her teammates surrounded her.

"Baseball magic, Fennoc," she yelled over the tumult. "Baseball magic!"

"Oh, Miss Em," Fennoc said. "You're an excellent spell-caster."

It was, she decided, the most fun she had ever had.

CHAPTER TWENTY-NINE

A disjointed air of awkwardness surrounded Callie McMasters in the hours after the tag-out.

First, she sat alone on the near end of the bench as the Small Folk charged the field. Then, as the celebration calmed to a revelrous acceptance of the moment, a sense of imposture followed in her wake as she patted Small Folk players on the back or gave little high-fives to the pixies.

She had done nothing, of course.

This win wasn't her doing.

Indeed, sitting on the bench during a game with such meaning had been the most excruciating pain Callie McMasters had ever felt. Worse than fixing the one cavity she'd had when she was nine. Worse than falling off her motor scooter. Worse than wrenching her knee stealing second base like she did when she was a Sophomore. That last had cost her absence in two games, an absence that had, again, been more irksome than the injury itself.

Joining the team's celebration as if she were an insider felt like she was stealing the team's glory. Yet, Emily had pulled her along, making sure she was invited to the post-game dinner, which was held in an open glade in the woods outside the Other Field, and was hosted by masses of what Callie saw were "commoners." Waves of gnomes and half-dwarves came to arrange the tables they'd made of raw lumber and the silk-draped counters of foodstuffs that ranged from aromatic bread puddings to beautifully prepared roasts, all cooked and served by a phalanx of brownies and tinker-bells. As they ate, lines of Small Folk fans processed before members of the team, and Fennoc, in particular, was so busy pressing his horn print into celebratory signature molds that he was barely able to eat.

When Emily pulled Callie aside and insisted they share a plate of cinnamon-flavored apples, she felt she had to accept.

"You clean up well," she told Emily, trying to avoid the game chatter that sprouted from every other mouth in the room. "That gown is amazing."

Emily shrugged. "Proof that Mellica and Jessebel are miracle workers."

"Don't do that, Emi—Miss Em."

"Do what?"

"You look great. Pretending you can't see it is just as bad form as pretending you've got something you don't."

Emily chuffed. "Hmm."

The two of them were both wearing outfits designed by the pixie pair — Emily's a flowing garment of cerulean blue lined with fine puffs of gauzy material that smelled of cottonwood, Callie's a darker brown hue that she would have considered ugly at home, but with its sharply cut lines and the wide black and maroon sash that cinched her waist, she realized it would catch eyes in any world, mortal or otherwise. Mellica's spell work with a makeup brush was equally different for her, but it had created magic with them both.

"Really, don't run yourself down," she said to Emily. "The pixies may be magic, but they can't make a masterpiece out of river mud. You look lovely."

"Thank you."

Sitting in the quiet copse of trees, they ate their apples. They were delicious, because of course they were.

"I'm sorry you weren't able to play," Emily said.

"Me, too."

"We'll try it again tomorrow, I'm sure. Fennoc is a good negotiator. Maybe he'll win the day."

"Maybe," Callie said as she watched the dancing small folk continue their celebration.

Inside, though, she felt the spider's thread of a bond already forming, and along that bond she could feel the slavering horde gathering for their run, smell the acrid burn of torches in the night air, and taste the sharp flavor of blood on the air. Inside, Callie knew that no argument Fennoc of the Small Folk put forward would ever result in her playing for *this* team.

No point in arguing with Emily, though.

DeWitt had her own ties to manage and her own problems to deal with.

But, as she stood with Emily and watched the party unfold, Callie realized there was something she *could* do. Something beyond sitting in the dugout and offering advice. Something beyond cheering hard and then — assuming there were any more — being a parasite at these celebration parties.

Something that, as a free agent, perhaps she was the only person with the wherewithal to pull off.

There was more at stake here than simply winning the Fairy Series.

At that moment, Izusa appeared in their little nook, dressed resplendently in a green vest and dark pants that fit tight over the trim, wiry muscles of his dancer's legs. His delicate pixie wings glimmered against his back, where he kept them tucked elegantly.

He bent at the waist to Emily, folding himself over one gracefully bent arm.

"May I have this dance, Lady Em?"

Emily blanched. "I don't know how—"

"She would *love* to dance," Callie interrupted. "Don't mind me."

She put her hand against the small of DeWitt's back, and, ignoring spluttered protests, pushed her into the fray.

She watched as Izusa spun her one-time rival into the firelight of the open glade, and let a real sense of accomplishment settle over her as DeWitt's stiffened posture turned joyous.

There, Callie thought. *That's one thing I've done here.*

And as the wild music of the Small Folk washed over her, she leaned back against the tree and formed a plan to do something more.

CHAPTER THIRTY

The next day had dawned overcast with a dome of clouds that rolled across the Fairy Realm, broken only by a brilliant sliver of golden-framed sunlight on the horizon. Last night's frivolities already seemed distant as Emily breathed in the sharp coolness of the springtime chill, the air wet and rich with an earthy aroma that only heightened her anticipation about the impending game.

She could not tell if that anticipation was built of excitement or dread, but it had clung to her all day.

Now the clocks had turned to evening time, and, as the grandstands at Unseelie Pitch filled with a churning mass of Fairy Realm denizens, the darkly macabre lights of the pitch had grown in strength. Clouds of noxious fumes seeped from the rotted seaweed that newly marked a set of twisting foul lines. Drummers pounded an unsettling rhythm that Emily thought might be some kind of goth jazz.

It made her think of Patsy Pell and her Unicorn teammates.

Focus, DeWitt, she admonished herself, hearing Callie McMasters' voice in her head this time rather than her mom's.

Emily stood on the mound, tossing warm up pitches to Nash, who seemed to be trembling behind the plate. Game four of the series would be starting in minutes. A big game made even bigger by the bruise her Small Folk ballclub had left on the Unseelie Queen. Everyone knew the Court would come out fervently ready to play. And, of course, fervently ready to cheat. As she threw a lazy practice curveball, the Designated Hitter's warning came back to her.

You will not like the result of a single win, better yet an effort to actually take the Web Gem.

She glanced into the Unseelie dugout to find the shadow-draped figure of the Designated Hitter, then the hazy outline of the Unseelie Queen, who was also seated in the darker area of the team's bench. Her features were sharply etched with the silver-white glow of the Web Gem, which she held tucked tightly against her side as if it were a precious infant. As always, she absently stroked it with the tips of her long, limber fingers.

Last night's bravado had faded, leaving only desperation to churn within her Small Folk teammates, and to be fair, Emily felt it, too — as, obviously, did the attendees, who chirped and bantered about the impossibility of the Small Folk winning again.

"Can't happen," one golden-brown centaur said in a booming voice loud enough Emily could hear it as clear as a foghorn on the ocean her parents had taken her to as a kid. The Pacific Northwest had been magical in its own way but was mostly wet as she remembered it. The centaur continued, quaffing ale from a pewter cup and calling a gnome to fetch a fresh batch of roasted walnuts along with a plate of dried fruits. As the centaur pontificated about the queen's reluctance to lose again, Emily cringed, seeing the gnome bow multiple times while barely ducking a wild backhanded whack from the centaur. As the gnome scampered away, Emily was fairly certain she'd seen the little guy in the limbo contest last night.

"*Plaaay baaall.*" the foul-smelling Dullahan umpire called as she approached home plate, cradling her grotesque head in the crook of one elbow.

It was not going too far to say that the thing Emily had the most problems adjusting to here in Fairy World was the Unseelie Queen's choice of umpire. The creature's ghastly presence, complete with eerie voice and its severed head — carried around like it was a football — gave her the willies, and probably always would. She took a breath and adjusted her cap, using the time to settle herself down, then she got to work.

The first two Unseelies grounded out: one to Greeven at third (whose wrist had healed well enough with the aid of one of Shady Marie's natural elixirs), and another to Delananey at second base. The Designated Hitter drilled a line drive right back up the middle, hitting it so hard Emily was lucky to avoid taking it right off the skull. That made her mad, though, and she struck out the next hitter on four pitches to end the inning.

Returning to the dugout, Emily sat back and tried to calm herself. This was going to be a tense game. She needed to conserve strength.

"Great job!" Shady Marie said, throwing herself onto the bench beside Emily.

"Way to go Lady Em!" little Essie sang as Greeven scooped the brownie up and deposited her back into his pocket.

"Thanks," Emily said.

Her eyebrows furrowed as she realized something was missing. A corner of her mouth twitched in a question. Leaning over to make sure she had a good view of everything, she scanned the dugout, first to her right, then the left.

"Is something wrong, Miss Em?" Fennoc asked. He was dressed immaculately again. Chewing a fresh blade of grass. His expressive eyes carried a sudden concern.

"Um..." Emily hesitated. "Where's Miss Rival?"

The whole team paused for a moment, then Maddoc replied.

"I don't know. I saw her during warmups. Since she can't play, perhaps she's off getting refreshments?"

"Or maybe the pressure is getting to her?" Nash added. "Maybe she couldn't bear to watch?"

Emily twisted her lips in dissatisfaction. Callie McMasters wouldn't miss any part of a game simply to grab popcorn, and Neverland or not, there was no way she would cave to nerves.

"Maybe," Emily said, trying to bury the question now that she'd already asked it.

Luckily, tensions were high enough that the proposals worked for the rest of the team. There was a game to play, and the Small Folk were setting about to play it. A moment later, Delananey led off for the Small Folk, striking out on three pitches that emerged from the Unseelie Queen's whiplike hand in clouds filled with crackling lighting and popped into the catcher's mitt with scintillating blasts of golden fairy dust.

Emily stifled a groan.

Yes, she thought. It was going to be a long, tough game.

A PAIR OF INNINGS LATER, the Unseelies scored two runs when the Designated Hitter blasted one of Emily's best curveballs into whatever served as outer space here. As he rounded the bases, he gave her the Unicorn salute, which at first made her mad with its sense of one-upmanship. But by the time he'd returned to the mausoleum-like dugout, Emily knew that was wrong of her. She couldn't say why, exactly, but the salute made her feel closer to him. The fact that it was a motion known only to the two of them made it feel like a secret language, and that intimacy said that, rather than being a symbol of his victory over her, the sign was made to honor her. As if he was telling her she had thrown a good pitch — which she had. The problem was simply that, with a hundred years of practice under his belt, he was a very, very good hitter.

Regardless of that game within the game, the Designated Hitter's home run left the Small Folk with another problem: a 2-0 deficit that, with the way the Unseelie Queen was pitching, now seemed as vast as the Pacific Ocean she'd been thinking of before today's game started.

Emily didn't want to give the queen the satisfaction of staring at her, but she did manage to catch the queen's dark form out of the corner of her eye — noting that the queen exuded even more extreme confidence than she always did as she was seated on the bench, still next to her coveted Web Gem. *Probably not even thinking about hitting*, Emily thought bitterly. *Nothing but a century of pitching, pitching, pitching. No wonder she's so good now.*

But Maddoc led off the next inning by hitting a home run that seemed to surprise even himself, making the tally sit at two for the Unseelies, and one for the Small Folk.

Emily loaded the bases with Unseelies the next inning but managed to get out of it without surrendering any more runs when Delananey and Shady Marie turned a perfect double play.

Then Emily goaded the Queen to throw a mistake and wound up on second base with a double. Greeven bunted her to third, and Izusa hit a wicked two hopper that took a lucky bounce off the horn of the satyr at first base, sending her across home plate.

The game was tied 2-2 as the last inning started.

The stadium was on edge as Nash, squatting lower and lower to reduce the size of his strike zone, led off the Small Folk's half of the inning with a walk.

Could a miracle happen twice? The spectators wanted to know.

Mellica grounded into a force play at second but flew down the line fast enough to beat out the throw at first.

Emily came to the bat then, and with the count full hit a ball as hard as she'd ever hit one. The crowd gave a sigh of anticipation as the ball flew into the nighttime sky. It was a homer. A huge, huge homer. Or at least it *should* have been a homer.

But as the white sphere arced through the black night, the park's walls shifted as if on their own, the forest parting to give the walls space to slide outward and outward until finally the descending ball hit off wood planks and rolled back toward the Unseelie outfielder.

"They're cheating!" Emily called as she rounded first base, knowing she was only going to get to second. "They're cheating!"

But though Emily's home run was denied, Mellica had been running on light feet, her fairy wings beating rapidly to speed her along.

As she rounded third, a bramble line of sharp thistle suddenly sprang up between her and home plate. But she never missed a beat, leaping and flying over them in a loop so graceful she didn't even break stride.

The thistles flailed uselessly behind her as she slid safely into home plate, earning the Small Folk the leading run.

The spectators went berserk, mugs raised, screams and cheers and moans mixing.

Several Small Folk did a line jig in the aisles.

"They're cheating!" Emily called to Fennoc, motioning him to go argue with the headless umpire, but the manager simply raised a hand and gave her a motion to rein herself in. She could imagine his voice, even though he wasn't talking. *"Be easy on it now, lassie,"* he would say if he were standing beside her. *"Don't be raising clouds when things are good."*

That it wasn't bad advice served to make that gesture sting a bit more.

The Small Folk were up a run.

It could be enough. It would have to be.

She used her open palm to dust her uniform off.

Two strikeouts later, the inning was over, and Emily jogged back to the dugout to grab her mitt. The score was Small Folk 3, Unseelie Court 2. If she could get the Unseelies out just one more time, her team would force a fifth and final game.

She strode to the mound, determination burning in her bones.

The Designated Hitter would be up fourth.

If she could retire the side in order she wouldn't have to face him at all — which would be good because in addition to the home run earlier, he'd pelted two doubles and a triple. Given the way the walls were moving on their own accord now (part of their nature, the crooked Dullahan had ruled between innings), she was pretty sure what would happen if she let the Designated Hitter get to the plate.

Emily was so pumped that she threw three straight strikes to the first hitter, striking them out almost as fast as the queen herself would have.

One gone.

The next hitter tapped weakly back to Emily, and an underhanded toss to Maddoc was more than on time.

Two outs.

The Designated Hitter stood on deck.

Emily stalked back up the hill to toe the rubber, noting that the Unseelie Queen had risen from her perch next to the Web Gem to now stand at the edge of the dugout. Her black gaze danced with fire. Her thin fingers moved with spindle-like gyrations that made the pit of Emily's stomach roll.

The whole stadium was on their feet, hooves, or paws. Tensions rode even higher than they had before. In the Small Folk dugout, Emily saw little Essie sat with her fists balled up and pressed to her eyes. Fennoc's jaw was stock still, muscles standing out in stark relief, the blade of grass locked down and motionless.

Emily vs. the Designated Hitter for all the marbles.

It was what they had all come to see, and that's what was on the line if she couldn't get this hitter out.

Emily threw a strike.

"Balllll oooone!!!" the umpire said, rubbing her detached eyes with the back of her hand.

"Ball?" Emily spat.

A gust of rancid wind swirled from the queen, and Emily understood what those finger gyrations meant. She knew better than to argue, though. Complaining to the umpire when the umpire likely owed its very existence to the dark queen was a loser's game. Dad had always been clear about one thing, and one thing only. The game is always rigged. Just do your best. Fight the good fight.

She pitched three more times, all of them across the plate, but none called strikes.

The hitter took her place at first, and the Designated Hitter came to the plate.

Emily gave him the Unicorn salute.

He tipped his cap and took his stance.

Just looking at him, Emily knew she was done for. The Designated Hitter was the best batter she had ever faced. He was going to lace her first pitch out of the park.

Then the Fairy Series would be over.

She was going to lose. And, more important (as she scanned the stands to see the expressions of longing etched on the faces of gnomes and elves and pixies around the park), the Small Folk would go back for another season of servitude and abuse.

Fight the good fight, she said to herself.

But as she peered in at Nash, she could not help but focus on the Designated Hitter. His bright eyes glittered in the fiery light of the Unseelie Pitch. His stance was of such perfect form. In her mind, Emily watched him swing and admired the smooth, almost effortless way he generated power with the whole of his body. A hundred years of practice would do that. A hundred years of being nothing more and nothing less than the Designated Hitter.

Until now, Emily realized.

It wasn't the Designated Hitter who'd been stolen from the Unicorns to play here, who'd been kidnapped, whose family had been jilted, who'd been robbed of a full life where he could grow up and make something of himself before finally growing old.

It was Adrien Thorn.

Adrien Thorn.

She drew a sharp breath, and a fresh sizzle of power made her spine feel like it was going to explode. It was so strong, she called time out to pace the area behind the mound.

Adrien Thorn.

It was the Designated Hitter's true name. The secret the Unseelie

Queen had guarded so jealously, because here, true names had power.

Hair raised on her forearms. Her lungs seized in cold power. For an instant, she almost cried.

She stared at him as she strode back up to the pitching rubber, and as she moved, their gazes locked.

He smiled then. It was a warm smile. An accepting smile. Or one that was forgiving. One that said he understood what was going to happen.

He whipped his bat in a whirlwind of a warmup swing, then stepped to the plate.

Without further thought, Emily took her position, holding the ball in her glove, and her glove up to her mouth. Words came to her, and she whispered into the wind, feeling them flow from her breath to encircle the baseball and seep into its threaded surface.

Spin little ball, spin and spin,
And off the bat be born,
A simple infield fly hit in,
From player Adrien Thorn.

She threw the pitch, and as she released the ball to spin obediently away, a tingle of real magic flowed along her arm, up into her shoulder, down into her heart.

The ball dipped downward as Adrien Thorn's bat looped around to connect with a weak, warbling thunk.

The ball rose almost straight upward into the night. Nash whipped off his mask, head back and beady eyes wide as he peered into the darkness to track the ball's flight. He took a single step in towards the mound, and then settled under the ball.

Then, as the entire pitch held its breath, it fell into his mitt.

The game was over.

The crowd erupted.

A second miracle had occurred! Small Folk three, Unseelie Court two!

Emily's teammates swamped her again, pounding her on the

back and cheering as wildly as the Small Folk in the stands were. Nash was jumping up and down, waving his catch in everyone's faces. Mellica and Jessebel were in each other's arms, sobbing in delight. Izusa was turning cartwheels so fast he was nothing more than a sparkly blur.

But she didn't miss the huge, disbelieving grin that spread over the Designated Hitter's–Adrien Thorn's–face as he stood still at home plate, leaning on his bat and shaking his head slowly.

The spectators stomped and shouted so forcefully the stands quaked, the cacophony rising and rising to approach deafening levels.

Until ...

"Cheaters!"

The trill that rose over the grounds was as sharp and deadly as a pike to the chest.

It was the Unseelie Queen, striding from her dugout. The dark hue of her uniform had grown pearlescent with her rage, and she pointed a now gnarled index finger at Emily specifically. A black cloud of magic sparked behind her progression.

"You cannot cheat the Unseelie Queen! You cannot take what belongs to me!" she called, raising both hands to mold a breath-taking sphere of roiling power between them.

Emily's body went stiff. Her back arched, and her arms fell loosely to her side as she rose into the air, hands dangling uselessly, legs feeling like they were melting. Her breathing stopped, leaving her in gasping pain so deep it might never end, and the only thing that seemed to exist was the scintillating sphere of energy between the Queen's cupped hands and her own energy that seemed to be drawing away and seeping into that dark sphere. The wind roared. A storm was brewing with sharp flashes of lightning and fire.

"Let her go!" someone screamed through the fury.

Instantly, the power let up, and the pressure on Emily's chest lightened.

A breath came, Oh, sweetness, an actual breath of air so cold it burned.

"What?" The queen's voice wavered with disbelief. She crooked her fingers again, but the power of her spell faded, and Emily fell heavily to the ground. Bruised, but not seriously hurt, she raised herself up to discover who had commanded the Unseelie Queen.

It was Callie McMasters, standing at the edge of the Unseelie Court's dugout, jaw set, eyes blazing.

In her hands, she held the Web Gem.

"You're the cheater," Callie called, striding forward. "And it's time you faced the music."

CHAPTER
THIRTY-ONE

A hush descended over the stands of Unseelie Pitch as Callie strode forward, aggressively presenting the Web Gem before her like a vampire hunter holding a cross. Warmth flowed from the trophy up into her arms to spread through her whole body. She felt like she could obliterate a baseball into powder if she were at bat right now.

"Looks like I've got the power now, don't it?" she said.

The Unseelie Queen hissed like a cornered snake. "Mortal fool. You think you can claim a boon from me merely because you hold the Web Gem in your filthy hands? You have not won it properly."

Callie shrugged but did not lower the trophy. "Maybe not. But I figure there's enough power here to do some serious damage, anyway."

Her knuckles tightened around the base of the trophy, and she dipped her gaze from the queen to the crystal cup that formed the top of it. A silvery glow building around the lip boosted that idea inside her, and Callie's heart pounded with newfound certainty.

The Queen hissed again, more distressed this time. "There is no need for such unseemly threats, child. I am not unreasonable. Name your demands."

Callie smirked and lowered the Web Gem a fraction of an inch. "That's more like it. Not so high and mighty when you're the one facing the business end of justice, are you?" She glanced over at where Emily was still lying on the hideous purple grass and trying to catch her breath after the queen's assault. If Callie had been just a few seconds slower... "You okay, Miss Em?"

Emily, perched now on one elbow, waved a hand. "I'm fine. You?"

She sounded casual, but Callie saw the uncertainty in her eyes. DeWitt wasn't asking if Callie was okay. She was asking if Callie knew what the hell she was doing right now.

But Miss Em didn't need to worry. Callie hadn't spent her entire childhood marinating in her dad's business philosophies to not press her advantage now. She knew exactly what she was up to.

"My demands are simple. One, the oppression of the Small Folk ends now, no matter who ultimately wins the Series and proper control of the Web Gem. And two, myself, Miss Em, and your Designated Hitter all go home to the human world safe and sound as soon as this Series is done."

Callie cast a glance over to home plate, where Adrien still stood. He looked rather thunderstruck, his lips pressed thin and his eyes wide as dinner plates, as if he didn't dare hope, yet could not stop himself from doing it anyway.

Poor kid. A hundred years of the queen's bull crap couldn't have been easy to deal with.

The queen laughed like a socialite at a party. The sound echoed across the entire pitch until it felt like there were ten queens politely giggling.

Callie tightened her shoulder muscles against the urge to hunch in on herself.

The Queen cut herself off so sharply it left Callie's ears ringing. "My dear Designated Hitter would never desire a different home than the one he has at my side. Who could give up an eternity without a care in the world except to play baseball for the best team in the Fairy Realm every single day?"

She turned a simpering smile on Adrien.

But Adrien did not smile back. His expression grew dark, but his posture seemed suddenly to release its tension. "My Queen, respectfully, who do you think put the Web Gem in such a place where the Small Folk might find it and use it to call their own mortal player to the realm?"

The queen's smile melted into a scowl that promised blood. She whipped back around to face Callie, her eyes flaring with barely contained power. "It does not matter. You've bitten off more than you can chew, mortal. You'll fit right in with those mongrels of the Wild Hunt next season." She paused, then pulled herself into a posture of regal confidence before gliding towards Callie, a fresh smile on her blue-painted lips. "Your mortal blood means you haven't the power to compel me so far as all that without having earned the bid. And your attempt to take more than you deserve opens your quaint little demands to my own additions."

She was right beside Callie now, her lips mere inches from Callie's cheek as she spoke. Her breath ghosted cold as a winter gust against Callie's skin, smelling of snow and fire stoves, and dry, dead wood with brittle branches. Callie could not have moved if she'd wanted to. Fear left her so chilled as to be paralyzed.

The queen lifted one finger and pressed it to the crystal of the Web Gem. The silver light rippled like liquid at her touch.

"A chance you shall have, my foolish little mortals. A chance to *earn* one of those demands, not both. Hear this: if the one who goes by Miss Em strikes out my Designated Hitter and scores a home run off one of my pitches, at that very instant, the three of you shall be returned to the human world. If she does not, why, her precious Small Folk will — of course — stand a chance at winning the freedom from oppression you requested by taking the Fairy Series in its five games. But the three of you will remain here in the Fairy

Realm for all eternity. And your souls, as well as your contracts, will belong to me."

Power burned through the Web Gem, flowing back and forth between Callie and the queen to tie them into a contract of binding.

Callie screamed at the pain, understanding now that these were not her father's negotiations, and that she could not let go of the trophy to make it stop. The power had them both in its grip and was using them as conduits to flow down into the soil of the pitch, and from there up and out to encompass every creature within the stadium's walls.

The Small Folk groaned.

The Unseelie players clutched their heads.

Emily DeWitt tried to stand, her arm flung out towards Callie as if she thought she could help, but she was just as much a prisoner of this new curse as everyone else.

The only one who seemed at all unfazed was Adrien Thorn, the Designated Hitter, who stood stoically at home plate, waiting for it to end. Callie had seen her mother look like that during some of her dad's tirades against competitors back before her mother asked for the divorce.

Finally, all at once the brutal magic stopped.

Callie drew in a breath that rasped against her raw throat. She couldn't feel her hands, and, suddenly afraid for her future, couldn't make herself look to see if the magic had affected them physically.

Beside her, the queen clapped and laughed in delight, the socialite once again.

"What fun! What fun!" she called with breathless anticipation. "Let's begin immediately, shall we?"

She snapped her fingers, and another pulse of power spread through the gathered people. Everyone flinched as one.

The headless umpire stood, her skeletal frame creaking, and held one pale hand up.

"Plaaaaay ballll."

CHAPTER THIRTY-TWO

"I can't believe you did that," Emily said to Callie. She stretched her arms and back, trying to reduce the dead pain she still felt after the Unseelie Queen's spell work.

They were sitting in the dugout, waiting for Nash to lead off the game. It was the first moment they'd had alone.

"Someone had to do something," Callie said. "It's not like I have any other reason to be here."

On the field, the queen threw her first pitch.

Nash ducked a high fastball.

All around, Emily felt ungainly discomfort blanketing her teammates. She watched Shayla and Twy leaning silently against each other and saw how Greeven and Essie were silent at the end of the bench. Maddoc sat in equal stoicism, simply staring at his first base glove and turning it over and over.

They were afraid. Afraid and worried.

Feeling their disquiet made Emily suddenly angry.

This *should* have been their most exciting game of all times.

It was, of course, still the most important match the team could play. The Fairy Series championship was on the line — and with it would come control of the Web Gem and the ability to manage the whole of the Fairy Realm. The queen's bargain, however, was a wicked dilemma that changed everything for them. If Emily played well, she and her mortal cohorts would be free, but that would leave the Small Folk on their own.

She felt their unspoken concern and the pressure of sideways glances and hushed whispers as they went about their preparations.

Did she care about winning? Did she care about lifting every Small Folk around the realm out of their servitude, or was she in it just for her freedom — a freedom that would result in her leaving her team behind to fend for themselves?

Would Miss Em abandon them at their time of greatest need?

Their concern was not unfounded. The discordant pull of Emily's situation had permeated every moment since Callie and the queen had come to their contract. She had promised her dad she would come home as soon as she could, after all. And now two additional lives — Callie McMasters' and Adrien Thorn's — were at stake. At the same time, though, Emily's heart pounded with camaraderie and concern for her teammates and for the Small Folk at large.

On the field, Nash struck out.

Along the bench, the pall deepened.

Emily sighed, and Callie made a subtle grimace.

It was going to be a long, uncomfortable game.

THE SMALL FOLK having gone scoreless in the top of the first inning, it was now the Unseelie's turn to bat. Emily, not completely over the residue of the queen's attack earlier, calmed a final zing of excitement as she watched the Designated Hitter come to the plate.

Lead off, she thought as the Designated Hitter stepped forward. The queen was really showing off — hitting Adrien Thorn in the slot, where he was sure to get the most plate appearances, was nothing less than flaunting a lack of respect for Emily. *Go ahead*, that lineup slot said. *Take your best shot.* Emily scowled but forced herself to keep her gaze on the catcher rather than give the Unseelie leader the satisfaction of a glare.

He looked worn down, though. Haggard in a way he hadn't earlier this evening.

Through the haze of her painful memory, Emily recalled the moment he admitted to a part in Essie's theft of the Web Gem, and to his discomfort with his binding to the Unseelie team. She wondered if that worn expression came from the queen's wrath. Possibly.

Still, he was a dangerous hitter.

And with three contracts on the line, Emily knew the queen wasn't going to be messing around too cavalierly.

Callie McMasters had struck again, and now everything was moving so fast. Emily felt completely out of sorts.

The whole game felt weird now.

A double header. For the championship.

She gripped the ball hard and considered using the Designated Hitter's true name again, but she couldn't bring herself to do that.

Not now.

Not since she knew he had taken a role in helping the small folk.

Instead, she reached up and gave him the Unicorn salute. The gesture brought a toothy smile.

She decided then and there: she could not let Adrien Thorn spend another moment under the queen's control. But the first step on her path to bring him — to bring them all — home was to strike him out, a feat which would be even more impossible now, with the queen surely commanding him to hit his absolute best.

She would have to pitch the best she'd ever pitched in her entire life.

She got to business.

Her first throw was too high. Her heart filled her throat.

The Designated Hitter swung, though, and he missed.

"Strike one!" the umpire bellowed.

Excitement crashed through her. She got the ball back, and after the Designated Hitter dug his back foot into the ground again, Nash called for a waste-pitch changeup, and she reared back and whipped her arm around again.

Thorn swung again, grunting hard, but completely fooled, missing by at least a full meter and drawing chuckles from the spectators.

"Strike two!"

Emily pumped her fist, then circled the mound a moment preparing for her next pitch.

One more strike and the first hurdle would be cleared.

Getting that one out of the way early would really shove the Queen's face into the dirt.

The cacophony of her teammates' chattering mixed with the buzz of the crowd. She watched the Designated Hitter dig in once again, but found herself having a hard time not thinking of his true name. The moment was getting to her. She felt her breathing grow tight.

Nash signaled curveball. Her best pitch.

Well, all right.

She snapped it off too hard, though, and even as it left her fingers Emily knew it was a bad effort. Indeed, the baseball dipped too early, hitting the ground well before the plate and bouncing to Nash.

The Designated Hitter swung, though, and when little Nash popped up from behind the plate and tagged the batter on the thigh, the umpire cried "strike three!"

For an instant, Emily rejoiced, pumping her fist with a gruff sound that was half scream half groan. But that instant was short.

As the team threw the ball around the infield, Emily began to stew.

Something was wrong.

That strike out was way too easy.

After the ball returned to her, Emily stared into the Unseelie dugout only to find the queen gazing straight at her, dark eyes challenging. "Looks like you're winning, little Miss Em," the queen's voice echoed in her mind, dripping with irony. The queen languidly caressed the trophy, sending purple and pink flashes running through it.

Emily furrowed her brow, but didn't have time to think it through.

The next hitter grounded out to Shady Marie at shortstop. The third batter, an athletic, bronze-toned sidhe if there ever was one, managed a single, but Emily struck out the cleanup centaur to end the Unseelie threat. Only then did she scratch the back of her neck, a similar motion to the one Dad used when he was thinking to himself, as she returned to the dugout, her team preparing to hit.

She would be third up, though, so her time to contemplate was limited.

She grabbed a bat and watched the Unseelie Queen warm her own arm up, throwing an impressive string of pitches that, if magic hadn't been involved, Emily might call curves, sliders, and knuckleballs.

Her teammates called them all simply "twisters," and stared with eyes as wide as saucers as the pitches all danced over the plate with velocity that seemed unhittable.

The queen's fastball was even bolder.

When Shady Marie and then Izusa both struck out, Emily came to the plate. She took a deep breath, then adjusted the wooden dome of the bowl-like helmets Shady Marie had brought her for their first game and dug in, whispering to herself.

"She's not getting that cheese by me," she whispered to herself. *"Fastball up. That's what's gotta come. Relax. Relax. Quick bat."* It was from one of Mom's favorite old-time movies. Or something close, anyway. Time had worn so much of her past away, and she was only eighteen.

She whipped her bat around in a slow practice swing, mostly just to loosen her muscles.

Then she was ready.

The pitch came. Slow this time, and fat. She couldn't miss.

Emily swung with all her might, knowing she had to hit the ball a mile and a half to get it out of a ballpark where the walls would move. The ball cracked off the bat with the sound of a shotgun blast. The ball rose high and far — probably the hardest hit ball Emily had hit in her entire life. Her heart soared. She danced down the line.

Then stopped as the ball hooked sharply foul.

Too far ahead of it, she thought as she picked her bat up again. *Calm down, meat!*

But as she stared out at the queen, she saw not anger at having been beaten. Instead, she got the distinct impression that the queen was disappointed in the hit going foul. *That one got out of here in a hurry, didn't it?* the queen's voice echoed again inside her head.

Emily froze.

It was something like another quote from that same movie.

She narrowed her gaze. A sense of violation burned in her heart.

She gripped her bat, then stepped into the box again. This time she waited and watched as another easy to hit pitch drifted past her.

"Strike two!" the umpire wailed.

Emily wrinkled her nose at the reek that came from the umpire's breath, but realized that it wasn't the only foul thing in the park right then.

The queen wanted her to hit this homer.

If Emily hit it now, the Small Folks would be ahead by a run, but the game was long, and a one run lead was nothing. If all three mortals were removed from the pitch, the Unseelies would be an even stronger favorite to win in a landslide, even losing their Designated Hitter. Assuming they did win, the queen would keep the Web Gem, retain control over the Fairy Realm, and, as far as Emily was able to guess, might then even use the Web Gem to retrieve her Designated Hitter once the dust settled.

Emily felt something else, too.

If the queen retained control of the Web Gem, her wrath against the Small Folk would be intense.

So inclined, now, Emily glanced at the queen and saw this truth reflected in every part of her — from her relaxed posture to the scintillating waves of magic that seemed to roll over the threads of her sharply cut baseball uniform. Even the logo seemed to pulse with the queen's resolution.

Stunned, Emily stood still in the box. She had to think about this, and the best place to do that was in the dugout.

The next pitch was similar to the last, a weak batting practice fastball high over the plate.

Emily tapped it to first base, grounding out on purpose.

Callie was spitting angry when Emily came to the dugout to get her pitcher's mitt. "What in the hell are you doing? That was our chance! You should have plastered that one."

"The queen is trying to get us out of here," Emily replied, pounding her fist into her glove.

Callie's demeanor calmed and her expression grew more perplexed than angry. "Yeah. Queenie grooved those pitches." Her expression turned contemplative, and she looked out to the field. "I see the game she's playing now. You're the pitcher. If you're not here, the Unseelies will score a bunch."

"I think you're right," Fennoc, who was standing nearby, said. "The Designated Hitter also struck out quite easily. I don't think he would have done that without being so commanded."

"That fits what I was thinking, " Emily added.

"Hey!" Nash called from behind home plate, waving Emily onto the pitch. "We need to get started!"

"We'll talk about this more," she said with an exasperated grimace. "Gotta go."

"Strike them out, Miss Em!" little Essie called as Emily jogged back to the pitcher's mound.

Despite herself, Emily gave a delighted little laugh.

There was something wonderful about that voice. She hoped she would remember it for as long as she lived.

From the dugout, Callie McMasters watched the game's momentum seesaw back and forth, neither team scoring runs but both teams having chances.

Having already been struck out the requisite time, the Designated Hitter returned to form. Emily couldn't get anything past him, but managed to coax him into a sharp ground out and a deep line drive that Izusa chased down with an elegant sliding catch.

Callie sensed that the team still struggled with the agreement she had entered into. Mellica cast virtual darts at her early in the game. Little Essie refused a high-five. Everyone else gave her the cold shoulder. They were worse than freshmen in the lunch cafeteria.

Maybe they did have a leg to stand on.

At least she could see the argument that she'd made things worse off for the Small Folk no matter what. As far as they were concerned, Emily was now in a quandary: save the mortals or save the Small Folk. But it wasn't that simple. The Small Folk had a never-ending string of chances. She and Emily had only this one. Of course, if DeWitt didn't manage to win the challenge, the queen would have three mortals, and would, theoretically, never lose another game, ever.

But that was going too far now, wasn't it?

Did they have so little faith in their teammate that they'd worry about it that way?

If it weren't for her relationship with Emily, though, Callie was pretty sure they wouldn't have let her stay in the dugout at all. Despite the fact that she had only done what needed to be done. Despite the fact that her own mortal soul was now on the line because she'd tried to help them.

Despite the fact that their own beloved Miss Em was, once again, putting everyone else's needs before her own.

As the game went along, she decided she needed to say something — and that it had to be without Emily in earshot.

So, she waited until Emily's next turn batting, then stood up and called out.

"All right! Enough is enough," she called out, beckoning to the team. "Gather round, kiddos."

None of the Small Folk moved a muscle.

"I'm serious," Callie said. "I have some things you need to hear."

Still nothing.

"For the love of..." she muttered. "Listen, you jerks. If you love Miss Em, you want to hear it."

The sound of reluctant shuffling finally echoed through the grave-like dugout.

Out on the field, Emily took the queen's first pitch — another softly lobbed offering — for a strike.

Callie glared at the gathered Small Folk. "You all know that Miss Em chose to come back and play for you."

"Of course she did. Now you want to take her away from us," Greeven spat, his elven features twisted into something darker than Callie had ever seen on him.

Callie continued on. "She came because she had to. Because that contract you gave her — without her consent, I might add — pulled at her so hard that it made her miserable at home. She's been happy to be here, though. That's how she is, you know? She likes you all. And once she understood the situation, she was all in. She wants to help you all save your Small Folk families from being ground to nothing. And you can all see how much she loves baseball."

Heads nodded as Emily took a second strike.

"What you don't know, though, is that Miss Em's mother passed four years ago, back when we were just kids," Callie said. "And I don't think she's ever come to terms with it."

All around the ring of Small Folk, faces fell.

"I'm so sorry to hear that," Mellica said. "We didn't know."

"Passed?" Essie said. "What does that mean?"

"It means she died," Callie said, bluntly.

"Like forever?"

Fennoc let out a gentle cough. “Yes, Essie. Forever. It’s something that happens to humans. At least, it does when they live in their own world and not here.” His voice was distant as he looked across to the other dugout, where the Designated Hitter sat on the bench.

“Right,” Callie said. “Miss Em’s mom got sick and never could recover. So now Miss Em lives ... lived ... with her dad. He’s all alone now.”

“What does that have to do with us?” Greeven said.

“Miss Em has a second contract, doesn’t she?” Fennoc said, suddenly strong of voice again. As Callie nodded, he reached into his uniform pocket and extracted a baseball, rolling it distractedly over his fingers, then placed it back into his pocket and addressed the team directly. “I believe Miss Em promised her father that she would return to him.”

“That’s right,” Callie said, glad she didn’t have to spell it out so completely.

“We see,” Greeven finally said.

“I’m sorry our calling made this happen,” Fennoc added.

Callie rolled her eyes. “Don’t be sorry. She loves it here. It’s just that she needs to be in two places at one time.”

“That is a quandary,” Fennoc said, his hand returning to the baseball in his pocket, his gaze going distant once again, and the drooping blade of grass in the corner of his mouth churning.

“I understand why you’re mad at me,” Callie said. “Truly, I do. But I don’t think you’re looking at this the right way.”

“And what way is that?” Maddoc said.

“If — when — Miss Em wins the challenge, the Unseelie Queen will lose the Designated Hitter, and things will be even again. You won’t need her the way you do now. With all her training, you’re all really not bad. You’ll be able to win on your own.”

“I’m not so sure of that,” Maddoc said.

“Seriously,” Callie said. “I’m not just blowing smoke. You should see the numbskulls and lollygaggers I’ve been coaching.”

A queasy silence settled over the team.

"'Tis true we are a sight better than we were," Fennoc said, rubbing his well-coifed beard.

It was clear to Callie that, on the whole, the gathering wasn't quite convinced. But it was also clear that at least she'd gotten them thinking.

On the field, Emily took her third pitch for a strike.

CHAPTER THIRTY-THREE

The game came to its last inning with the score knotted at nil each.

The field seemed both frozen in time and like it would endure forever, but it wasn't anything to do with Unseelie Pitch's uncanny nature. It was the nature of all baseball fields, the timelessness of baseball itself.

The night sky was black as ink. A breeze spiced with the warmth of oncoming summer whirled in growing intensity. On the mound, the queen took her final warmup tosses.

Emily watched from the bench, tired from two games of pitching, but still wired on the moment. She was engaging in a little baseball math. Being due up sixth this inning meant that if she hit, the Small Folk would likely have scored, or at worst have the bases full, giving her a chance to rack up multiple runs. Given the queen's pitching acumen the chances were not high that Emily would come to bat, but they weren't zero — and baseball magic had its own way of working.

She couldn't bring herself to leave the Small Folk in a lurch and hit a home run, no matter how tempting the queen's offering. But she could scale down and simply drive in a run or two. And if that baseball magic worked in her favor, she'd pitch the bottom of the inning, keep the Unseelies from matching and surpassing that score, and win the game.

This was what she had missed for all those years on the Unicorn roster — playing in big games and dealing with big moments. Now that one was here, she couldn't help but smile.

At least she'd have something she could look back on with pride during her endless servitude under the queen. Maybe sometime, when the excitement of this season had died down, she, Callie, and Adrien could come up with another plan to escape. It would fill the time, anyway.

There came a pull on her sleeve.

She turned to find little Essie standing on the bench beside her, Fists planted on her tiny hips and a piercing scowl on her tiny face, and the rest of the team lined up behind her as primly as if they were taking a team picture.

"What's going on?" Emily said.

"So you don't think we can win without you?" Maddoc said, crossing his arms.

"What do you mean?"

"That's what you're saying, right? Striking out on purpose like that? That we're not good enough baseball players to win one game without you?"

Emily blushed with embarrassment. "That's not—"

It was Shady Marie who interrupted this time. "Because if that's what you're saying, it's pretty annoying." The dryad stepped beside Maddoc and mimicked his defiant posture down to the crossed arms.

"That would be off-putting, it would, Miss Em," Nash added, planting his feet firmly and jutting his jaw out.

Emily couldn't believe this was happening. "It doesn't matter if we score a ton this inning if the Unseelies surpass it. We need a pitcher."

Fennoc gave a sharp nod that made his grass blade wave. "True. Which is why Twy is in the bullpen, you'll notice."

He indicated the fenced-in space at the end of the dugout, where the nymph who'd spent the season singing her own version of baseball magic was indeed throwing warmups.

Emily gaped. Some of those pitches — a lot of them, if she was honest — looked solid. She'd been practicing, apparently.

"Like a wise baseball player once said," Greeven started.

"It can't all rest on one player," Maddoc added.

"It has to be a team effort," Shady Marie finished.

"Lass," Fennoc said, stepping forward and putting a hand on Emily's shoulder. "We cannot take our freedom by exchanging it for yours. You're as Small Folk as the rest of us. Either we all go free, or none of us do."

By now, Emily was crying. "I... I don't know what to say."

"Don't ye now, lassie?" Fennoc said firmly. "The team has spoken. To a person, we expect ye to play your best. If that means you go home, win or lose, we'll all be happy for you."

Play your best, Mom said in her memories. *Play your best for a team you love.*

"Yes. Yes, I do see," Emily said. "And I... just... thank you. But it's a long way to my spot in the lineup."

"Don't you be worrying about that, Miss Em," Nash said resolutely. "We'll find a way. Just you see."

"Ye need to be hitting that homer, now," Maddoc added. "So get yer mind in order."

Tears stung the backs of her eyes again. "I will."

A deep breath later, Emily looked out to the wall around the outfield. Letting the air out relaxed her. "We'll see what kind of magic the Queen has up her spindly little fingers this time."

Fennoc beamed. "That we will," he said, one hand drifting to his pocket again. "That we will."

Nash, leading off, this time managed a walk.

It was his specialty, and as Emily had predicted, he had led the Fairy Realm season in the tally of such free passes.

Now he stood at first base, grinning, and — since he was the slowest runner on the team — expecting Fennoc to pinch run for him. Except, of course, he was the catcher and if Nash were pulled from the game no one else could play his position well.

"Stay there!" Fennoc called.

Shady Marie struck out, but Izusa managed a bloop hit to right field that put Nash to second and left the pixie behind at first. Maddoc hit a grounder to second base that initially made everyone gloomy as it bounced. A perfect double play ball. But the Unseelie second base glove botched it, and the ball caromed off her chest to roll harmlessly into the infield grass.

The bases were loaded and there was only one out. A hit from Greeven would leave the Small Folk ahead. Alas, he swung his thin branch of a bat at the queen's first pitch and managed only a weak popup. When the queen herself caught the ball, Emily was next.

A home run now — a grand slam — could plate four runs.

The idea sat on Emily's mind heavily as she went to the plate.

Four runs could be enough.

The entire stadium was on fire in anticipation. Spectators who should have been drained from two tense games were nowhere near so drained.

They stomped. They chanted. They filled the eerie stands with their own kind of baseball magic. Emily thought she could smell blood in the air, and realized it was the aroma of Fairyland bets being thrown down across the entire realm.

Could it happen?

Could she win her rival's challenge with the queen, free all three human mortals from the Fairy Realm, *and maybe* even win the game for the Small Folk?

Never in modern history of the Fairy Series had there been such a moment.

And as Emily gripped her bat, she realized the weight of the moment had fallen on the Unseelie Queen's shoulders just as well as everyone else.

She, too, had picked up on the change in the Small Folk. She'd seen Twy in the bullpen. She'd felt their tightening teamwork as they'd meticulously loaded the bases. Beyond that, the game was now deep in. To give the Small Folk runs would be too risky.

"I will not be humiliated!" the queen's voice rolled down from the mound like a wave.

"We'll see about that," Emily replied before she could rein in her bravado.

Oh, yes, how she'd changed in her time here.

The queen's first pitch dipped and dove and spun in a corkscrew right, then left. Magic seeped from its hide as it approached the plate.

Emily swung hard and missed.

That's okay, she told herself as a shot of nerves jangled through her. *Two more chances left.*

The next was no better.

Two strikes.

The audience stood, clamoring and shouting. From the corner of her eyes, Emily saw Small Folk shielding their gaze, the tension so tight they could not watch.

The queen, feeling the turn of the tide against her, was taking no chances on letting Emily get that home run. She may have wanted to eject the mortal players and keep her place of power earlier; now, though, she saw danger on the horizon. A home run ran the risk of losing it all. Instead, she was pitching all out, knowing that even if Emily managed to score a run, the queen would only be risking losing the Web Gem for taking the consolation prize of gaining two more skilled mortal players, thus allowing her to make a practically unstoppable run at the Series to reclaim her lost trophy next season. Better yet, Emily thought, the queen intended to win it all. At this point, a straight-out Unseelie Court victory would solve all her problems.

And now Emily felt the pressure of her own commitment. If she did not hit a home run, she would be locked here forever. And if she were here forever, she would never fulfill her commitment to Dad. The idea stuck like a bone in her throat. The queen's gleeful yearning was too much to take.

Her hands shook as she adjusted her grip on the bat.

"Time!"

It was Fennoc.

The faun stepped from the dugout to approach the umpire. "I believe you need to check the queen for illegal magic, madam," Fennoc said, looking the umpire in the crook of her arm.

"Excuuuse meeee?" the umpire said.

The Small Folk manager drew closer, putting one hand on the small of the Dullahan official's back. "I believe no ball could move like that without the application of external magic," Fennoc said.

"Shuuuuuutttt up!" the queen raged. "I'll not have such besmirchment of my skills!"

"No besmirchment at all, Your Majesty," Fennoc said, holding his composure so firmly that Emily couldn't help admiring him. As the umpire turned to the queen, she saw Fennoc's deft hand slipping away from the bag of spare baseballs the umpire wore.

"The Smaaaall Folk's manager is within riiiiiights of the ruuules for me to check youuuuu, my Queen," the umpire said.

"Or would you prefer we play under protest and tie the ending up in a league of red tape?" Fennoc said.

The queen glowered, then removed her cap and proffered it to the gaze of the umpire's severed head. "Get on with it."

Fennoc took a step to stand next to Emily as the inspection proceeded from ballcap to glove to other parts of the queen's uniform. *"Foul off her next pitch,"* he whispered to her.

Emily's brows knit.

"Trust me, lassie." Fennoc winked.

She gave him a wordless smile in return, then raised her bat as the umpire returned.

"I fiiiiind noooo souuurces of exterrrnal maaah-gick," the Dullahan said.

"Fair enough," Fennoc said, tipping his cap to the queen as he left the argument.

The fans, who had been roundly enjoying such drama, increased their excitement to fever pitch.

A moment later, the queen took out her resentment by throwing her hardest fastball.

Emily swung late, but made contact. The crowd oohed and aahed as the ball flew into the air, but out of the park down the right field line.

The umpire threw another ball to the queen.

And, for Emily, time stopped.

CHAPTER
THIRTY-FOUR

She would know the ball anywhere.

She knew it by the pull it had on her, by the sense of time she'd spent with it — a sense that registered here in the Fairy Realm so strongly she almost gagged on it. The image of it filled her mind. Pristine white cover, red stitching perfect everywhere but a single stitch pulled too far to one side. It carried a logo on it, and a signature. One place, she knew, was scarred so gently that no one else would see it. But Emily knew it was there. A tiny bruise, Mom would say. A little scar to show where it had been.

Her mom's ball.

This understanding took her breath. She stood outside the batter's box and blinked.

The ball changed everything.

It was her price omen. The thing she'd give to return here of her own volition. And it was baseball magic, Emily knew. The ball would protect her. It would dispel anything the queen could bring at her.

She glanced at Fennoc, who gave her the wide-toothed grin that only he could give.

She glanced at Callie McMasters, who seemed oblivious to the substitution Fennoc had finagled.

Then she looked at Adrien Thorn, and pressed her lips together. Get ready, she thought. Adrien responded with a salute.

"Are you getting into the box or are you just giving up now?" the queen said.

"Bring on the cheese, Meat," Emily said, stepping into the box.

The queen wound up.

The ball flew through the air, shedding the queen's spell work as it flew.

It impacted Emily's bat with a sound as pure as spring growth.

Rose up. Higher and higher, into the air. Moving faster than the expanding walls of Unseelie Pitch could stretch. Reaching its apex and still traveling. Disappearing far into the darkest regions of the forest beyond. Emily, running down the first baseline, felt it land as the entire stadium of fairy folk erupted in astonishment.

She raised her fists in triumph.

She had done it!

She'd won the challenge! She was going home! The power of the moment washed over her, and she screamed with joy as she approached first base.

But as she came within two steps of the bag, it transformed into a huge snake, thick and bulbous at its viperlike head. Its scales gleamed golden green as it coiled, then rose to hiss at her.

Surprised, Emily bolted backward, stumbling to fall smack on her backside.

"Not sssssssoo fast, little Miss Em," the snake hissed, swaying back and forth as if dancing to hidden music. Its tongue slid out, then back in again. "First bassssse you cannot passsssss."

"But—" Emily paused, hearing the queen's tone in the snake's admonition and recalling the exact words the queen had uttered. *Hear this: if the one who goes by Miss Em strikes out my Designated Hitter and scores a home run off one of my pitches, at that very instant, the three of you shall be returned to the human world.*

The words *and scores a home run* ate into Emily's thoughts.

I have to touch the plate, she thought.

Just so, the queen said in her direct speech. *Touch the plate, or your contract belongs to me.*

Emily picked herself off the ground, staring hard at the dark-eyed snake as it hissed in her direction, determination burning hotter than her fear. She felt Mom again. But this time it was not the baseball magic version of Mom. This time the image that came over her was the one sitting on the edge of a hospital bed, finishing a chemo drip, weak and drained, but sitting as firmly upright as she could, then smiling as she saw her daughter enter the room.

Emily clenched her fists as the image grew solid.

"Come here, baby," her mother had said, making space for her.

That's when Mom had gotten direct with her for the first time. She remembered the entire talk. Every word. She remembered the hospital smell of the room. The roughness of the hospital sheets. The clear liquid that snaked through the clear tube to run into Mom's arm. Mom's touch on her shoulder, and on her cheek. *"This monster might beat me, but I'm not giving up without a fight. And come what may, you will always be my little girl, all right? Promise me that? Promise me you'll remember that, okay."*

Emily had cried that day.

But she did not cry now. Instead, Emily gritted her teeth and took a firm stance to face the snake before her.

"All right, then," she said. "Let's do this."

She didn't walk resolutely forward — she charged. The snake lunged for her, fangs bared and already dripping venom that burned holes as it fell onto her uniform. But the snake was too slow.

Emily dodged it and grabbed with both hands its scaly body right behind the flared sides of its arrow-shaped head.

The snake writhed madly, thrashing and flinging venom that fell in hissing, steaming gobs all around the place where first base should be. But Emily held on, squeezing tighter and tighter, twisting it in anger as she stepped firmly into that space.

She screamed out uncontrollably, bursting out in tears of anger and crushing the snake's head down to the ground again and again, releasing all of her pain and fear and anger in one long burst.

And in that instant her cleated foot touched the dirt where first base had been.

The snake went limp, then melted to its proper form as the base.

Emily rose to stand, panting. First base successfully touched.

Behind her, Nash toddled across home plate to score the Small Folk's first run. The crowd cheered and stomped their feet.

"Next monster up," Emily quipped, feeling powerful now as she turned all her attention to second base, which was waiting serenely for her to approach.

No sense in waiting, she thought.

She charged again, running full tilt as if she needed to avoid a tag-out.

As she came halfway down the baseline, the bag wriggled and lurched. A canine snout appeared, covered in coarse gray fur and twisting from side to side as it emerged, clawing its way up and out. It was a wolf, Emily thought. Huge and muscular. Its paws, tipped with mold-caked claws, tore through the fabric of the base. A pair of powerful shoulders thrust outward, sending the last shreds of thread and dirt showering down. Snarling and growling, smelling more rank than the Wild Hunt itself, the wolf stood in the place where second base had been, its yellowed fangs too long to fit inside its mouth, and its green-gold eyes filled with sharp hatred, malice, and starvation as it turned them on Emily.

It lowered itself to pounce.

Though her heart hammered with fear and adrenaline, Emily did not slow her pace.

Instead, when the wolf leapt, she slid down.

Pain lanced up her thigh and hip as the friction burned her. But the wolf arced overhead, and Emily's outstretched foot crossed all the way to the center of where the base ought to be.

As she dug her cleat into soil to pop upright, she pushed hard against the wolf's belly. The beast jerked itself in midair, twisting like an acrobat so it landed facing her, snarling and ready to pounce again.

Emily pushed herself up out of the dirt, keeping her foot firmly "on base" as if she were playing a game of childhood tag. She made herself face the wolf fully and kept her eyes open and her fists clenched. "The base is the base. And safe is safe," she called as the wolf came again, teeth gleaming, breath stinking. With a growl, it soared through the air and stretched out its front paws, claws fully extended.

Emily held firm, despite every instinct screaming at her to move.

She braced for impact, arms crossing, muscles straining.

The instant the wolf touched her, it dissolved into smoke. And as the smoke coalesced back into the stuff of second base, Izusa pirouetted across home plate, bringing the score up to 2-0.

Taking a moment to catch her breath, Emily felt the roar of the crowd wash over her, a wave just as she'd always imagined it. Her side ached from the slide, bruised at least, possibly scraped raw. Her hip hurt to run.

But she couldn't take the time to doctor herself. Not yet.

She turned to third base.

Like the others before it, the white bag sat there looking innocent and unthreatening, its casing pristine.

That was a facade, though. She knew that now.

Gathering her strength, Emily dashed towards it, clearing her mind as she ran, feeling the pounding in her veins as if it was a distant drumming of power.

The base began moving almost immediately, though what horror it was becoming was unclear. It remained perfectly white, though. Spreading itself wider and wider, the two sides tapering and lifting, the front of it elongating upwards, lolling sideways and around like a thin roll of dough.

The tapered appendages sprouted long, glowing white feathers, and the thin roll sprouted an orange beak and black, avian face.

A swan.

A massive swan, standing in place of third base, its wings mantled, its beak open in a low, throaty hiss.

Unlike the wolf, it remained in place, guarding its base like a treasure.

Emily's breath sawed in her lungs. She didn't slow, but she rounded her shoulders and spread her arms wide, trying to make herself look bigger, more intimidating.

The swan merely hissed louder and stood its ground.

Fear nearly cut off her breathing as she realized what she would have to do.

She was two steps away from the base. In range for the swan to bite her.

The moment its graceful head darted forward, Emily leapt.

Her fingers grabbed the swan's neck, and her momentum carried her to land on the swan's back. Even before she settled, Emily hooked her second hand around the swan's neck as she'd done with the snake.

Except the snake hadn't been just as big as Emily, and its thrashing had been easily subdued. The swan, instead, fought like an earthquake.

It bucked her forward and back. Its wings buffeted her so hard her head rang.

The beak gave a dry snap nearby her ear.

Somehow, she kept her hold on it.

She straddled it, her knees pressed into the bird's body, her fisted hands pressing its neck downward as hard as she could. Slowly, agonizingly, the swan's head moved towards the dirt at third base. When it was a mere breath away, the swan gave its mightiest thrash — and its head whipped upward with blinding quickness. A sharp pain flared along Emily's cheek as the yellow bill tore into her skin, cutting a slice a hair's breadth from her eye.

She let out a yelp, but did not let go.

Blood trickled down her cheek to drip off her chin, but she wrestled the swan back down, arms and shoulders burning with the effort, finally, into the dirt.

Instantly, Emily was kneeling on all fours, alone and panting with exertion on the bag of third base.

Maddoc crossed home plate.

The stands erupted again, not a wave this time, but a constant, unending torrent.

A whirlpool of excitement swirling around her.

3-0.

Slowly, painfully, Emily got to her feet. Everything hurt. Her side throbbed so hard she assumed everyone could see it swelling. Her head pounded from the still-ringing blows of those massive wings. Her cheek burned, and every muscle in her entire body felt like it was on fire.

She lifted a wrist to swipe the dribble of blood from her chin.

In the middle of the field, the Unseelie Queen stood like a pillar of pure fury. Emily had bested all three bases. Now, only one single obstacle remained.

Home plate.

If she touched home plate, the home run would be scored. The contest would be over, and the runs would all tally into the official scorebook.

What monstrous thing would the queen summon to stop Emily from taking everything away from her?

Could Emily face it?

Hurt as she was?

Energy from the crowd fed into Emily. It surged through her and around her, pouring into her heart. The spectators felt the power of the moment, too, feeding it back to her. The edge of history was cutting a new path now. They roared and whistled and blew their horns, hoping and wishing and yearning for her to succeed.

If she scored, it might well be the most exciting thing to happen in Fairyland for many an eon.

The whole of the Small Folk team had come to stand outside the dugout, jumping and waving and screaming support at Emily. Twy even had on Emily's pitcher's mitt.

Callie was there, too, looking somehow both overcome with pride and overflowing with expectation. *Come on, DeWitt,* her eyes said. *Time to kick ass.*

And Adrien Thorn, too, the Designated Hitter, was there. The shadows of the Unseelie Court had pulled away from him, leaving him nothing more than mortal, just a boy who was better than average at baseball, and who was ready to finally go home.

Emily closed her eyes and let all this fill her up.

Magic. Pure, clean magic. Even here at Unseelie Pitch.

She opened her eyes. Drew in a breath.

Ready to perform one more miracle.

Her cleats crunched against the dirt of the third base line, heading for home. The crowd chanted in time with her steps. Power surged through her muscles, and the pain faded as she ran.

Faster and faster.

Closer and closer.

She was five steps from home. Then three. Then two.

Home plate didn't so much as twitch.

Not until she was one step away.

Then it changed. Transmuted from its hard, bone-colored surface, to a pool of blackness with caustic coils of smoke and ash rising from its red-hot surface.

A blast of forge heat slapped Emily so hard she gasped and stumbled backwards, turning her ankle as she stopped her momentum, barely catching herself as she dropped to one knee. She knelt there and stared with horror at the seething pool of molten iron. From her left, the queen's laughter rang.

In front of her, the faces of the Small Folk, of Adrien Thorn, of the whole crowd fell. The cheers went silent, the air taut with uncertainty.

She had to touch this. Had to step into it to score the run.

The scorching heat and floating cinders told her everything she needed to know. To do that would be to burn herself to ash. To save Callie and Adrien, she needed to sacrifice herself.

Emily recalled sitting on the library bench with Callie — thanking her rival for taking actions to save her and doubting her ability to do the same if her turn came. Here it was, though. Her chance. And yet...

Emily choked back a sob. She couldn't tell if her blurred vision was due to tears or the unbearable heat awaiting her.

"It's not fair!" she called out to the still cackling queen. The price was too dire.

"Everything is fair in love and baseball, Miss Em."

She felt Adrien Thorn nearby, and Callie McMasters, too. And she felt her contract to the Small Folk, who needed her to score the run that might then free the whole of their people. And she knew what she had to do.

Dragging herself painfully to her feet, she stepped to the edge of the pit, lifting one foot out over the middle, where home plate would be.

Then, as if out of that rippling curtain of heat stepped Callie McMasters.

Literally, despite the wisps of smoke that trailed from her clothes and hair, she stepped across the molten pit of home plate.

She was, quite obviously, unburned.

On the mound, the queen screeched and spat. But everyone in the entire stadium ignored her.

Emily stared as Callie approached her with a smug little smile. "Wh-what— How—?"

"Thought so," Callie said. "It's an illusion. Read all about it at the library. Fairies can't work with iron, cold or hot."

"I don't understand."

Callie replied. "If you believed it was real, you'd burn. At least that's what the books said. But now that you know, it can't hurt you."

Her smug smile grew into a goading grin, and she held a hand to Emily.

"So, unless you're too scared..."

"Like hell I'm too scared," Emily smiled as she took Callie's hand.

By then, Adrien Thorn had also come to stand beside them, calm and cool after his own pass through the illusory heat. He, too, held out his hand, though his smile was less goading and more encouraging.

The crowd went berserk.

Emily turned to the Small Folk, lifted one finger to the brim of her hat, and gave them all the Unicorn Salute.

Together, little Essie included, the Small Folk returned the motion.

Then she took both Callie's and Adrien's hands, held them tight, and stepped onto home plate.

4-0.

CHAPTER THIRTY-FIVE

For a single breathless eternity, she was weightless in a sea of light.

A squeeze came to her left hand. A tug to her right.

She squeezed back, then leveraged the tug.

All at once she was standing on home plate, not at Unseelie Pitch, not in the Other Field, but at Unicorn Field.

It was a bright, sunny day without a cloud in the sky. The stands were entirely empty.

Except for one section, near the dugout, where a small collection of people sat in eager anticipation.

The current Unicorns — Jake, Patsy, Benji, Jamal — clambered down in a field-rush worthy of a championship celebration. Emily hugged each in turn, letting them slide past her to give their enthusiastic welcomes to Callie also.

"Who is this?" Jake asked, looking at Adrien.

"Adrien Thorn?" Benji said in a tone of wonder, holding the long-lost Unicorn hero at arms distance for a brief moment.

"That's me," Adrien said, staring with some confusion at the entirety of the world around him, not the least being the business skirt and dress shirt Benji wore, or the striking makeup that almost covered the thin Fairyland glow that was radiating from them.

His stunned reaction to Patsy's dark makeup design was priceless.

"We're so glad to see you!" Patsy said to Emily, dabbing at one thickly mascaraed eye.

Emily looked at each of her friends, then to the empty stands where they had been sitting.

Where they had been waiting.

As if ...

"I don't understand," she said, almost stammering. "How did you know we would be here?"

In unison, every last one of them beamed as brightly as Benji Amberman could ever beam.

The sound of scuffing shoes came from the dugout behind Emily.

It was a man. Tall and thin. His hands pushed into the pockets of a White Sox windbreaker.

Ignoring the pain in her ankle and her hips, and forgetting the ache that seared her muscles, she ran across the open expanse of the field.

"Daddy!"

He met her halfway.

They crashed into each other with a power stronger than anything she'd felt from the Unseelie Queen's magic.

A long hug later, they finally separated.

Their moment complete, her Unicorn teammates came closer.

"How?" Emily repeated her question. "How did you know we were coming?"

"Your dad's been sitting in these stands every day since you left," Patsy said unable to keep her excited admiration from her voice.

Emily glanced back at her dad.

He got a sheepish expression, and then raised his head. "Just waiting for a sign."

"A sign?"

"Yesterday, this dropped into my lap."

He dug into his pocket and pulled out a baseball, then gently placed it onto Emily's open palm.

It was perfectly white with red stitches in perfect lines — with one familiar exception. Now, the ball had not one, but two tiny bruises. Two tiny scars that showed how it had been. She closed her fingers tightly over it.

Emily would know it anywhere.

CHAPTER

THIRTY-SIX

Emily stood in front of her bedroom mirror, holding her hair up on her head experimentally and swiveling her hips to make the skirt of her purple sundress flare. Mellica's gold highlights were still there, which made her happy. Was the outfit too much for a remedial history tutoring session at the library? Probably. But Adrien's eyes had gone flatteringly wide last weekend when she'd come to take him to the movies wearing a pale green dress of a similar style.

Besides, she felt comfortable with this look. Confident, even. All that was missing was Mellica's gold dust for her eyes, but Emily had done a more than passable job with the new palette of eye shadow she'd picked up.

Satisfied with the hairstyle, she moved to the vanity to grab some pins.

"Knock knock."

Dad's head poked out from around the doorframe.

"Oh, my gosh. You look so much like your mother," he said as he took her in. His smile turned warm.

Emily felt herself blush. "I know."

Dad came fully into her room, his hands in his pockets. “So. I suppose all this is for Rip?”

Emily stifled a groan. How on earth had she let her dad get Callie’s stupid nickname stuck in his head? But, unlike everyone else, she’d told her dad everything this time, and Adrien certainly was a bit of a Rip Van Winkle. Hence the remedial history sessions.

They’d returned with a full month of summer vacation left before Emily’s second senior year would start. Adrien intended to attend as well, though he required a more substantial cover story. He’d been torn to discover that his family’s descendants still lived in Pattersonville, both delighted to meet them and devastated to realize that everyone he’d known and loved as a kid was gone.

He’d presented himself on the Thorn Family doorstep as a distant cousin who’d been named after the family’s lost son, and had been staying with them while he arranged his education.

“He’s a good guy,” Dad continued. “A little odd. But I like him. Think he’ll try out for the Unicorns?”

Emily finished pinning her hair as she contemplated the idea. Adrien hadn’t been back to the field since their return, but she knew he still thought about it, just like she did. She had every intention of rejoining the Unicorns. The team had made it all the way to the final game of the State Finals before ultimately losing to the Bulldogs, so the championship trophy remained elusive.

Repeating senior year meant she had one more chance to claim it.

Not that that was why she was planning to join. She simply couldn’t imagine not playing.

“He might,” she finally answered.

“He might,” Dad agreed. Then he pulled one hand out of his pocket to point a thumb over his shoulder. “Anyway, I came up to let you know you’ve got a visitor, if you’ve got time before, uh, *history lessons.*”

This time Emily did roll her eyes. “Daaaad.”

But she was smiling as he walked out and Callie McMasters came in. She was dressed in full baseball kit, a light windbreaker over her jersey, her cap pushed up high on her forehead.

"Thanks, Mr. DeWitt," Callie said as they passed each other. Dad clapped a hand on Callie's shoulder and gave her a nod.

"Hey," Emily said by way of greeting.

"Nice dress."

"Thank you. Getting ready for a pickup game somewhere?" Emily said, waving a hand at Callie's getup. This late in the summer, there weren't many games going on at all, just kids getting together in the park now and then.

But Callie's thin smile and the distance in her eyes told Emily the truth before Callie voiced it.

"Nah," Callie said, hesitating.

Emily gave a slow nod. "You agreed to play with the Wild Hunt, didn't you?"

Callie nodded back.

"It's time. The summer season is winding up in the Fairy Realm, and now that I missed summer camps, too, I'm not exactly off to play college ball, am I?"

Emily opened her mouth to argue.

"Don't worry," Callie cut her off. "I negotiated my contract so I'm only bound to play one season. I get to go home no matter the outcome. I'll be back by fall. Maybe walk onto a college team then."

"Whenever that is," Emily retorted.

"I'll be fine."

"Still," Emily said, not convinced. "Be careful."

"I will."

A moment passed, suddenly awkward. They'd become friends — of course they had, how could they not? But their connection was still new, still less familiar than their old antagonism. Sometimes they had moments like this where they weren't certain what to say to one another.

Callie broke it by digging into her trouser pocket.

"Anyway, I was going to come to say goodbye in any case, but I came now because I got a message last night. For you. I think it came to me because the fairy connection is stronger for me than it is for you right now, what with getting ready to get yanked over and all."

She pulled a scrap of paper — parchment, really — from her pocket and held it out to Emily.

"Here."

The moment Emily's fingers touched it, she felt a spark of magic. The scent of the forest wafted from the paper, together with the aroma of good clean dirt and fresh summer rain.

Carefully, Emily unfolded it.

A tiny fragment of something rolled out. She caught it before it hit the floor.

Miss Em,

It was a very tough inning, but we won!

I trust you have already found your freedom, but please find enclosed your share of the other part of our winnings.

If you ever have need of us, only call on it and know the Small Folk will answer. We're free to do so now, thanks to your help.

Fennoc

P.S. Keep the baseball magic alive, eh, lass?

A chill crossed her spine, and for a moment she thought she might cry.

They'd done it. The Small Folk had won the Fairy Series, the Web Gem, and their freedom.

She'd never felt so proud of anything in her entire life.

Emily lifted the thing she'd caught into the thin stream of evening twilight that was slanting into her room, and gasped as she recognized the glint of crystal. A piece of the Web Gem.

The light became something powerful as it passed through the facets.

She turned to share her joy with Callie, but her rival was already gone.

Emily got the feeling it would be a while before she saw her again, but it didn't matter. Callie had made her choice, and Emily had a history lesson to get to.

First, though, an important task lay before her.

Folding Fennoc's note back into its neat little square, she moved to her desk and the trophy shelf that hung over it. She placed the note on the far side, leaving just a little space for whatever might happen during her true senior year, then arranged the shard of Web Gem crystal next to it.

She put Mom's ball on top of it all.

Standing back, Emily nodded in satisfaction, then gathered her history books. Time for the library.

Maybe Adrien would be up for ice cream afterward.

And maybe a walk to Unicorn Field.

Time worked weird in Fairyland, after all.

She wanted to be there when Callie came back.

ABOUT BRIGID COLLINS

Brigid Collins is a fantasy and science fiction writer living in Michigan with her wonderful wife and her irritating cats. (Just kidding, the cats are pretty wonderful, too.)

Her fantasy series *The Songbird River Chronicles* and *Winter's Consort*, her fun middle grade hijinks series *The Sugimori Sisters*, and her dark fairy tale novella *Thorn and Thimble* are available wherever books are sold. Her short stories have appeared in Fiction River, Feyland Tales, and Mercedes Lackey's Valdemar anthologies.

Sign up for her newsletter at www.brigidcollinsbooks.com/newsletter-sign-up/ and get a free copy of *Strength & Chaos, Mischief & Poise: Four Cat Tales*, exclusively available to her subscribers!

Website: https://brigidcollinsbooks.com

ALSO BY BRIGID COLLINS

<u>Novels</u>

Songbird River Chronicles (4 books)

Winter's Consort (4 books)

<u>Novella</u>

Thorn and Thimble

<u>Collections</u>

The Sugimori Sisters series (3 volumes)

Three Tales of Faeries

Three Tales of Powers

Three Tales of Monsters

Strength & Chaos, Mischief & Poise

ABOUT RON COLLINS

Ron Collins is a best-selling Science Fiction and Dark Fantasy author who writes across the spectrum of speculative fiction. You can find his work at all major online retailers.

His short fiction has received a Writers of the Future prize and a CompuServe HOMer Award. His short story “The White Game” was nominated for the Short Mystery Fiction Society’s 2016 Derringer Award.

He holds a degree in Mechanical Engineering, and has worked to develop avionics systems, electronics, and information technology before chucking it all to write full-time.

Website: https://www.typosphere.com

Get Free Books!

Ron’s Reader List: Newsletter: http://typosphere.com/newsletter

ALSO BY RON COLLINS

Novels

Stealing the Sun (9 books)

Saga of the God-Touched Mage (8 books)

The PEBA Diaries (2 books)

The Knight Deception

Wakers

Collections

Tomorrow in All the Worlds

Picasso's Cat & Other Stories

Five Magics

Collins Creek (3 volumes)

Nonfiction

On Writing (And Reading!) Short

Poetry

Five Seven Five

CPSIA information can be obtained
at www.ICGtesting.com
Printed in the USA
JSHW021917220323
39340JS00003B/24

9 781946 176462